plan b

plan b

jenny o'connell

POCKET BOOKS   MTV BOOKS
New York   London   Toronto   Sydney

POCKET BOOKS, a division of Simon & Schuster, Inc.
1230 Avenue of the Americas, New York, NY 10020

ISBN-13: 978-1-4165-2033-7
ISBN-10:   1-4165-2033-3

This MTV Books/Pocket Books trade paperback edition March 2006

10   9   8   7   6   5   4   3   2

For information regarding special discounts for bulk purchases, please contact Simon & Schuster Special Sales at 1-800-456-6798 or business@simonandschuster.com.

For my daughter,
because she's my most
favorite girl ever.

acknowledgments

First and foremost, my agent is responsible for suggesting the idea that I try my hand at the life of a seventeen year old, and for that, I thank her. And Lauren McKenna, Megan McKeever, and Louise Burke at Pocket, for giving Vanessa a home and helping me make her the kind of girl I'd love to hang out with. Vanessa Palomo, Sarah Palomo, and Paige Penrod provided the insider information and suggestions only brilliant high school girls could offer. I can't wait to see what fantastic things you girls achieve. Stacey Ballis, who brought me backstage at the Goodman Theater and taught me all there was to know about what goes on behind the curtain. Finally, the amazing author Norma Klein, who wrote books that kept me mesmerized during my teens, made me a voracious reader, and watched over my shoulder while I wrote *Plan B*.

prologue

I knew it was too good to be true. Only nine months. Forty weeks. Two hundred eighty-four days. If I wasn't so busy getting ready for the first day of my senior year, and I'd remembered to buy the calculator required for my AP calculus class, I could have had it down to the exact hour. The day I graduate from high school. Then a summer traveling around Europe with Taylor, where hopefully five years of conjugating French verbs would finally pay off.

Anyway, I had life all figured out. In one short, hopefully relatively painless year, I'd be on my way out East to college, where I'd join Patrick and things would be exactly like they were last year when I was a junior and Patrick was a senior. Only better. Because we'd be away from home and on our own (in a manner of speaking, of course, considering our parents would be footing the entire bill for our college experience and the road trips Taylor and I were already planning to Boston).

That was the plan, anyway. But then came the phone call. I was waiting to hear from Patrick, the cordless phone sitting silently beside me on my bed so my parents wouldn't get to it first. But when I picked up the phone it wasn't my college-bound boyfriend calling to tell me he couldn't wait for me to visit. It was a woman asking for my father in a voice that was so polite, so practiced, I thought she had to be a telemarketer trying to get him to switch our long-distance telephone service or, at the very least, renew his subscription to the *Chicago Tribune*.

If I'd known then what I know now, I might have just told her she had the wrong number, replaced the receiver quietly on its cradle, and unplugged all the phones in our house. Maybe even called the phone company and asked to disconnect our number all together. But I didn't. I brought the phone over to my dad, who was in his study reading a book while my mom worked on the laptop at his desk. And that's when everything changed. In that single moment when my dad said hello and I watched his face transform from a look of practiced calm to a look of petrified shock, I realized that life as we knew it was about to change.

And that's when my carefully laid plan went out the window.

chapter one

"Has Patrick called you yet?" Taylor asked me for what seemed like the tenth time today.

"He just left on Wednesday," I reminded her, flipping through my *Let's Go Europe*. "Besides, he's only had a day to settle in and meet his new roommate. I'm sure there are tons of things incoming freshman have to take care of," I added, not sure whether I was trying to answer Taylor or convince myself.

Taylor shrugged and sat up, swinging her legs around until she was sitting Indian style on the sunken cushion of the armchair we'd staked out in the language section of Barnes & Noble. The girl had become amazingly limber since she read about Madonna's addiction to Bikram yoga and decided to replicate the same conditions in her bedroom with a space heater, an electric blanket, and a DVD she bought off some swami's website. "Still, I would have thought you'd hear from him by now. He has a cellphone, you know."

"He'll call," I assured her, repeating the silent mantra I'd been reciting to myself for the past two days.

"Aren't you afraid of cheating?" Taylor asked, not even looking up from the book in her lap as she traced a map of Germany with her finger.

I shook my head and dismissed her absurd suggestion. "No way. I'd never cheat on Patrick."

This time she looked up. "I meant, aren't you afraid of him cheating on you?"

"Nope." I touched the small gold heart charm hanging around my neck, a birthday present from Patrick. I rubbed it for good luck and then discreetly checked my fingers to see if the gold came off. He'd said it was fourteen carat, but you never knew.

Taylor wasn't as convinced. She wasn't exactly Patrick's biggest fan and I knew she was glad to finally be rid of him. "I don't know. Last year when Courtney Maxwell and Brian Bonham left for college he cheated on her in less than two weeks with some girl who had a barbell through her tongue."

"Brian Bonham was a prick."

Taylor frowned at me as if to say, aren't they all?

"Can we please not talk about this now?" I asked.

"Sure. I didn't mean to imply that Pat—I mean Patrick—will cheat on you." She shrugged. "Just that, well, you know."

Yeah, I knew. The look on Taylor's face was the same look everyone gave me when I told them Patrick and I were going to still date after he left for Yale. A look that said, who are you kidding?

"*Ich brauche ein Abführmittel,*" Taylor slowly mouthed, trying out a line from the book in her lap. "That means, 'I need a laxative.' "

"Let's hope we won't need that one," I noted and traded my *Let's Go Europe* for her *Lonely Planet Europe Phrasebook*. Even though it was barely Labor Day, Taylor and I were already planning next summer's vacation. We were also trying to convince our parents that two eighteen-year-old girls would be fine trekking across Europe by themselves, which was proving more difficult than last summer's task, when we persuaded them to let us go camping for the weekend at Starved Rock State Park. Apparently having their daughters pitch a tent amidst 2,630 acres of thick forest was preferable to setting them loose in a foreign country.

But focusing on next summer made the next nine months seem bearable and gave me an added incentive to kiss up to Madame Rodriguez in French class. At least I had something to think about besides the fact that Patrick was 874 miles away in Connecticut, moving into a new dorm room, on a new campus, meeting new people. He was probably waiting in line as we spoke, getting his ID photo taken or having his phone and computer hooked up so he could e-mail his girlfriend back home to tell her how much he missed her.

Still, when Taylor kept quizzing me about what Patrick was doing every hour of the day, it just reminded me that whatever he was doing, he was doing it without me.

"We *are* going to Germany, right?" Taylor asked.

"That's the plan."

"Ech will eine heue Frisur."

"Let me guess: 'I've got the runs'?"

"I want a new hairdo," she translated. "Maybe dark brown or black."

"Your mother will kill you." Taylor's mother, with a little help from L'Oreal, went to great lengths to achieve the golden auburn tone Taylor was able to achieve naturally. After all, as she always reminded us, she was worth it.

"But I want *etwas exotisches,*" she told me, sounding like there was peanut butter stuck to the roof of her mouth. "Something exotic. Look." Taylor riffled around in her backpack, pulled out the latest *People* magazine, and flipped to the Star Tracks page. It showed celebrities caught in everyday moments just like the rest of us—climbing into their Ferraris, sunbathing on the deck of their yacht in Cannes, eating lunch at the Ivy. "Everyone's doing it—Reese, Renée, even Nicole," Taylor clarified, as if that should explain the sudden interest in going from her natural tawny red to inky black. And it did.

Taylor is obsessed with anything to do with celebrities. She can tell you who's dating who, which stars are teetering on career suicide, and what former "it" girl is in rehab.

"See there." She pointed to a photo of two stars from *Wild Dunes,* her favorite show. "Reed Vaughn is shopping for groceries with Rebecca Stewart, and what color is her hair?"

"It's the color of the filter in my parents' espresso machine—dingy brown. Besides, the photo is obviously just a publicity stunt."

"Why?" Taylor asked, concerned. She never doubted the voracity of the information she read in *People.* It would be like questioning the Bible—the world as she knew it would cease to make sense.

Taylor received a subscription to *People* for her ninth birthday and has saved every issue that's arrived in her mailbox every Friday for the past eight years. That means she's saved over four hundred issues of *People,* and her mom finally had to take her to The Container Store and buy plastic shelving units to hold her growing library. Taylor even gets *Us Weekly, Entertainment Weekly,* and *Teen People* now, but she claims she's a purist; that even though those magazines are fine imitations, it's *People* she wants to write for when she graduates from college.

That's why I don't think anyone was surprised when Taylor suggested that our school paper, the *Cabot Chronicle,* include an entertainment section. Of course, she also volunteered to be the section's first reporter and editor. Taylor covers the school-sanctioned entertainment at Cabot, like last year's half-assed production of *Les Miserables,* a title that described both the performance and what it was like to sit in the audience. She also provides running commentary on how Hollywood's trends find their way into the halls of our esteemed school.

I took the magazine away from Taylor and inspected her evidence. "We're supposed to believe they're shopping for farm-fresh produce? Rebecca looks like she hasn't eaten in months and I thought Reed was in rehab."

It barely took Taylor a second to scan her mental encyclopedia of entertainment facts. "He was at Casa Hope in Malibu because he blacked out and drove his car into a Starbucks on his way home from a cast party for the new season of *Wild Dunes.*"

What was I going to do, disagree with her? The girl knew the comings and goings of Reed Vaughn better than Reed Vaughn. His alcohol-induced blackouts were probably more distressing for Taylor than they were for him—after all, if Reed couldn't remember what he did, how was she supposed to read about them?

If I didn't put a stop to the conversation now, Taylor would have me running down the list of famous alcoholics and drug addicts who attended Casa Hope—some more than once, which I didn't think was a resounding endorsement, considering the place was supposed to cure people. But I wasn't about to get into it with Taylor, who was surely in need of her own 12-step program to treat her addiction to *Access Hollywood*.

"Hey, it says in *Let's Go* that we should take a good self-defense class so we can react to unwelcome advances." Taylor held up the guide and pointed to a photograph of a girl giving some guy a swift kick in the balls.

"I don't think I'll bring that up to my parents. As it is, unless we get them to change their minds, the only thing Greek we'll be see-ing next summer is the gyro stand at North Avenue Beach."

"Tell me about it." Taylor slumped down in her chair and closed her *Let's Go* in defeat. "I can't believe your mom and dad aren't into the idea. I was counting on them convincing my parents to let us go."

I shrugged. What was I going to do? My parents were consistently inconsistent. They liked to think they're quirky theater people, chalking up their eccentricities to the fact that they're *in the arts*. But my mom hasn't designed a set since she became an interior decorator and traded in curtain calls for plantation shutters, and the only thing dramatic about my dad's job as artistic director for the Bookman Theater were the hissy fits he had to deal with from aspiring actresses who thought they deserved more attention.

Granted, they were more tolerant than the other parents at Cabot, but it wasn't like I gave them a whole lot to get uptight about. Even if my mother did have a tendency to rearrange the furniture on a weekly basis and my father can manage a cast of thirty performers yet can't manage to keep his beloved sheep dog from crapping on my mother's shantung silk curtains, at least I had my act together. While other kids were sneaking out at night and hiding pot in their underwear drawers, I didn't have much to rebel against. My parents took a perfectly pragmatic approach to child rearing.

Teen pregnancy—it's called the pill. Use it.

Clothes—my mom once wore a see-through gauzy thing to an opening-night performance and gave the audience more of a show than the actors on stage. We have the picture in our family photo album to prove it, so who was she to complain?

A curfew—only for parents who didn't trust their kids. ("We trust you, Vanessa, until you give us a reason not to," they always told me.)

And I always got the feeling that if they caught me smoking dope, they'd just give each other a knowing look, one that said, been there, done that.

So what was I going to rebel against? The fact that they made me volunteer to hand out programs at matinees?

No, my parents weren't concerned with the classic things most parents worry about, but coming to terms with the idea that their only child was about to leave the nest, that freaked them out. That's why I think they're so set against our trip to Europe. No matter how many articles I strategically place on the kitchen counter, articles that proclaim the numerous benefits of multicultural experiences, they haven't budged: "If you want a multicultural experience, we can take you to the Latin American film festival next summer." They just didn't get it.

"Maybe if we got jobs this year and earned enough to stay in hotels instead of hostels," Taylor suggested halfheartedly. Neither of us wanted to get a job.

I hated that word—"hostel", not "job." A job I could deal with, just not while I was dealing with my senior year of high school. But the word "hostel" sounded too much like "hostile," like we'd be sleeping in our dumpy cots and wake up with some knife-wielding psycho hovering over us with a deranged look in his eye. Why couldn't they call them something nicer—like "cozies." Think of how many parents would sleep better at night knowing their kids were staying at a cozy?

"I think the cultural angle is still our best bet," I told her. "We need to play up the benefits of living among natives, so to speak."

"Shit, we should have thought of this last year. We could have used the whole college application thing as an excuse—no college wants an applicant who writes her essay about a summer job at the Shoe Carousel. They want someone who learned how to make voodoo dolls at the knee of some African medicine man while attempting to discover an alternative energy source and restore peace to the Middle East."

College applications. "Let's not go there. We have five days before school starts. Can't we just think about sitting at some sidewalk café in Paris eating warm, flaky croissants while we sip cappuccino?"

"This is depressing, we're probably never going to convince them to let us go." Taylor started collecting the stack of entertainment magazines splayed out on the coffee table. "I'm heading over to the magazine racks to return these."

She took off and left me with the task of returning six travel books and one map of the London Underground back to the bookshelves.

After I'd put back the books, and spent a few minutes organizing several others that were also out of place, I found Taylor basking in the glossy glow of *Premier, Wow, InTouch,* and *Star.* Back when it was a tabloid that shoppers would flip through while waiting in line at the checkout, Taylor snubbed *Star.* But now that it was a glossy magazine placed on the rack right next to her revered *People,* it had become fair game.

"Aren't you going to buy one?" I asked, as she returned the magazines to their displays.

"No. There's a new Reed Vaughn calendar I was thinking of buying instead." In Taylor's mind, twelve months of Reed Vaughn trumped four Hollywood weeklies.

Unfortunately for Taylor, when we found the calendar section, Reed Vaughn wasn't in sight.

"Excuse me," she asked the salesperson as she paid for the *Lonely Planet Europe Phrasebook* and *Europe by Rail.* "Do you have the new Reed Vaughn calendar?"

The salesperson shook his head. "Nope. All sold out. We should be getting more next week."

"Can I get put on a waiting list or something?" she asked.

"Waiting list? It's a calendar," he pointed out, making the idea of a waiting list for a calendar sound as ridiculous as if she'd asked to make a reservation at KFC.

I knew Taylor wouldn't let his comment slide. Running out of this season's best-selling calendar, that she could understand. But letting some salesperson live with the misbelief that twelve color photos of Reed Vaughn sweating it up in front of a camera didn't deserve a waiting list? That was an egregious error she felt compelled to correct.

"It's not just a calendar. It's a Reed Vaughn calendar," she explained, calmly. "Now, do I have to ask for your manager or will you please put me on a list to be called when you get more calendars in?"

What was the cashier going to say? He took her number, even though I was sure he'd toss it in the trash the moment we walked out the door.

I stepped forward to pay for my *Let's Go*.

"You want to go see a movie tonight?" Taylor offered while I waited for my change. "There aren't many days left before school starts, we may as well take advantage of it."

"Can't. My parents are taking me to some opening night at a gallery their friend owns. A new show called 'The Human Canvas.' "

"What's that mean? Does the artist paint with his toes or something?"

I shrugged. "Who knows. All I know is that they think this guy is the next Picasso."

"I thought they said that organic sculptor was supposed to be the next Picasso."

"No, he was going to be the next Calder, but it doesn't matter anymore. His stuff was crap."

"That bad, huh?"

"No, I meant it was crap—literally. Turned out the guy was carving dried cow manure."

Taylor laughed and grabbed the bag with my *Let's Go*. "That's a good one."

I took my change and followed her out of the store. "My mom didn't think so. She convinced one of her clients to buy a piece. I guess they should have known something was wrong when he named all his pieces *Sculpture Number Two*."

"Maybe the next Picasso will be better," Taylor offered hopefully.

"Maybe," I told her, but, given my parents' track record, I wasn't very optimistic.

chapter two

Up until my freshman year, I attended a school that was supposed to foster individuality and independent thinking. The kind that forgoes grades in favor of thoughtful comments about personal growth, and shuns uniforms for fear that plaid jumpers and paisley ties will stifle creative expression. But two weeks before I was all set to return to the Sharingham School and begin ninth grade, the parents' association learned that Williard Thomas, the school's *primary scholar*, was exhibiting a little creative expression of his own. Apparently our esteemed primary scholar (that would be the principal in schools unconcerned with hierarchical labels scarring the psyches of their students) was embezzling tuition to fund some rogue group attempting to rescue Australian dung beetles from impending extinction.

So with the Sharingham School caught up in the very public, very Robin Hood–like dung beetle scandal, my parents thought it was the perfect time to let me discover a new bastion of social experimentation and egalitarianism. Public school.

My parents loved the idea of their only daughter mingling with kids from all over the city. The thought fed the liberal ideals they fought so hard to maintain even as contractors were retrofitting our kitchen to accommodate a wine cooler and a stainless steel, four-thousand-dollar Viking stove—perfect for cooking garden burgers and tofu dogs. I could practically see my mom and dad humming "We Shall Overcome" as they envisioned a utopia where students from all walks of life could convene on the cracked cement steps of Lincoln High School and join hands in social harmony.

But I guess even visions of utopia are easy to abandon when Celia Carlisle's only baby must pass through a metal detector before homeroom bell. And so that's how I ended up at Cabot Academy.

Cabot Academy was a long way from Sharingham. Students were expected to address teachers as Mr. and Mrs., not Ted and Sheila. A vegan alternative was conspicuously absent among the all-American lunches that included cheeseburgers and pizza. We had a good old headmaster, Mr. Whitney, instead of a primary scholar, and I got the feeling that our daily moment of silence was intended to provide the teachers with a rare quiet minute rather than give students time to visualize world peace.

Cabot students weren't obsessed with winning NASA's science contest for the tenth year in a row like the hyperachievers over at Chicago Lab School, but we weren't studying the finer art of Native American basket weaving like the students at Sharingham. We were somewhere between future Nobel Prize–winning mathematicians and those street corner musicians in scratchy wool ponchos trying to sell homemade CDs they recorded on their iMACs.

At Lab I'd be just another smart girl jockeying for a place at the head of the class. At Cabot I was currently running second behind Benji Coburn. And that was fine with me. We all knew he'd end up at MIT or Stanford. We also knew he was destined to live in some dilapidated shack in the woods, only to emerge as the next Unabomber in a few years. Taylor was already planning to cover the story for *People*.

Besides, everyone knew that colleges only accept so many people from the same school. At Cabot I had a better chance of getting into Yale. Last year Patrick was the only one to apply, and he got in. Not because he was especially brilliant, but because he's one hell of a lacrosse player and both his parents went there.

Even though my parents decided that Cabot was better suited for me than a school where search and seizures took place between homeroom and first period, they were a little concerned by Cabot's limited artistic outlets. Apparently they thought there'd been a huge void left in my life when I transferred from Sharingham, as if the lack of courses dedicated to a vast array of papier-mâché techniques would leave me ill-prepared for life as a functioning member of society. And so they encouraged me to join them for gallery openings, music fairs, and theatrical productions—and forced me when their encouragement didn't work.

"This is going to be amazing," my mother assured me while we waited for my father to pay the cabdriver. "Clark Clark is a rising star in the art world."

I turned toward the large plate glass window spanning the front of the gallery and peered inside. The gallery was one of those long, narrow hallwaylike spaces with polished hardwood floors, blank white walls, and track lighting. Inside the gallery, a small cluster of people were gathered around a short, stubby man in a black kilt, black tank top, and pink Chuck Taylor high-tops. The group watched the animated fashion victim gesture wildly toward the frameless photographs mounted on the walls, and from the looks of awe on their faces, I assumed that he was the rising star.

"I thought Clark Clark was a painter," I commented, stepping into the gallery behind my parents.

" 'The Human Canvas' is just a metaphor for Clark's work. He paints directly onto the human form and then captures the image on film," my dad explained before stopping to look at the first print in the series.

I stood beside him and tried to figure out what it was exactly that Clark Clark was capturing. All I saw were red, white, and yellow circles painted inside one another like a bull's-eye. It wasn't what I'd call groundbreaking—I'd seen this logo tons of times outside Target.

But then I noticed that the center of the bull's-eye wasn't flat. In fact, it was actually raised, like a little mountain rising up from the surrounding prickled landscape. And that's when I realized that I wasn't standing four inches away from a painted replica of a store logo. I was staring at an up close and personal photograph of a woman's . . .

"It's brilliant," my mom gasped.

"It's a nipple," I practically shrieked. I didn't care what they called it—art, vision, whatever—it was a nipple!

"Vanessa!" my mom quickly swiveled her head to see if anyone had heard me. "Don't be rude. Clark has a unique vision, and we need to respect that."

Funny, when Clark Clark slaps some paint on a woman's private parts and snaps a photo, we're supposed to respect his unique vision. If some guy in eleventh grade art class did the same thing, he'd be suspended.

"These are all blown-up photographs of naked body parts," I pointed out, diverting my eyes from the next picture, a male body part painted yellow like a banana. "This is porn, not art."

"You can't be so literal, Vanessa," my dad scolded before turning to my mom. "I swear, I don't know where she gets it from."

My mom shrugged, not willing to take any credit.

"Celia! Will!" Neiman rushed toward us, his arms outstretched as he prepared to embrace all three of us at once. I was nose deep in Neiman's armpit before I could think of a way to escape.

It was like this with all my parents' friends. There wasn't a normal one in the bunch. In addition to collecting art, Will and Celia Carlisle collected starving artists, melodramatic gallery owners, method actors, and street musicians.

"Neiman, this is fabulous," my mother observed, her voice muffled against Neiman's chest. "I think I have a client who would love Clark's work."

Neiman pulled back and grinned. "Anything but the banana and the two oranges over there, I already sold them. The interest in the show has been phenomenal."

"I can see why, such an imaginative use of texture and line." My mother proceeded to caress the banana photograph. Neiman and my dad decided to join her.

Could I really be the only one mortified by this? Was that really possible?

And they wondered why I never wanted to join them at these art gallery gigs? I was currently standing next to my parents while they admired a painted penis.

Neiman turned around and I thought he was going to ask me to join them in their reverence of the sublime fruit. "Look at you," Neiman cried instead, clasping his hands together dramatically. "Vanessa, you are just lovely. Really. Just like your mother."

Either he was severely nearsighted, or Neiman was sucking up to my mom in hopes of selling a few of Clark's pieces. I tended to think the latter.

My mother and I look nothing alike. I'm blond, her hair is blacker than black. I've been trying to grow my hair out for the last three years without much success, and my mom has always sported a short Mia Farrow pixie cut that makes her look a little like Peter Pan. I'm almost five seven, she's barely over five feet tall—again, contributing to the Peter Pan effect. My mother also tends to have a split personality when it comes to fashion, like tonight's get-up. She was probably the only woman in the world who could get away with wearing a butter yellow Chanel suit with handmade jewelry crafted by an indigenous tribe from some third world country. She said that the combination allowed her to balance her karma without sacrificing her fashion sense.

"You must be getting ready to start school," Neiman noted, making conversation with me. "Are you starting to think about what you'll do next year?"

"Hopefully Yale," I answered, thankful to have their attention away from Clark's work.

Neiman nodded. "Great art museum."

"And drama school," my dad added.

Of course, neither of which I had the least bit of interest in.

"Actually I was thinking about majoring in economics."

"Really?" Neiman wrinkled his nose. "Economics?" he repeated distastefully before looking to my parents for an explanation.

But they simply shrugged, as if to say, we're hoping she'll grow out of it.

Yes, while parents across America were discouraging their daughters from a life in the theater and urging them to study something more useful, like accounting or engineering, my parents were still hoping I'd walk through the door reciting a soliloquy from *Hamlet*. Which is why I "volunteered" at the theater this past summer after the store I worked at, Groovy Smoothie, went out of business. My parents wanted me to work at the theater all summer—"You need to experience some culture," they'd insisted—but I also wanted to make some money. Culture doesn't buy you much at Abercrombie.

When Groovy Smoothie closed its doors in July, I was quickly recruited by my parents and for the rest of the summer I joined the ranks of other theater volunteers—"the saints," they'd called them, which I figured was probably nicer than calling them what they really were: people with lots of free time to kill.

"Well, shall I introduce you to Clark?" Neiman offered, taking my mother by the hand. "There are hors d'oeuvres on the table in the back, Vanessa. Help yourself."

I accepted Neiman's offer and parked myself next to the stuffed mushrooms and spinach dip for the next two hours. Thankfully, once she'd expressed interest in actually purchasing one of Clark's soft-core porn-o-graphs, Neiman monopolized my parents the rest of the night. And that was fine by me. The last thing I wanted to do was contemplate the meaning of a tie-dyed belly button—even if, according to my mother, the artist's use of naval lint was truly groundbreaking.

By the time we got home, it was almost eight o'clock. I'd been gone for almost three hours, and still no message from Patrick. Sure, I told Taylor he'd call, but what else was I going to say? He'd been gone for almost three days!

Let's make that *only* three days, not almost three days. He was probably just going through hours of orientation, I shouldn't freak out. I wasn't one of those clingy girlfriends who dialed her boyfriend's phone every two minutes until he answered. I was one of those cool girlfriends who picked up the phone, thought about dialing, actually dialed the first six numbers, and then hung up before she looked like aforementioned clingy girlfriend.

I decided to take my mind off Patrick's new school by preparing for the start of my own school year. Without Patrick it was going to be a pretty uneventful nine months until graduation. Short of waiting for my acceptance from Yale, and convincing my parents that a summer in Europe was the perfect graduation gift for a daughter who never caused them any grief, there wasn't much to break up the monotony of another year at Cabot. I grabbed a pencil and settled on my bed with the summer reading questions I had to finish before classes started on Tuesday. Senior Seminar in Women's Fiction. Uneventful indeed.

When the phone finally rang the shrill sound was so unexpected my hand jumped across the page and snapped the tip off my pencil. It had to be Patrick. I cleared my throat and prepared to sound like the sexy girlfriend he remembered. I even closed my eyes and pretended I was wearing some short, strappy sundress instead of my navy blue Cabot gym shorts and an I ❤ THE BOOKMAN THEATER T-shirt. Like I said, I didn't give my parents a whole lot to get uptight about.

I was all psyched to hear Patrick's smooth voice, just thinking about it made the blond hairs on my arm stand on end, but as soon as I looked down at the handset I knew it wasn't him. Instead of his familiar cell number, the digital caller ID displayed an area code I didn't even recognize. Shit!

I punched the talk button and answered the phone with a very irritated hello designed to let the caller know that every second on the phone with him was keeping me from talking with my boyfriend.

"May I speak with Will Carlisle, please," a woman asked politely. Normally it was pretty obvious when a telemarketer was calling for my dad. They'd ask for William Carlisle or Bill Carlisle, and sometimes they'd even butcher his name completely by asking for *Will-i-am Car-ly-sol,* trying to pronounce every single syllable in hopes of getting it right. But this woman used my dad's correct name and knew the "s" was silent in Carlisle. I figured, even if she was just going to ask him to switch to MCI, she'd earned her moment of rejection.

I asked her to hold on a minute and headed down the hall to my dad's study. As per their nightly ritual, my father was lounging in the brown leather chair my mom surprised him with for his forty-fifth birthday, his sock-covered feet resting on the matching ottoman. He'd asked for a raincoat, a pretty practical present if you ask me, but apparently new furniture was more important than keeping dry. Besides, she couldn't stand the old nubby orange La-Z-Boy my father bought when they were first married, and his birthday gave her an excuse to replace it with a chair that didn't clash with the new palate of sage greens and taupes that she'd chosen as this season's trendy colors.

I held out the phone. "Dad, it's for you."

"Who is it?" he asked, peering at me over his wire-rimmed reading glasses.

"I didn't ask."

He frowned but removed his glasses and put down the leather-bound book he'd been studying. "Couldn't you tell them I wasn't here?" he asked, and then grudgingly took the phone.

My mom was typing away on the laptop on my dad's desk. I watched over her shoulder as terms like "trompe l'oeil," "tumbled marble," and "Venetian plaster" filled the screen. My dad wouldn't take more than a few seconds to tell the woman on the phone that he wasn't interested in a new calling plan that provided unlimited calls to Indonesia, and I wanted to take the phone back to my room so I could wait for Patrick's call. "What's that?" I asked.

"A letter to an editor over at *Architectural Digest*. They're interested in featuring the Kohn's house in their January issue."

I was about to ask if the magazine was going to interview her, too, when I noticed that my father was still on the phone. He wasn't talking to the woman, but he was doing some very intent listening, staring straight ahead at the built-in bookshelves against the wall, his face frozen in the same combination of scared concentration that you'd expect to see on someone receiving instructions on how to dismantle a bomb. Maybe MCI was using some new scare tactic to get customers to switch from Sprint. Whatever it was, it was working.

After about five minutes of silence, my father mumbled something about getting back to her tomorrow. That was one hell of a saleswoman. And I wasn't the only one who noticed.

My mom's fingers were no longer pecking at the keyboard. "Will? Is something wrong?" my mother asked, standing up.

Something definitely wasn't right.

"Vanessa, can you leave your mom and me alone for a minute," he muttered, his voice uneven, like he was out of breath.

From the look on my father's face I thought their conversation would take more than a minute.

"Sure," I answered, and turned to leave just as my mother made her way over to my dad.

"Will? What is it?" I heard my mom ask, her voice fading away as my dad pushed the door closed behind me.

I stood on the other side of the doorway staring at the paneled cherrywood with its brushed nickle handle, one part of me wishing I was inside to hear his answer. But there was another part of me that was thankful I didn't know what he told her, because that call was obviously not from a woman promising long-distance calls for three cents a minute. This had to be bad. This had to be very, very bad.

chapter three

My parents didn't believe in arguing behind closed doors. Everything in our house was conducted out in the open, for better or worse. As a matter of fact, I can only remember one other time my parents asked me to leave them alone, when Grant Farley, the theater's lead set designer and my mother's former boss, finally died of AIDS.

The thought made my heart jump. Someone died. The woman on the phone was probably a nurse. Who else could be so poised and professional when delivering such horrible news? After all, she was probably used to people dying all the time. I quickly ran down the list—my grandpa Harry in Florida, my mom's parents. My aunt Jane? But she was four years younger than my dad, there was no way it was her.

The waiting was excruciating. I tried to read over my school supply list to make sure I had everything, but the words on the page kept blurring together until they were a jumble of indecipherable letters. All I could think about was who'd died. Eventually I gave up trying to do anything productive and just sat there on my bed and waited. The minutes ticked away on the clock on my night table as I scrutinized the details of every piece of furniture, every photograph, every picture in my room until it was committed to memory—the sheer lavender curtains falling beside my windows in soft folds, the bright white crown molding following the outline of my ceiling like a picture frame, the way my night table lamp projected a shadow that resembled a sunny-side up egg onto the pale yellow of my walls. I took it all in, because I wanted to remember what it was like before I heard the terrible news. Whatever it was.

"Vanessa, can you come here a minute, please," my dad called out down the hall after what seemed like hours but was really only twenty-seven minutes. He didn't sound like he'd been crying, but then again maybe he was just trying to be strong for my mom.

This time when I entered the study, my mom was seated on the leather ottoman, her elbows resting on her knees, leaning forward as if anticipating my reaction. No red-rimmed eyes, no tear-stained cheeks. They were both so brave!

As I made my way to the couch against the wall, I kept telling myself that whatever it was, I wouldn't cry. But even as I dug my nails into the palm of my hand and focused on the sharp pain making its way to my fingertips, a lump was growing in my throat.

My dad stood there leaning against the front of the desk while my mom watched me with an expression that almost looked . . . hopeful? "Your mom and I just received some unexpected news," he began.

I squeezed my eyes shut and dug my fingers in deeper waiting for the news. I wish I didn't bite my nails. It would have been more effective.

My mom jumped in, putting on her best game face. "We know

this is unexpected, but we hope that you'll find this as exciting as we do."

I opened one eye and noticed my mother's foot nervously tapping the floor, which made me think that whatever it was I was about to hear, it wasn't exactly as *exciting* as she was making it out to be. She looked more anxious than ecstatic.

My dad inhaled deeply and then let out the news in one long breath that seemed to sweep across the entire room. "You have a brother."

At first I thought my father must have said I *had* a brother, like there'd been a baby who died at birth or something. Or maybe he'd been born with some rare birth defect and they'd sent him away to a home where doctors could take care of him.

I shook my head, trying to push aside the thoughts stampeding against my brain so I could remember exactly what my dad just said. He didn't say I *had* a brother. He said I *have* a brother.

"What do you mean, I have a brother?" I demanded. My mind raced trying to fill in the blanks. Was he locked up in a mental hospital somewhere, rocking himself to sleep in a straight jacket? Was he a runaway with a needle stuck in his arm in some crack house? Was he kidnapped by some cult and forced to live on a farm and wear a toga? "Where is he?"

"California."

The breath I didn't even realize I'd been holding in came rushing out. "Oh my God!" It was the cult!

My dad came over to the sofa and took a seat on the cushion beside me. "Even though we think this is good news, we do realize this is probably a surprise for you."

A surprise? Getting your period a week early is a surprise. Finding a five-dollar bill inside your winter coat pocket is a surprise.

Discovering you can still fit into last year's bikini is a surprise. But finding out you have a brother? That's a freaking bombshell.

My mom moved over to the sofa and joined us. "We always wanted you to have a sibling," she added. "And now it turns out you do."

I jumped up and left them sitting alone on the couch. I watched as the cushions where I'd been sitting quickly fluffed up to fill the void, one reason my mother always told her clients to choose synthetic fibers over down. "What's going on here? This is crazy, why didn't I know this?"

"We didn't know," my mother offered in their defense.

"How do you not know you have a son?" I demanded, my voice rising. This was insane.

My dad cleared his throat before declaring, "Well, it's quite simple, really."

Simple? No. Finding out you have some long-lost brother is lots of things—simple wasn't one of them.

My father reached for my hand and held it while he provided his simple explanation. "Your mother and I separated briefly after we were married. I was directing an especially difficult adaption of *A Doll's House*—you remember that, don't you Celia?" He looked over at my mom, seizing the opportunity to change the topic for a moment.

She nodded and seemed to relax for the first time since I'd entered the room. "It was grueling. Maintaining the integrity of Ibsen's work while highlighting the plight of Native Americans was very courageous, Will."

He smiled warmly at my mother and she smiled back. "I certainly tried to illuminate the Native American aspect, but I also wanted to explore the gender inequities present in our own culture."

My mom pondered this for a moment before continuing down this path of momentary denial. "That's why I always thought setting the piece to the music of Sonny and Cher was such an inspired choice."

Were they kidding me? I was waiting to find out how the hell I ended up having a brother, and they wanted to offer theatrical critique?

"Enough!" I finally shouted. "I get it. The play was some Herculean task. So what?"

"Well, I was consumed by the play and your mom was tired of set designing and was trying to get her interior design business off the ground."

The recap of their diverging career paths was fascinating, but I still didn't see how this had anything to do with the fact that I had a brother—what, work was so stressful they separated and forgot they had a kid?

"During our separation I had a brief relationship with one of the show's actresses, and apparently . . ." He let his voice trail off as if I could figure out the rest myself. And I could. My dad knocked up some wannabe actress while my mother was off helping some client reupholster a love seat—chintz or polka dots?

"You had an affair?" I turned to look at my mother. "Mom?"

I wanted an explanation, but she was occupying herself with what appeared to be the most important hangnail ever facing womankind.

"We were separated, Vanessa. We didn't know what was going to happen," she finally offered, placing her hand on my dad's knee in a show of solidarity. "Besides, being apart made us see how much we loved each other, so it all worked out for the best."

Unless you considered the small fact that my dad fathered another child.

"How long ago was this?" I asked.

"Almost eighteen years," she stated matter-of-factly.

I didn't need a calculator to do the math. I was five days away from starting AP calculus, after all. "He's my age?" I screamed, my voice shrill. "I have a brother who's my age?"

My dad nodded. "Well, he's four months older."

"An older brother," my mom chimed in, giving me an encouraging smile.

Four months older, as if that made a difference. I didn't just have a brother, apparently I had a big brother.

"So, what? Was that him calling to track down his long lost father?" *His father?* My father!

"No, that was his mother. She's worried about him. He's been getting into trouble and she's afraid something bad is going to happen to him if he stays in Los Angeles."

"So, what? He's coming to visit us?" Were we supposed to have some sort of perverse family reunion, like an episode of a reality show—*Meet My Illegitimate Son?*

My mom glanced at my dad, as if contemplating whether or not they should continue this conversation with their daughter without the help of a professional's intervention. "His mother would like him to spend his senior year with us," she explained calmly. "She thinks it will have a normalizing effect on him if he can be part of a family. Marnie never married." Marnie? My mother was on a first-name basis with the mother of my father's love child? This was total madness—and we were supposed to have a normalizing effect on this guy?

My dad nudged himself forward to the edge of the sofa and I could tell I hadn't heard the whole story. There was more. Maybe my brother had a twin. "Vanessa?"

"What?"

"There's one more thing. Your brother, you already know him in a way."

I was waiting for them to tell me that even though he was only my half brother, we were probably a lot alike. That we probably had a lot in common, the same dirty blond hair and gray eyes or something ridiculous like that.

"How could I possibly know him?" I snapped. "He's a total stranger."

"Not a total stranger," my mom interjected.

"It's Reed Vaughn," they both blurted in unison, like they were announcing the winner of this year's Tony Awards.

"Reed Vaughn?" I repeated, the lump in my throat dissolving as I thought about the absurdity of it all. Reed Vaughn? My hysterical laughter filled the silent room. "This is a joke, right? Is this some sort of senior prank Taylor is pulling for the *Cabot Chronicle,* because it's a little early in the year, isn't it?" I waited for them to point out the hidden cameras or, at the very least, expected Taylor to burst through the door.

My dad shook his head. "This isn't a joke, Vanessa. I had a brief relationship with Marnie Vaughn and then she moved to L.A. after the play closed."

I turned to look at my mother, who was apparently above freaking out over something as trivial as her husband having a child with Marnie Vaughn. Marnie Vaughn, for God's sake! My dad didn't sleep with some wannabe actress, he slept with Marnie Vaughn! Academy Award–winning actress and mother of Reed Vaughn.

Oh my God. My hands flew to my stomach and I could feel the stuffed mushrooms and warm spinach dip make its way up toward my throat. "I'm going to be sick," I mumbled before running out of the room toward the bathroom, both hands covering my mouth just in case I didn't make it. Throwing up was one thing. Throwing up on the Italian granite my mother painstakingly handpicked piece by piece was another.

When I reached the bathroom I fell to my knees, the dull thud sending a shot of pain up through my legs. But the sharp pain in my knees was nothing compared to the throbbing in my head. I laid my forehead on the cool seat and tried to catch my breath.

My dad had an affair. I had a brother. My dad had an affair and now I had a brother. And my brother was Reed Vaughn. This was just too much. It was sick. The whole thing was sick.

And then, in one fluid motion, I lifted my head off the seat, and I was sick, too.

chapter four

"What happened?" Taylor stood in front of her bedroom door, blocking my exit as I paced around the room. "You look like crap."

She really didn't need to point that out. I hadn't slept at all last night, even though my parents had insisted that a nice warm glass of soy milk would calm me down, as if my problem wasn't the fact that Reed Vaughn was my brother—it was lactose intolerance.

I shook my head, still out of breath from running the six blocks to her apartment.

"Did you and Patrick have a fight?" she asked. "Is something wrong?" Taylor reached behind her and pulled the door closed while she waited for me to stop hyperventilating. But it was practically impossible to catch my breath, and I was seriously beginning to question whether coming over to Taylor's was such a good idea after all. Everywhere I turned, Reed watched me. Over Taylor's bed, a poster-size Reed leaned against a tree in faded jeans and a white T-shirt. Scenes from *Wild Dunes* formed a collage beside her desk. On her night table, Bad Boy Reed straddled a Harley in a black leather jacket.

I grabbed the picture frame from the night table and held it out to Taylor. "You want to know what's wrong?" I breathed, still short of air. "He's what's wrong!"

Taylor looked like she couldn't decide what to do—let me finish my rant or remove her beloved Reed's photo from the clutches of a madwoman. "Why don't you hand me the picture and we can talk about it." She cautiously reached for the frame, but before she could grab it I glanced one more time at Reed's hairless chest peeking out from beneath the leather jacket. Was this what it felt like to want to scratch your eyes out?

"I can't even stand thinking about it!" I screamed, launching the picture frame at the wicker garbage basket by the door.

The frame missed the basket and crashed against the wall, where Taylor's horrified eyes fixed on the cracked glass creating a jagged starburst across Reed's leather-clad chest. "You better tell me what's going on. And you better have one hell of an explanation."

How do you tell someone that after seventeen years you've discovered you have a brother? How was I supposed to explain that, for the next nine months, the guy plastered on the walls of my best friend's room was going to wake up in my house. Was going to see me with morning breath. And eye boogers. That his shaving cream was going to share bathroom space with my tampons.

"Reed Vaughn is my brother."

"What are you talking about?" Taylor frowned, clearly convinced at this point that I'd lost my mind. "That's crazy."

"No, that's what happens when your father sleeps with Marnie Vaughn while he's separated from your mother." I flopped down on Taylor's bed and stared up at her ceiling. A horizontally mounted Reed stared back at me from the set of *Wild Dunes*.

"You're kidding me, right?" Taylor pushed my legs aside and sat down next to me. "Right?"

"If I was kidding, would my mother be planning how to redecorate the guest room for Reed's arrival? Would my father be calling Mr. Whitney about enrolling Reed for his senior year?"

Taylor just sat there, staring at her hands while she processed my news.

"Say something," I demanded.

"Oh my God," she practically whispered. "I don't know what to say. It's too unbelievable."

"He'll be here on Sunday."

"So he's going to go to school with us?" she asked slowly, as if she couldn't quite believe she was even saying the words. "Reed Vaughn, *the actor*, is going to Cabot Academy?"

"Not just Reed Vaughn, *the actor*," I mimicked, losing my patience. "Reed Vaughn, my fucking brother!" Every time I said it, my stomach dropped like I'd just plunged down the Viper at Six Flags.

"What about the show? What are they going to do about Gray?" she asked, calling Reed by his *Wild Dunes* character's name.

I propped myself up on my elbows and stared at Taylor. She had to be kidding.

"I tell you that I found out I have a brother, that my parents were separated, that my father has a son he never knew about, and you want to know what's going to happen to some fictional character on a TV show?"

"Oh my God, Vanessa, that's not what I meant," Taylor insisted. "I just can't believe he can pick up and move here like that. Or that your parents would want him to live with you. Or that you have a brother you never even knew about. No wonder you're freaking out." She sat silently for a minute, just shaking her head at the carpet. Finally, she seemed to get it. "I still can't believe it."

"Believe it. They've already shot the first six episodes of the new season and Marnie said the producers told Reed if he didn't straighten up they were going to write him out of the show anyway, so he really didn't have much of a choice. Getting sent to live with my family is his mom's version of scared straight."

"His mom . . . is Marnie Vaughn." Taylor's mouth dropped open, as if realizing for the first time that my dad slept with *the* Marnie Vaughn. "This is way too much."

"You're not making this any better," I told her, making a concerted effort to avert my eyes from all the Reed-related paraphernalia scattered around Taylor's room. "I know it's too much. The question is, what am I going to do?"

"Well, let's think about this." Taylor bit her lip and concentrated on figuring out a solution to a situation that didn't have one. "I guess you could tell your parents that Reed can't go to Cabot. That sounds reasonable, right?"

"Yeah, except, what other school would have him at the last minute? Besides, he's nothing but trouble."

Taylor didn't try to dispute this fact. Instead she looked me straight in the eye and told me the cold hard truth. "You. Are. Screwed."

"I know. And you can't tell anyone about this, Taylor. My parents and Marnie don't want a bunch of reporters making a scene at the airport. Reed's supposed to be coming here to get away from all that."

"That's fine," she agreed. "But you do know that the story is going to get out the minute Reed shows up here. Everyone is going to know."

"I realize that," I admitted, wishing she wasn't right. "But at least they don't have to know until he gets here."

Taylor laid a hand on my shoulder and attempted to give me a reassuring squeeze. "I'm so sorry this is happening to you. I can't even begin to imagine what it's going to be like."

"Imagine it? That's all I've been doing since my parents spilled the fabulous news."

"Come on, maybe it won't be that bad," she offered. "Maybe it will actually be fun."

I rolled my eyes at her. "Who's side are you on here?"

"Yours, of course," Taylor told me, and then nudged my leg. "But maybe you're looking at this all wrong. Try looking at it like the hottest guy on TV is going to be living with you."

"As my *brother*, Taylor," I reminded her. "Not a prospective prom date."

"Let's look at all the positives," she tried again, and then started rattling off all the positive aspects of having, one, a brother, and two, Reed Vaughn in the starring role.

She just didn't get it. I knew Taylor meant well, but there was no way to spin this into a heartwarming human interest article in *People*. This wasn't like some made-for-TV movie where the long-lost son comes home to live with the father and sister he never knew, and everyone rediscovers the true meaning of family in the process. As much as Taylor wanted to help me believe that things would end up okay, I knew better. This was one story that wouldn't have a happy ending.

I only stayed at Taylor's another fifteen minutes. No matter how bad I made my situation sound, she tried to get me to look on the bright side, to cheer me up. And I think that Taylor actually almost convinced herself that there *was* a bright side to all this, like maybe I'd discover I had a cool big brother. A big brother who just also happened to be a TV star.

Was I the only one who saw "disaster" written all over Reed's touching homecoming?

When I got home, my dad was in the kitchen cleaning up the remnants of his breakfast. Usually he'd be at the theater by now, but he'd spent the morning on the phone with my school making sure my brother's transcripts could be transferred, that everything was in place for the arrival of the prodigal son.

In the two hours I'd been gone, all the details of Reed's *visit* had been ironed out (on the walk home I'd decided to call his presence a "visit," in hopes that my word choice would hasten Reed's return to Los Angeles). Reed Vaughn was officially a member of Cabot Academy's senior class, and I was officially on the verge of a nervous breakdown. According to my dad, Mr. Whitney was thrilled with the idea of having Reed join the Cabot family, although I had a feeling my headmaster's enthusiasm was bolstered by the thought of Reed's alumni contributions and the fact that my dad conveniently left out Reed's impressive history in rehab.

"I hope you'll take the time to show Reed around school and help him feel at home," my dad told me as he washed out his coffee cup and placed it in the dish rack on the counter. "It's not always easy being the new kid." He actually sounded sympathetic.

"I seriously doubt Reed will need any help from me," I replied, my own voice containing no hint of sympathy or any other emotion indicating I empathized with Reed's situation. "It's not like every single person doesn't already know who he is."

"Still, it would probably make Reed's transition a little easier."

I shook my head. He couldn't be serious. "Why are you so worried about Reed? What about me?" I asked, my voice rising. "I'm the one whose life is being turned upside down without asking for it. I haven't done anything wrong, so why am I the one who has to bend over backward to make his time here any easier? Why isn't anyone trying to make it any easier for *me?*" I yelled.

My dad just stood there by the sink, watching me as he tried to figure out what to do next. That's one of the things about always being the rational, responsible daughter. When you actually have an outburst that doesn't quite fit with your normal operating procedure, parents don't quite know how to react.

Finally, he reached for the dish towel and wiped his hands before coming over to me. "You're not the only one whose life is affected by this news," he told me, the tone of his voice a mix of impatience and commiseration.

"Then why are you and mom acting like this is all a good thing?" I wanted to know. "Why do we have to open our arms and pretend we want him here?"

My dad's answer wasn't the complex explanation I was expecting, an analysis of Reed's unconventional upbringing and his need for acceptance by the father he never knew. Instead, my father told me, "Because we're his family."

"I'm not buying it."

"You're a very intelligent girl, Vanessa. I'd think you'd at least give Reed a chance to get to know you before you decide you want nothing to do with him," my dad continued, trying to appeal to my sense of reason. "Besides, you may discover you actually like him."

Like him? As far as I could tell, there were a billion reasons *not* to like Reed, and I'd never even talked to the guy. How could I even begin to like someone who was:

A) gorgeous, thereby making me, someone who until now was considered pretty decent looking, seem, at best, perfectly average, and, at worst, like the sibling who got beaten with the ugly stick;

B) paid huge bucks to roll around in the sand making out with equally gorgeous girls while I donned a hideous fluorescent orange apron, an equally hideous lime green baseball cap with an assortment of stuffed fruit dangling from the center in a makeshift pom-pom, and honed my smoothie-making skills for six bucks an hour;

C) a veteran of rehab, probably attended more 12-step programs than all the boy bands from the nineties combined, thought nothing of totaling a hundred-thousand-dollar sports car, and even managed to expose his pearly whites in his mug shots so that he looked like someone making a Dentyne commercial instead of a criminal about to begin two hundred hours of community service, while I followed the rules or never caused my parents a day of worry, and yet they wouldn't even let me spend one lousy summer in Europe, for God's sake.

No. I was sure that the only thing I'd discover upon meeting Reed Vaughn was that he's probably even more unbearable in real life.

I didn't bother telling my father this, of course, and instead went to the refrigerator for a bottle of water. We didn't drink tap water in our house. Not that Chicago's water system was bad, it's actually pretty good. It's just that my mother believed that paying more than a dollar a bottle for water claiming to dribble slowly from some Swedish iceberg was somehow better than the stuff that went through the scientifically engineered filtration plant stuck out in the middle of Lake Michigan. And the labels were pretty, she'd also explained.

"Where's mom?" I asked.

"In the guest room."

I didn't even have to ask what she was doing in there. In times of stress, my mother sought refuge in the one thing she had total confidence in—her ability to decorate.

I left my dad in the kitchen and made my way upstairs. Our house isn't big, but, still, in the city, having a house is a pretty nice thing. I'd say most of the kids in my school lived in condos or apartments or town houses. And most of them have brothers and sisters they need to share a bathroom with, or even a bedroom. But our place has three bedrooms so I pretty much don't have to share anything with anybody. Except when the guest room is occupied by some member of the traveling circus my parents call friends—actors stopping in for a few days on their way to L.A. from New York, artists trying to get a show at a local gallery, even chefs looking around Chicago for a new restaurant in which to flex their culinary muscle (that was Glenda's line). My mother's best friend, Glenda, had just come back from three years perfecting her pastry-making skills in Paris when she moved into the guest room for two months while she interviewed for a job. She moved out and ended up opening her own pastry shop, but it actually wasn't so bad having Glenda around, even though we did have to share a bathroom. She told me all about her travels around Europe, how she'd buy a Eurorail pass and just get off at some random stop and explore. That's when Taylor and I started talking about spending a summer over there. Unfortunately, even with Glenda's glowing recommendation that every young woman should experience Europe on her own, my parents weren't buying it. Yet they were buying the idea that Reed Vaughn would make an excellent addition to our family. Go figure.

I stepped over our sheepdog, Daisy, who was sleeping on the hall runner in her favorite spot where the sun came in and created a bright patch of light against the Oriental pattern. She let out a soft groan but otherwise didn't bother acknowledging my presence.

I stopped in the doorway of the guest room and silently watched my mother arrange green and yellow candles on the bedside table. If my mom had a motto it would be, When in doubt, decorate.

"What are you doing?" I asked, leaning against the doorframe.

My mom looked up and ran a hand across her forehead, as if exhausted by the energy required to artfully assemble a few stacks of wax. "I thought I'd feng shui your brother's room."

"I really wish you'd stop calling him my brother."

"I could do that, Vanessa, but it wouldn't change the fact that he is." My mother reached down and rearranged the display of candles, as if moving around the pillars gave her something to focus on while she talked about Reed. "Besides, I thought that this would be a good time to experiment with feng shui. I have a lot of clients who have expressed interest in it."

"Why did you move the bed?"

"I'm balancing the energy. Don't you feel the difference? Neither the feet nor the head should be pointed directly at the door of the room," she told me, probably reciting from some article in *Architectural Digest*. "I'm correcting the flow of chi."

I considered pointing out that just on the other side of the guest room's wall, my bed was directly aligned with my door, but then I decided not to. It would only encourage her and reinforce the idea that our house was filled with some sort of invisible energy. Besides, if tomorrow's arrival of my half brother couldn't be considered bad feng shui, I didn't know what would.

My mom was off and running about the principals driving her redecorating decisions, and somewhere between feng shui's four pillars, five elements, and eight aspirations, I started to realize, to truly realize, the close proximity of my bedroom to the room that would become Reed Vaughn's new sleeping quarters.

Standing in the doorway of the guest room—my *brother's* room—I had to admit for the first time that this wasn't just a bad dream. This was really happening. Reed was going to be sharing my bathroom, he'd be eating at our kitchen table and sitting in our family room watching our flat-screen TV (yes, although my parents didn't approve of TV, per se, it was another form of artistic expression, and as long as we were going to succumb to the programming whims of popular culture, we may as well do it with a state-of-the-art media center and surround sound).

I couldn't imagine what it would be like once Reed was really here, in my house, separated from my bedroom by a single wall. All I could picture was his character on *Wild Dunes*—an outsider who becomes a rebel in a rich seaside town. Or the out-of-control celebrity Taylor followed in the pages of her magazines. Neither sounded especially appealing. But as much as I couldn't imagine Reed, at least I knew who he was. He had no idea what to expect from his new sister, although he probably already figured I was boring. I mean, how could the life of a normal high school senior compare to his? There was no way Reed could think I'd compare to the girls he was used to—my teeth were nice and straight thanks to braces in eighth grade, but they weren't bleached to within an inch of being fluorescent under a black light. The idea of wearing a bikini didn't mortify me, but my stomach wasn't concave, my ribs didn't show, and my 32Bs weren't the work of some Beverly Hills surgeon. My expectations of my new sibling weren't high, but his had to be positively below low.

"Did your dad tell you that Pat called?" my mom asked.

I snapped to attention. "No."

"This morning while you were at Taylor's. Pat said that he'll be pretty busy all day, but he'll try to call you tonight."

I must have made a face, because my mom quickly corrected herself. "Oh, sorry, I meant *Patrick* said he'll try to call you tonight."

I appreciated her effort, but that wasn't why I'd made a face. It was true I'd reminded my parents and Taylor a hundred times that I hated it when they called Patrick Pat, but right now that seemed like the least of my problems.

"Did he say what time he'd call?"

She shook her head. "I had to call Marnie this morning to find out Reed's birthday," my mom went on, placing a bubbling fountain under a set of wind chimes in the corner of the room. "I didn't even know your brother's birthday, isn't that weird?" she asked.

Yeah, that's what's weird. Not the fact that my mother was coordinating artificial water elements for her husband's child. Or that she'd hung wind chimes in a spot where the only breeze available to jangle the hollow metal chimes would have to come from the air-conditioning duct.

"Doesn't it bother you?" I wondered out loud.

"Doesn't what bother me?" she repeated, arranging three turquoise pillows on the bed.

"The fact that dad had a kid with someone else," I told her. "Why am I the only one who seems to think this whole thing is out of control?"

"Look, obviously you can't ever prepare for something like this, but it's all in how you choose to look at it. Besides, there isn't anything we can do about it now, is there?"

I thought I detected an opening, like my mother was waiting for me to tell her what we could do about it.

I listened to make sure my dad wasn't coming upstairs, and then waited a minute before answering. "We could always tell Marnie that we don't want Reed to come here," I suggested, feeling for the first time like maybe my mom was on my side, like maybe she wasn't any happier about this than I was.

"Don't be ridiculous," she snapped, obviously not even willing to consider the possibility.

"You know what's ridiculous?" I snapped back. "The idea that we're supposed to be thrilled with the idea of a total stranger moving into our house."

My mom stopped fluffing the pillows and turned to me. I waited for her to tell me that I was acting like a spoiled brat or that I should just go to my room and calm down. Instead she said, "We told his mother that he was welcome to come live with us, and that's that."

His mother. The woman my father had an affair with.

"What's she like?" I asked.

"Marnie?" my mom asked, turning back to the pillows and not looking up. "I always liked her, actually, which is ironic if you think about it. You know, even back when Marnie was working with your father, you could tell there was something special about her. Whenever she walked onto the stage, it was as if everyone around her faded into the background."

"Was she nice?"

"Sure. Of course, once I left the theater I didn't see her much, and by the time your father and I were back together again she'd already left for Los Angeles, but from what I remember she was very nice. And beautiful," my mom added, stepping back and admiring her work. "Looks pretty good, doesn't it?"

Her changes were an improvement, but I failed to see how they were supposed to make our situation any better. "Are you doing the rest of the house?"

"I thought we'd wait and see how this works first." She ran her hands along the chimes and listened to them tinkle. "Can you feel the chi?"

I shrugged. "Feels the same to me."

My mom looked around as if double-checking to make sure she did everything right. "Maybe it takes a little while to kick in."

If there really was something to this feng shui stuff, I hoped not. With Reed arriving in less than two days, time was of the essence.

chapter five

That night as I tried to fall asleep, my feet and head directly facing my doorway in flagrant disregard of the chi supposedly filling our house, I waited for a call from the only person who could understand how I felt. The phone was resting on top of my chest, and even with my eyes closed I was aware of it rising and falling every time I inhaled and exhaled. Instead of lulling me to sleep, it only served as a reminder that, while I was waiting in the dark for him to call, Patrick was probably out partying with his new friends.

It wasn't supposed to feel like this. *I* wasn't supposed to feel like this. All those movies with girls who looked at their boyfriends all doe-eyed, the adoring hangers-on who sat by the phone waiting for it to ring, I hated them. I hated how the girls were always so desperate. Go out with your friends, I always wanted to yell at the screen. Get a life. Yet here I was, starring in my own pathetic little scene. I didn't want to be desperate, but that was exactly how I was feeling.

When Patrick and I started going out last year, I never thought about the fact that he'd graduate and go off to college while I'd still be here going through the motions of senior year. I never thought about what it would be like to say good-bye to him the night before he left, or how the sheets on my bed would still smell like his musk-scented Speed Stick deodorant, and my pillowcase like his kiwi shampoo, for days after he was gone. You know what's more pathetic than a girl laying in her bed with the phone on her chest while she waits for a phone call? Said girl actually smelling her pillowcase just so she can get a whiff of the guy she's hoping will call.

When we first started sleeping together, I actually worried that my mom would realize that my pillowcase smelled like Patrick. It never occurred to me that:

1. My mom doesn't change my sheets, our housekeeper Rosa does;
2. My mom wasn't going out of her way to sniff Patrick's hair like I was.

I knew she wouldn't freak out if she discovered we were having sex, but my parents were not so enlightened as to encourage their daughter to swing from the rafters while they were out attending gallery openings and experimental theater. They were still my parents, after all, and even if they knew it was within the realm of possibility, they weren't looking for play-by-play analysis.

Although my sheets still held the faint aroma of Patrick, I knew his sheets didn't smell like me at all. And the thought of his new bed, his new room, and his new friends wasn't just scary. It was downright petrifying. All I could think about was Taylor bringing up Courtney Maxwell and Brian Bonham. They'd gone out for two years and all it took was a few days away from each other to make a barbell-wielding tongue look appealing. And they'd both gone off to college at the same time, which, now that I thought about it, should have made it easier than having one of them sitting at home staring at the phone jack wondering if the spindly copper wires connecting to the cables outside were even working.

I glanced at the clock: 10:30. Eleven-thirty in Connecticut. What if Taylor was right, and at this very moment some chick with a piece of stainless steel through her tongue was lying under Patrick's sheets, making them smell like patchouli and clove cigarettes?

I had to get a grip. Four days and I was already crazy. Nine months of this would kill me. To take my mind off Patrick's new, hopefully empty bed, and take up time until he called, I decided to rehearse our conversation in my head. Here's how it went:

PATRICK: Vanessa, I'm so sorry I haven't talked to you. I've been in the library every day studying. All I think about is organic chemistry and you. Mostly you.

ME: That's okay. (See how breezy I sound? This is not the response of someone laying in her bed freaking out.)

PATRICK: I wish you were here with me right now. I miss you.

ME: Me, too. (Ah, still the picture of cool.)

PATRICK: I have the picture you gave me next to my bed. Think you could get that made into wallet size, or maybe even a poster for my wall? My roommate thinks you're hot, too. (Okay, so maybe I'm reaching here.)

When the phone finally rang at midnight, here's what really happened:

PATRICK: Hey, what's up? Hope I'm not calling too late.

ME: Where have you been? (So much for not sounding desperate.)

PATRICK: I'm sorry I haven't talked to you. They're keeping us pretty busy.

ME: I miss you so much. (Wasn't he supposed to say that first?)

PATRICK: Me, too.

ME: Really? (Make that desperate *and* needy, not a winning combination. Not exactly someone you'd want a poster of on your wall.)

PATRICK: Of course, really.

ME: (Feeling a little better at this point.) So tell me about Yale.

I snuggled down under my sheets, pulled them around my neck, closed my eyes, and pretended Patrick was next to me as he talked all about orientation, his roommates, and everything he'd been doing to get ready for the first day of classes.

Laying there listening to Patrick, everything was fine. Everything was just like I'd planned, just like it was supposed to be. Patrick's voice sounded so close, so familiar, that he could have been in his family's apartment on Lake Shore Drive instead of halfway across the country. And that's why it wasn't until we hung up twenty minutes later that I realized I'd actually forgotten to tell him about Reed.

The next morning the countdown to Reed's arrival began in earnest. I awoke to an unfamiliar odor wafting upstairs from the kitchen. There was no way I could have slept through the assault on my sense of smell. It was horrible. Which could mean only one thing. My mother was cooking. I had two choices. I could either pull my comforter over my head and try to block out what would probably turn into a black cloud of smoke in a few minutes (my mom tends to burns things more often than not), or I could go downstairs and try to put a stop to it before the smoke alarms went off, in which case my mom would be yelling and shouting for my dad to get the step ladder and pull the damned First Alerts off the walls.

I threw off my covers and headed downstairs.

"What are you doing?" I asked, walking into the kitchen to find an apron tied around my mother's waist. An apron! This was a woman who wouldn't know how to turn on her Cuisinart if it wasn't for the step-by-step instructions my dad wrote out for her on a laminated Post-it note. And here she was standing at the kitchen counter doing her best Betty Crocker imitation.

She took her eyes off the wire whisk in her hands just long enough to smile at me. "Making a gluten-free carob cake for Reed," she answered.

Even more disgusting than the fact that my mother was trying to win Reed over with her baking was the congealed substance she was currently beating in a mixing bowl.

"You're baking?" As far as I knew, every single cake that's ever entered this house has come in a yellow cardboard cake box and had Glenda's bakery logo on it.

"I thought I'd give it a shot. Here, taste this."

Before I could object, she shoved a spoonful of batter in my mouth.

"What do you think?"

I attempted to form words, even though my tongue now had a layer of what felt like rubber cement on it. "I think you should give Glenda a call."

At two o'clock, Glenda rang our bell and saved us all from certain indigestion, or, if history was any indication, an afternoon hunched over the toilet.

"So, Vanessa, how's it feel to be a little sister?" she asked, sitting down on a stool at the breakfast bar while we waited for my mom to come downstairs.

I rolled my eyes. "Ugh."

Glenda laughed. "That good, huh?"

"Have you mentioned anything to my mom about this summer?"

Glenda nodded, but didn't look very optimistic. We'd decided that she would try to grease the wheels with my parents, but so far she wasn't having much luck. "I keep trying, but she's not going for it. I'm not giving up yet, though, so don't you."

I held up crossed fingers. "What'd you bring?" I asked, lifting the lid off the cake box.

"Flourless chocolate cake iced with chocolate ganache."

"Mmm, my favorite." I reached into the box to swipe some ganache, but I wasn't quick enough. Glenda swatted my hand away.

"You're not the only one. I guess Marnie told your mom that it's Reed's favorite, too."

"Really?"

Glenda shrugged. "That's what she told me."

So my mom had talked to Glenda about her conversation with Reed's mother. I thought about my mother's off-handed comment about Marnie: *She was very nice. And beautiful.* Maybe that's why my mother was channeling Martha Stewart in the kitchen this morning. Maybe she wasn't as immune to the idea of her husband having a child with a beautiful actress as she pretended.

"Did you ever meet Marnie?" I asked, thinking maybe Glenda could fill me in on Reed's mom and help me make some sense of all this.

But Glenda just shook her head. "I was in culinary school at the time. Why?"

"In seventeen years my mother has never once attempted to make me a cake," I pointed out. "I was wondering if Marnie had something to do with the carob mix clogging our kitchen sink."

Glenda hesitated before answering. "It might."

"Do you think it's normal for everyone to act like they're so happy about Reed?"

"Your parents aren't normal, Vanessa."

"I've noticed."

Glenda frowned. "That's not what I meant." She had a tendency to do that, to seem like she was on my side, like about the Europe thing, and then turn around and switch sides. "They're trying to make the best of an awkward situation."

"So you don't think they're as gung ho as they seem?"

"I think they're excited to meet Reed, but they're probably just hoping for the best. They don't know what to expect any more than you do, but at least they're willing to give it a chance. Perhaps if they thought you felt the same way, they'd be more open to your ideas."

She raised her eyebrows at me and I knew what Glenda was implying. Perhaps they'd change their minds about Europe.

"Maybe," I agreed. If giving Reed a chance would increase my chances of spending next summer in Europe with Taylor, it was something I had to consider. After all, any guy who loved flourless chocolate cake couldn't be all that bad. Could he?

chapter six

Sunday at two o'clock my parents and I were standing in the baggage claim area of United Airlines. The scuffed linoleum floor and fluorescent lights weren't exactly the red carpet Reed was used to. Not to mention the fact that instead of taking a private plane, Reed was flying commercial, just like us regular folk. I liked the idea of him slumming it, and figured it somehow put us on equal footing.

We couldn't meet Reed at his gate without a boarding pass, so we settled for waiting at the bottom of the escalator in the baggage area. We stood in the same spot usually clustered with limo drivers holding up cardboard signs with their passenger's name on it. The irony wasn't lost on me. Especially not when my mother handed me one end of a rolled-up, long thin sheet of paper.

"Here, hold this," my mom instructed.

As she moved away from me, the roll unwound until we were standing about six feet apart, the paper banner stretched taut between us.

"What do you think?" she asked, looking down at the white craft paper.

WELCOME HOME, REED! the banner read in large aqua blue and emerald green block letters.

"I think you're still quite the artist," my dad complimented, and then got a pensive look on his face. "Hey, Ceil, I was thinking Reed might like to visit the theater and see how we do things. Do you think he might consider a role in the spring production?"

My mom smoothed out a few creases in the paper. "I think that's a great idea, but you should probably give him some time to get settled in and used to us before you mention anything."

"Maybe you're right. We don't want to overwhelm him too soon."

We didn't want to overwhelm him? Did my father not see the six-foot-long banner strung out across the landing of the escalator?

"I am not holding this," I told them, thinking that a banner with his name on it wasn't exactly the best way to keep Reed's arrival under wraps. Actually I was surprised there weren't any covert photographers lingering around us, snapping photos of Reed's new family. I guess Marnie had done a better job of keeping quiet about Reed's arrival than I expected.

"But we want him to know he's welcome," my mom explained.

"I don't care." I let go of my side of the sign and it rolled back up toward my mother like a window shade.

My parents stood there watching me, once again unsure of how to respond.

"Your mother worked hard on this," my dad told me, walking over to her and taking hold of the limp paper.

"I'm not holding that banner," I insisted, holding my ground. "I didn't sign up to be a member of the Reed Vaughn welcoming committee."

I could almost see my mother mentally sorting through all the chapters of the parenting books at home on our bookshelf as she searched for advice on how to handle a daughter who decides to be a pain in the ass in the very public arrivals area of one of the busiest airports in the world.

I guess she finally gave up looking for the politically correct way to handle the situation, because the next thing she said was, "Oh, yes you are."

At this point passengers from an arriving plane were coming down the escalator, and there was no way in hell I was going to hold that sign and look like a complete idiot.

I crossed my hands over my chest, and then quickly moved them to my side when I realized my pose looked exactly like the cover of the book *Girls Will Be Girls: Surviving the Teenage Years*.

Now the escalator was practically full with arriving passengers and my dad had had enough. "You're holding the sign and that's that!" he told me, and stuffed the crumpled paper in my hand.

I reluctantly held the banner, but let my end droop down along the dirty floor so there'd be no mistaking how I felt about it.

I figured Reed would be the first one from his flight down the escalator—the star of *Wild Dunes* would obviously be flying first class, which would mean he'd be leading the stream of passengers as they exited the plane. But at 2:25, three other groups of arriving passengers descended toward us, and Reed still hadn't appeared.

And that's when I started feeling hopeful. Maybe Reed had decided to stay in L.A. and enter some sort of halfway house for wayward stars. Or maybe Marnie had decided that sending Reed to stay with my family wasn't the optimal environment for someone seeking normalcy.

But just when I'd convinced myself that Reed wasn't coming, that I could breathe a big sigh of relief, I heard it. The people calling his name and bursts of white lights followed by the sound of camera lenses snapping in succession.

"There he is." My mom pointed to the top of the escalator, where my brother, Reed Vaughn, stepped into view.

I'd hoped that maybe Reed's good looks were the result of talented makeup artists and lighting effects, but in real life he looked exactly like he did on *Wild Dunes*. The same sandy blond hair falling across his eyes, the same cheekbones that Taylor once described as "the best damn cheekbones in the business." Reed's black T-shirt was just tight enough to play up pecs he probably earned with the help of a personal trainer, and his camouflage cargo pants just baggy enough to hang from his slim hips. Despite the sick feeling growing in my stomach, I couldn't take my eyes off him. And I wasn't the only one.

When Reed stepped onto the escalator and started his descent toward us, everyone within view stopped what they were doing and watched. Of course, Reed didn't even seem to notice and just stared out over our heads looking bored. Make that *completely* bored. And completely gorgeous.

Oh. My. God. I grabbed my stomach and hoped I wasn't going to be sick again.

Is it wrong to think your brother is gorgeous? And if so, is it also inappropriate to throw up on the down escalator in the baggage claim area of United Airlines?

When Reed reached us, my father stepped forward and held his hand out, waiting for his son to take it. "Reed."

I wondered how many times my dad rehearsed this moment in his head over the past three days, going over it in his mind like he was staging one of his productions—Reed would arrive stage left, lit by fluorescent bulbs overhead, my father hovering downstage in the red glow of the Avis sign.

Reed reached for my dad's hand, and when their palms pressed together my father pulled his son into him for a full-on bear hug.

I held my breath and dreaded what would happen next, while I waited for my father to tell Reed to call him Dad. But instead my father turned to us.

"This is my wife, Celia, and your sister, Vanessa," my dad continued once they'd pulled apart.

We all watched Reed and waited for a hello or some other greeting befitting this joyous family reunion. Instead he turned and looked over his shoulder at the snapping cameras. "Can we get out of here? They're all over me."

Reed and my dad led the way out of the terminal toward short-term parking. All Reed had was a carry-on, which I thought was a good sign that he wasn't planning to stay very long. And then I heard him tell my dad that Marnie had shipped everything else. Apparently that's what Reed called his mom—Marnie. No wonder he had issues. But at least that meant he wouldn't be calling my father Dad.

"How'd all those photographers get to meet him at the gate if we couldn't?" I whispered to my mom as the glass sliding doors closed behind us and we made our way across the crosswalk.

"I guess they bought tickets," she whispered back.

Sure, what's a few hundred dollars for a plane ticket when it could snag you pictures of Reed Vaughn.

Plane ticket to nowhere: $250. Camera with telephoto lens: $500. Picture of Reed Vaughn rolling his eyes in disgust as he's introduced to his new family: Priceless.

He'd probably make it onto the covers of *Us Weekly, People,* and the *Star* by week's end.

"Do you think he liked our sign?" my mom asked.

I thought it was obvious Reed didn't like anything about us.

There was no stretch limo waiting for Reed in the parking lot, no driver standing at attention to hold open the passenger door and point out the refreshments available in the minibar. There was just my parents' silver Volvo wagon.

Reed climbed into the backseat next to me, his legs a mere twelve inches from my own, our bodies separated by the armrest he'd immediately pulled down from the back of the seat.

Reed wasted no time staking out a spot on the armrest with his tanned forearm, and I let him have it. For the next nine months I was going to have to pick my battles, and who got the armrest wasn't one I felt like fighting right now.

Except for the *tick-tocking* of the blinker and the sound track from *The Phantom of the Opera* drifting out of the speakers, the car was silent on the ride home. Occasionally my parents attempted to make benign conversation, but Reed felt no apparent compulsion to register interest in what they said. His responses ran the range of "uh-huh" and "sure", to his most enthusiastic "I guess so," while he stared out of the window and watched the scenery go by. And he looked completely unimpressed.

I stared out my own window and tried to see what Reed saw. The strip malls lining the off-ramps, the rusted metal train tracks separating the inbound and outbound lanes of the highway, the dirty yellow cabs passing beside us. It was hard not to realize how boring it all must look to him. How flat Chicago would seem compared to the mountains surrounding L.A. How paltry Lake Michigan would look next to the Pacific Ocean. How our three-bedroom row house couldn't compare to Marnie's gated house in the Hollywood Hills.

Jesus. No wonder he didn't look thrilled. Now even I was getting depressed the closer we got to the city.

After a grueling forty-minute ride, my dad pulled the car down the ally behind our house and parked in our garage. Our one-car garage. I watched Reed attempt not to slam the back door into the garage wall as he opened it, saw him feel his way along the narrow space, and could swear he muttered something under his breath. Marnie probably had several garages—heated, of course, and with those black rubber floors so you didn't see the oil drips—to house Reed's collection of sport cars (now minus one Frappuccino-covered Porsche).

We all walked single file across our meager backyard until we reached the back door.

"Are you ready?" my mom asked Reed, her hand poised on the door handle like a hostess from *The Price Is Right*. "Reed, welcome to your new home."

My mom threw open the door for the grand unveiling of our house, but before Reed could step through the doorway, I pushed past him and raced to answer the ringing phone. Anything to avoid watching my parents fawn over my new brother.

"Is he there?" Taylor asked when I picked up, her voice barely a whisper, as if we were involved in some covert operation.

I glanced toward the front door, where my mother was now explaining the significance of the sculpture mounted to the foyer wall, and Reed was eyeing the doorknob like he was planning his escape. "Yeah. He's here."

"Well, what's he like?" Taylor wanted to know. "Tell me everything," she insisted, probably gripping a pencil and her reporter's notebook on the other end of the line.

I watched my mother giving Reed a tour of the first floor, and could swear I caught him glance at his watch like he was wondering how much longer he'd have to put up with us.

"He's what I expected," I told Taylor. "He's *exactly* what I expected."

chapter seven

As soon as my mom finished the grand tour of our home, Reed went upstairs to his room and closed the door. And that was the last we saw of him for the next two hours.

"He's kinda rude, isn't he?" I finally pointed out, just in case nobody else noticed. In fact, I think I was the only one who noticed. My mom and dad seemed to be the self-appointed leaders of the Reed Vaughn Admiration Society

"He's just getting used to us," my dad assured me. "You'd be the same way."

I took a page from my brother's playbook and rolled my eyes. There was no way my parents would ever let me get away with acting like Reed.

"Besides, he's probably just tired," my mom added, giving Reed the benefit of the doubt.

"Yeah, I'm sure all the pampering Reed received in first class was just exhausting. I mean, how could he be expected to rest with all those flight attendants falling over themselves to meet his every need?"

"Why don't you go check on him, make sure he's finding everything okay," my dad suggested.

"I'm sure he's adjusting fine. After all, he has all that good chi up there with him."

My mom let my comment slide. "Go up there and ask if he needs anything until his stuff arrives from California."

"What he needs is a personality," I answered.

My dad glared at me and pointed a very long, very stern finger toward the stairway. "Get up there," he ordered, and I knew I didn't have a choice.

I finally gave in, turned around, and slowly climbed the stairs one at a time, all the while thinking, I sure as hell better get a trip to Europe out of this.

I knocked lightly on Reed's bedroom door, and, when he didn't answer, pushed it slowly open, not knowing what to expect. What if he was practicing tantric yoga in the nude or some other weird actor's ritual?

"Are you finding everything okay?" I asked.

Reed was sitting on the bed, his fingers tapping out a message on a Sidekick. "I haven't really been looking for anything," he answered, without looking up.

I stood there in the doorway of his room and waited for something—an invitation to come in, or maybe a request to leave. "My parents asked me to see if you wanted some company."

Reed paused just long enough to wave me in, and then went back to tapping. "Not really, but if you want . . ." he let the sentence trail off without finishing.

If you want what? If you want to sit down, you're welcome? If you want to leave, that's fine? If you want to share your innermost feelings and bond like a real brother and sister are supposed to, come on in and we'll bare our souls?

I decided he meant I should come in, but figured all that bonding and baring of souls stuff was out of the question.

Once I stepped inside, I avoided his bed and pulled out the desk chair instead. Reed still didn't take his eyes off his Sidekick, so I just sat there and waited for him to finish up. And that's when I looked down at my bare feet and noticed the fuchsia polish peeling off the tips of my big toes. I've accepted the fact that I'm a nail biter and will never have perfectly polished fingers like all the advertisements say I should. But, just for the record, I am meticulous about my toenails. I hate chipped polish and go to great lengths to make sure my toes are pedi-ready at all times. But Patrick just left a few days ago, and so I figured I could go a couple of days before re-polishing for the first day of school. I tried to hide my toes under the chair and sat there hoping Reed wouldn't notice.

Of course, with my toes curled up and tucked under the chair, my knees stuck out. And that's when I noticed yet another minor problem where the smooth skin of my shins stopped and prickly blond razor stubble sprouted along my kneecaps. Ditto the whole speech about my toenails, but substitute shaving my legs. I should have remembered to shave my knees in the shower this morning, but I always ended up cutting myself and inevitably walking around with bloody Kleenex on my kneecaps until the bleeding stopped long enough to stick on a Band-Aid. Needless to say, I couldn't cover my knees with my hands without exposing the tips of my well-bitten fingertips, so Reed was going to have to either discover that his sister's razor stopped short of her knees or the state of disarray her fingernails were in at the moment.

I decided to take my chances, and laid the palms of my hands over my stubbly knees.

Unlike our ride from the airport, when I avoided looking at him at all costs, now I had the opportunity to inspect my new brother without worrying that he'd think I was some psycho stalker. Reed actually wasn't as much of a pretty boy as his posters made him out to be. Sure, he was good looking—okay, great looking—but he almost looked like he could be just a hot guy in my class. He wasn't *that* much better looking than Patrick, and he even seemed a few inches shorter. Reed's hair was longer than Patrick's, curling up haphazardly where the tips reached the collar of his T-shirt. And the stubble blanketing his chin and cheeks wasn't nearly as dark as when Patrick didn't shave for a couple of days.

I continued watching Reed as he pecked out messages on the miniscule keyboard, and noticed the rough skin around his unevenly bitten nails (yes, I'd been expecting a professional manicure). Maybe we'd both inherited the nail-biting gene. Wouldn't that figure? We couldn't share the genes that gave Reed the cheekbones, the sun-streaked highlights, and the perfect ass, but the same nasty nail-biting habit, *that* we get to share.

I noticed there was a two-inch-long scar just below his left elbow, and I smiled at the thin jagged line of raised skin that interrupted an otherwise smooth, tanned arm. A scar. A permanent flaw. So Reed Vaughn wasn't perfect after all.

I watched Reed and couldn't help wondering who he was messaging. Was it someone back in L.A.? A friend? Did he even have regular friends, or were they all costars and personalities? That was what Taylor liked to call them, "personalities," as if the rest of us poor slobs were sorely lacking in the personality department just because we weren't media magnets.

Finally, Reed hit the SEND button and looked up at me. "So, what do you want?"

Did this guy just not get when someone was being nice? Was Hollywood *that* unfriendly? "I don't want anything."

Reed didn't reply. Instead he sat there silently, like he was testing me to see how long I could take it. I was determined not to fold under the pressure, but after about fifty-three seconds he had his answer. I stood up and left Reed's room, but not before noticing that the water in the corner fountain had evaporated. So much for good chi. The Carlisle family's had just run out.

Taylor called three more times that afternoon to see how I was surviving. So when the phone rang a fourth time, I figured it had to be her. But I was wrong.

"Nothing new to report," I breathed into the phone, not even bothering to say hello.

"Vanessa?" an unfamiliar voice asked.

"Yes?"

"Hi, it's so nice to talk to you. This is Marnie Vaughn, Reed's mother."

Reed's mother. The clarification wasn't necessary. I was talking to Marnie Vaughn. The same woman who accepted an Academy Award. The same woman who hosted fund-raisers that were featured in the back of Taylor's *InStyle* magazines. The very woman who had designers lined up outside her door for the privilege of providing custom-made gowns.

"I was just calling to make sure Reed made it there all right," Marnie continued. I pictured her lounging beside a kidney-shaped pool sipping a martini while a staff of uniformed help fanned her. I just couldn't decide if she was wearing a caftan and large dark sunglasses or a string bikini.

"Yeah, Reed's here," I told her.

"Oh, good. Can you put your dad on? I'd like to talk with him for a minute."

So this was how it was going to be. It was like some grand experiment in bicoastal child rearing.

I told Marnie to hold on and went to get my dad for the first of what promised to be many calls to figure out how to work this out.

I think the trendy term for what they were attempting was "co-parenting." But the more appropriate term was "impossible."

Our first family dinner promised to be an interesting experience. I figured Reed had to be a vegan or adhered to a strict macrobiotic diet, or something equally freakish (in which case he'd fit in just fine at our dinner table). I waited for him to point out that he only eats things without lips or plants fertilized with the feces of virgin goats. Instead, he reached for a skewer of free-range chicken and red peppers and prepared to dig in to my dad's barbecue creation.

"I'm sorry," I apologized, making a point of placing my napkin on my lap while Reed chewed his dinner. "Would it take too long for you to wait until we're all seated?"

Reed stopped midbite and smiled at me, exposing his half-chewed peppers.

"That's okay, we're all here now," my mom offered, as she and my dad slid into their seats at the table.

Reed watched me as he wiped the barbecue sauce from the corners of his mouth like a proper gentleman in some old movie. I didn't think it was a coincidence that he chose to use his middle fingers.

"So how was your flight?" my mom asked for what seemed like the fifth time. I knew what was coming and prepared to mouth the words along with my brother.

Reed gave her the same answer he'd given her the other times, before biting into his chicken. "Fine."

My brother wasn't the talkative type—at least not without a script. Not that he could get a word in edgewise with my mother going on and on about how excited *we* were to have him here. How *we* couldn't wait to get to know him better. How *we* were thrilled with the idea of having an addition to our family.

"Reed's going to love Cabot Academy, right, Vanessa?" my dad prompted, and waited for me to agree.

Actually, I was pretty sure Reed would hate it. "I guess."

"Vanessa's very involved at Cabot. She's head of the student council this year, and she's editor of the yearbook, on Model UN, a member of Scholastic Bowl—last year Cabot was runner-up for the state championships, right, Vanessa?"

"What, no chess club?" Reed mumbled into his fork.

My mom puzzled over this question for a minute. "I think they only have chess club in the lower school, don't they, Vanessa?"

I nodded and silently wished that Reed would choke on his chicken. "Actually, maybe the lower school would be more your speed, Reed," I said, turning to him. "They still use flash cards."

"Cabot also has a wonderful theater program," my mom added. I could practically see her mentally redecorating the master bath. There was no other way she could possibly be staying so calm.

Reed turned to me. "I suppose you do that, too."

"No, actually, I don't," I told him.

"Why not?"

"I don't get up on stage."

"But you have to stand at a podium and talk for your other things, don't you?" he challenged, continuing this inane line of questioning as if he had something to prove.

My parents watched us, probably thrilled that their children were getting along so well.

"Let's just say I don't get up on stage and pretend to be something I'm not."

"Vanessa didn't inherit our family's passion for the arts," my dad explained.

Our family? How did I become the odd one out? I had seventeen years on Reed, so why was I being made to sound like the outsider?

"Speaking of the arts." My dad diverted his eyes from my mom and I knew he was about to do something she'd told him not to. "I'm directing this spring. It's a small production called *Running Out*?" My dad made it sound like a question, as if he was waiting to see if Reed had heard of it. "I thought maybe you'd like to see if there's a role that interests you." He waited for Reed to answer, but my brother just continued eating his shish kebab.

Finally Reed looked up long enough to see the three of us staring at him. "Were you talking to me?"

My dad nodded. "Well, yeah. Who else would I be talking to?"

Right. He only had a daughter sitting next to him, someone who'd made him proud the past seventeen years by being the model of responsibility and achievement. Of course he would be talking to the derelict sitting across the table from me.

I saw my mom crack a nervous smile. "Why don't we give Reed some time to get adjusted to his new home before he starts thinking about working again."

"It wouldn't be work, it's a great learning experience," my dad insisted, not willing to give up so easily. What was so important about having Reed in his play? He'd never tried this hard to get me to do anything. Of course, I never put up much of a fight.

"I'm not really a theater guy, but I'll think about it," Reed conceded, tossing my dad a bone.

"No pressure." My mom smiled. "We're just happy to have you in the family, Reed."

"As long as we're on the topic of our family, there's something we wanted to talk with you both about." My dad put down his fork and looked serious all of a sudden. "After talking this over with Marnie, we decided that there should be some house rules."

Ah, here it was. They were finally going to lay down the law for Reed. And I couldn't wait.

"We're going to start with a curfew," my dad began, before rattling off a list that included household responsibilities (laundry, cleaning up, walking Daisy), school work (homework completed after dinner, no skipping classes), friends (no going out on school nights, parents have to meet all new friends they don't know).

Reed just watched them, his eyes growing wider with every new demand. He was probably regretting ever screwing up. This was worse than some halfway house. This was more like juvenile detention.

My mom let my dad finish and then waited for one of us to say something. "So, do you think you can both live with those?"

"What do you mean, we can *both* live with?" I repeated. "You mean I have to follow these new rules, too?"

"Well, yes, Vanessa. It's only fair."

"But I've never had a curfew."

"Me, neither," Reed chimed in, and I glared at him.

"But I haven't done anything wrong," I added. "Besides, I thought you trusted me until I gave you a reason not to."

"We do," my mom reiterated.

"Then what you're saying doesn't make sense."

"It doesn't have to make sense. We're your parents."

Huh? "So, you know I shouldn't have to be subject to the new rules, but because my screw-up brother is here, you're doing it to prove a point?"

"You both have chores to do, and that's that," my dad concluded.

"Chores?" I repeated. "What is this, *Leave It to Beaver*?"

I thought I caught Reed laughing at me, his trademark grin and dimples on full show.

"What do you do when you aren't looking so pretty?" I snapped at him.

"Probably what you do every day," he shot back.

"Reed, that's enough," my dad scolded, finally stepping in to referee.

"We just thought it would be easier if you both had the same set of rules to follow." My mom stood up and started clearing her plate. "Flourless chocolate cake, anyone? Marnie told me it was your favorite, Reed."

My brother seemed to resign himself to the idea of a curfew pretty quickly, and went back to finishing off his chicken kebab. Maybe he was hoping to earn some time off for good behavior. Or maybe he just planned on ignoring the rules altogether. "Sure, I'll have a piece."

"Vanessa?" My mom waited for me to answer.

I wanted to say no. I wanted to tell her that I had no interest in partaking in Reed's favorite dessert. But I was already feeling shitty enough as it was. There was no reason to let Reed ruin dessert for me, too.

"Yeah, I'll have a piece," I told her, hoping that it was true that there was nothing so bad that a little chocolate couldn't make it better. Still, that was putting a lot of pressure on one little piece of cake. This was no ordinarily bad situation. "Actually, I'll have two."

• • •

After dessert, I went upstairs to my room for the rest of the night. When it was finally dark out, and I figured Patrick would be back in his room, I reached for the phone and dialed his cellphone. But instead of getting my boyfriend, I got his voice mail. I didn't necessarily expect Patrick to pick up, but at the very least I wanted to hear his familiar voice tell me that I should leave a message and he'd get back to me. Instead, I was greeted with an unfamiliar, "It's Pat, you know what to do."

He'd changed his message. And his name.

You know what to do? No, I didn't know what to do. Not anymore. This year was supposed to be uneventful. I'd already filled out the milestones in my day planner—SATs, a weekend trip to New Haven for an interview and to see Patrick, college application deadlines, April's acceptance letters. Now what? I didn't know what to expect when school started in two days, no less what was going to happen for the next nine months.

"Hi, it's me," I spoke softly into the phone's mouthpiece and tried to make my voice sound normal, which wasn't easy considering the lump growing in my throat. "Everything around here is completely different since you left," I started, but then realized there was no way I could tell Patrick about Reed by leaving a message on his voice mail. Or let him know how much I wished he'd call. Or that I felt like crying.

So if I couldn't be honest, there was only one other choice. Lie.

"I hope you're having fun." Lie number one. I really hoped Patrick was miserable without me.

"Everything's fine." Lie number two.

"Give me a call," I reminded him, but before I could tell Patrick I loved him, a beep cut me off and I was left holding a phone that had gone dead.

chapter eight

$\mathcal{I}$ don't usually get dressed before going downstairs to get myself some orange juice and breakfast. And I don't usually brush my teeth, either. Ever have orange juice after just brushing with some Tartar Control Crest? Not exactly pleasant. But since Reed's arrival two days ago, I not only changed out of my boxers and T-shirt, brushed my teeth, plucked my eyebrows, combed my hair, and rolled on some deodorant before heading downstairs, I actually stood in front of my closet and spent at least twenty minutes picking out an outfit to wear. To breakfast. In my own house. And the entire time I stood there, my stomach growling as it told me to hurry the hell up, I kept thinking about Reed sitting across the kitchen table from me, sizing me up. For someone used to waking up next to anorexic, spray-on-tanned, artificially highlighted costars (at least according to Taylor), I wasn't looking forward to the early morning comparison.

But this morning when I got downstairs the only person sitting at the kitchen table was my mother.

"It's his first day at Cabot, aren't you going to wait for Reed?"

my mom asked as I walked into the kitchen and headed to the fridge for some juice.

In the two days since he'd arrived, Reed and I have had exactly one conversation. And it went something like this:

REED: So who's Pat? Your boyfriend?
ME: It's Patrick.
REED: That's what I said.
ME: No, you said Pat. His name is Patrick.
REED: Whatever. (He shrugs and walks out of the kitchen and back to his room.)

I could have just said, yes, he's my boyfriend. But Pat wasn't exactly the most masculine name and I hated it when anyone called him that. Pat the Bunny, Pat Boone, Pat the androgynous character on the E! reruns of *Saturday Night Live* that Taylor made me watch. Not a stellar group. Last year I even asked Patrick if he'd thought of maybe shortening his name to Rick. I could live with Rick. Shit, people could call him P. Diddy for all I cared, just not Pat. I hated it. No girl ever dreamed of falling in love with a guy named Pat.

So, no. I hadn't been planning on waiting for Reed. "Do you want me to?" I asked, pouring myself a glass of OJ.

My mom nodded. "I think it would be nice. He doesn't know where he's going."

For some reason I liked the idea of Reed trying to navigate Chicago's transit system on his own. I pictured him sitting next to some crazy old man who talked nonstop about the conspiracy to coverup the fact that Elvis was alive and well and living in a double-wide in Arkansas.

"Fine." I glanced at my watch. "I'll wait, but if he's not down here in five minutes I'm leaving. He's not going to make me late."

"That's reasonable," she agreed. "I'll go upstairs and see what's keeping him."

I'm sure when people pictured a private school called Cabot Academy they envisioned boys in navy blue blazers and girls in knee socks and those kilts with bulky gold pins keeping them from flapping open. But Cabot's dress code isn't so much about what we *have* to wear as it is about what we *can't* wear. No jeans, sneakers, T-shirts, or miniskirts.

I figured my parents had told Reed about this sartorial requirement ahead of time. But when he walked into the kitchen wearing all the prohibited clothing except the miniskirt, I realized it was going to be up to me to set him straight.

"You're going to have to change," I pointed out. "Don't you have something else you can wear?"

Reed shrugged and poured himself a cup of coffee. "I do, but why should I?"

"Because you're not allowed to wear those to school."

Reed took a sip of his coffee before responding. "In addition to being on some academic all-star league, are you also a member of the dress code police squad?"

"I don't make the rules," I told him.

"You just enforce them, right?" Reed shook his head and turned to leave, but not before adding, "You know, my on-set tutor doesn't give a shit what I wear."

"Was that the same on-set tutor who produced such brilliant scholastic minds as the cast of *Saved by the Bell* and Macaulay Culkin?" I asked, and waited for Reed's answer.

But I guess his witty repertoire was used up for the day, because instead of tossing out a good comeback he left the kitchen. I stood there and waited for my brother while he went upstairs and changed for his first day of school.

"Good-bye, we're leaving," I called out to my mom, and started for the front door. But when I reached the foyer I already knew something was different. Instead of seeing a relatively empty sidewalk and some bushes out in front of our house, I saw people. Lots of them. And they weren't moving.

"What the hell," I muttered, and peered through the front window to see what was going on.

"What's up?" asked Reed, coming up behind me.

"There must be an accident or something," I told him, and moved aside so he could see.

As soon as Reed poked his face in front of the window I heard the screams; shrill, high-pitched shrieks that didn't stop until he pulled back and faced me.

"I'm the accident," he explained.

I thought it was pretty brave of him to finally admit what I'd been thinking. "I couldn't agree more," I answered.

"What I meant was, those people out there are waiting for me."

This time I poked my head in front of the window, which, of course, didn't elicit a single shriek or shout. In fact, I thought I heard a few disappointed moans. "They're all girls," I commented, pointing out the obvious. There had to be at least forty of them packed onto the sidewalk. "Is this what it's going to be like every morning? Your flunkies camped out on our sidewalk?" I glanced at the clock on the mantel in the living room. "And, more importantly, how are we going to get to the bus stop without getting mobbed?"

All of a sudden I pictured myself being trapped in my house for the next nine months, thanks to Reed. This situation required some intelligent thinking, and I knew I was the only one capable of that. I quickly devised an alternate plan.

"Come on, we can go out the back door and down the alley," I told him, and turned back toward the kitchen.

Reed grabbed my arm as I passed by. "Hold on. All they want is a few pictures. Let me go out there and sign their bras or whatever it is they want me to do, and they'll be on their way."

I frowned. "Wouldn't it just be easier to go out the back?"

"I've done this before," he assured me.

"Of course you have," I agreed, giving the former rehab resident an unimpressed nod. "And look how well it's turned out for you."

Reed reached for the door handle. "Wait here."

As soon as Reed stepped outside he was enveloped in a swarm of teenage girls. Some pushed black felt tip pens at him and screamed their names, while others shunned subtlety and lunged for him, attempting to plant kisses on his cheek. Before I could even see where they came from, photographers seemed to come out of nowhere, snapping pictures of the frenzy taking place outside my front door while Reed worked the crowd.

For the life of me, I couldn't understand what all those dopey girls saw in my brother. Besides his looks. And his fame. And his success. Okay, I got it, I just didn't like it. I couldn't even watch. It was pathetic, the way they all cried out his name and grabbed for Reed like just touching his skin was some meaningful experience that would warrant acting like an idiot on someone's front lawn. What would make any guy worth that? And what kind of girl would act like that?

As I turned away from the window, a bolt of panic shot through me, a fear so sudden and unexpected I could feel the blood rushing to my fingertips, making them tingle.

I knew exactly what kind of girl would act like that. Someone who was obsessed with Reed Vaughn. Someone who thought TV stars were more special than the rest of us. Someone who'd seen every episode of *Wild Dunes*. Twice. No, three times.

Someone like Taylor.

I peered through the window again, afraid of what I'd see, afraid I'd spot my best friend among the pack of morons currently flocking around my brother.

Of course, she wasn't there. Taylor would never do that to me. Sure, she pretty much worshiped Reed. But, I was way more important to her than some actor. I was her best friend.

As I stood there taking in the scene outside my living room window, I tried to see what Reed's crowd of fans saw. The floppy hair that kept falling across his eyes so he'd have to squint a little as he signed his name to yet another *Wild Dunes* T-shirt. The perfect smile. The confidence that seemed to ooze from every pore as he laughed at some stupid compliment a girl gave him. He was hot. He was a celebrity. And, unfortunately, he was my brother.

I guess Reed knew what he was talking about, because one by one the girls backed off, satisfied with their brush with fame. Soon there was just a small crowd, and they lingered until Reed waved good-bye and came back into the house.

"Now let's go out the back door and down the alley," he told me, walking toward the kitchen.

"But why? They're almost all gone."

Reed just smiled. "Trust me."

It was already 7:45 and if we didn't get going we were definitely going to be late.

"Is everything okay?" my mom asked, coming down the stairs. "I thought I heard something."

"Yeah, everything's fine," Reed assured her as he tucked his shirt in and ran a hand through his rumpled hair. "We were just leaving."

I followed Reed out the back door and down the walk until we reached the alley, where he looked both ways before stepping out into the narrow single-lane street that ran between the garages.

"There's no traffic," I told him, wondering what he was looking for. "Come on."

I heard the noise before I saw where it was coming from. It was the same rapid snapping that accompanied Reed's descent on the escalator at the airport. When I turned to find the source I spotted a photographer hunched down beside a garbage can a few yards away.

"Just keep walking," Reed instructed, his voice grim. This was an entirely different guy than the fan-savvy Reed I'd witnessed on the sidewalk out front. A scowl lined his face, but Reed didn't attempt to avoid the photographer or block his view. In fact, he almost seemed to pause just long enough to give the guy with the zoom lens a perfect shot.

"Are you coming?" I called back to Reed, listening as the shutter finally stopped snapping.

"Yeah, I'm coming," he answered, and looked over his shoulder at the photographer one more time before following me toward the street.

"Do you always take the bus?" Reed dug his hands in his pants pockets and stared down the street looking for the 156 bus.

"Yeah."

"Ever think of taking a cab?"

A cab? I doubted my parents would spring for a cab, even if the prodigal son had returned home. Public transportation would have to be good enough. "It's a lot cheaper to just use a student bus pass. Besides," I added. "It's only a ten-minute ride."

Even though Taylor lives six blocks away, she takes a different bus. She'd called me six times yesterday (twice to see if I wanted her to come over and help me get ready for school, twice to see if I wanted her to swing by and say hi, once to ask if I wanted to meet her at Starbucks—she probably figured my parents would make me bring Reed along—and once to ask if I was ever planning to introduce her to my brother). If I was really a good friend I probably would have surprised her with a visit from Reed when my mom made me take him to Walgreens to get school supplies. She'd kill me if she knew we were a mere elevator ride away. I was almost surprised she hadn't decided to walk the six blocks just to see Reed standing at the bus stop this morning. Then again, Taylor's twelve-year-old sister, Sadie, also goes to Cabot, and Taylor was in charge of making sure she got there in one piece.

Once we made it out of the alley, Reed and I got to the bus stop without any more interruptions, and now we were the only students among a small crowd of businesspeople waiting on the corner. I wasn't surprised that nobody at the bus stop recognized Reed. The other riders weren't exactly in *Wild Dunes*'s demographics. Still, I couldn't help wondering if Reed was questioning his star power. There wasn't a single sideways glance or lingering stare that would indicate someone recalled Reed's face from a magazine or TV show. He was just another kid on his way to school. On his way to *my* school.

"I bet your mom is going to miss you," I commented. With Reed about to enter my territory, to share my school and maybe even a few of my classes, I decided to make nice. Keep your friends close, your enemies closer—isn't that the saying? Reed might not exactly fall into the enemy category, but I wasn't taking any chances. He was certainly no friend.

"You think?" Reed's shoe collided with a stone and sent it skidding across the sidewalk and off the curb.

He may be a TV star, but Reed Vaughn wasn't much of a conversationalist.

"Are you glad it's your senior year?"

Reed shrugged. One of his favorite responses.

I continued on, unfazed by the fact that he seemed more interested in staring at the ground than listening to what I had to say. "Cabot's not so bad," I offered in a tone that could only be described as cheerfully optimistic. Look at me, reassuring Reed Vaughn.

"You like school, don't you?" he asked, looking up at me.

"Well, yeah."

"I can tell." He turned his attention back to the fascinating sidewalk beneath his feet.

"What's that mean?"

"Nothing."

Nothing always means something. "You meant something by it, so tell me."

"It's just that you're standing there with your backpack filled with new notebooks and fluorescent highlighters, all set for the first day of school. You probably have a protractor tucked inside a pencil case somewhere."

"I do not." I almost pointed out that you didn't need a protractor for AP calculus, but I didn't want to get into it with him. "I know it doesn't compare to some on-set tutor, but Cabot isn't so bad, you know."

Reed finally stopped moving and turned to me. "Look, you don't have to pretend to be all sisterly with me. I don't want to be here any more than you want me here. Probably less."

I doubted it.

Reed stood there waiting for me to come up with a reply. But what was I supposed to say to that? That I *did* want him here? That I'd always wanted a big brother? That sharing my senior year with the star of *Wild Dunes* was my idea of a good time? I'd have to be one hell of an actress myself to pull that off.

Still, he didn't have to be such an asshole about it. I may not want him here, but my parents were bending over backward to make Reed feel welcome.

"Fine, but the least you can do is act a little nicer to my parents. They're actually looking forward to having you here."

Reed fixed his eyes on me, the same gray-green eyes that Taylor had compared to a mossy riverbed at sunrise. As if, after growing up in Chicago her whole life, she'd ever actually seen a mossy riverbed. Or, after staying up to watch late-night reruns of *E! True Hollywood Story* she'd ever crawled out of bed early enough to catch a sunrise.

I stared back at Reed, refusing to let him beat me at his game of chicken. Did I mention I hate to lose?

We stood there like that for a minute, neither of us saying anything, but a street-side stare down wasn't as easy as I thought it would be. Reed never blinked. He must have learned the fine art of staring in some acting class.

"What's your problem?" I demanded, giving in. And hating it.

"I don't have a problem." Reed tipped his head to the side and smirked. "I'm just trying to figure you out."

"There's nothing to figure."

"I think there is."

"Is not."

The bus rumbled up beside us and opened its doors, letting out a burst of air-conditioning onto the sidewalk. Reed dramatically bowed to me and gestured with his hand. "After you."

If I didn't know better, I would have stuck my tongue out at him. If I didn't know better, I would have thought we were acting just like a brother and sister.

Reed didn't sit with me. Instead he walked to the back of the bus and picked a seat by himself. And that was fine with me. I'd wasted enough time thinking about Reed Vaughn. It was my senior year and I wasn't going to let him overshadow the next nine months. There were SATs and college applications and class ranks to worry about. In the grand scheme of things, we all had a lot more to keep us busy than the latest addition to Cabot's graduating class.

Cabot is small, both in the size of the campus (if you can even call it a campus—we have two three-story buildings, a courtyard, and an athletic field), and the size of its student body. Which means that in order to be in the top five percent of my class I have to be either number one or two, and we've already determined that the number one slot is taken and not likely to be relinquished anytime soon unless Benji Coburn decided to forego his pursuit of Stanford and move directly into a cabin in the woods.

It wasn't like I was expecting senior year to be some amazing experience. If anything, I was prepared for it to pretty much be a letdown. Everyone would be looking ahead to college and getting sick of seeing the same faces we've been looking at for the last three years.

But, as much as I didn't have any major expectations, I didn't need any distractions this year, either. And that's exactly what Reed would be—an unwelcome distraction. I couldn't let the boy from L.A. get to me. I couldn't let him intimidate me. And I sure as hell wouldn't let him win.

Every stop the bus made, every intersection we passed through, took us closer to my realm, and farther from Reed's. And by the time the bus stopped in front of Cabot's main building, I was starting to think that maybe my senior year could go exactly as planned. After all, Cabot was *my* school, with *my* friends who liked me and teachers who loved me (I was second in my class, right?). Why should I feel threatened by Reed Vaughn? If his anti-social behavior was any indication, he wasn't going to be spending a whole lot of time at school, and that was fine with me. It was the way I wanted it. He'd probably just end up being a nonissue.

In fact, I decided, maybe no one would even care about Reed Vaughn.

Of course, as soon as I walked through the double doors to begin my last year at Cabot Academy, I realized I was just kidding myself.

In fact, I was dead wrong.

chapter nine

Right away I knew something wasn't right. Usually everyone would be hanging out by their new lockers, catching up after the summer. But there had to be at least thirty students lingering in the school's lobby. The lingering was odd enough. The fact that they were all girls meant they were waiting for a reason.

"I'm so sorry. I swear I only mentioned Reed's name in passing," Taylor gushed, running to my side as soon as she spotted me. "And then all of a sudden everyone knew."

When I said Cabot was small, I wasn't kidding. News traveled fast.

"So where is he?" she asked, craning her neck to look behind me.

"He's coming."

And that's when Reed decided to enter. It was as if his arrival had been choreographed. The double doors swung open, and there he stood, the late-summer sun seeming to create a glow around all six feet of him. I swear there was a collective gasp from the crowd that assembled.

"Come on, ladies, get to your homeroom," Mr. Whitney's voice boomed above the silence. "Mr. Vaughn, will you please follow me. Vanessa, if you could come by my office after homeroom, I'd like to talk to you, too."

The girls grudgingly dispersed and made their way down the hallway, their jaws still hanging open at the sign of the *Wild Dunes* star. Reed followed Mr. Whitney to his office, not even bothering to say good-bye to me. And I was left alone, standing next to the glass-encased list of last year's honor roll, my name scrolled in calligraphy at the top of the list.

So much for nobody caring about Reed. If that was the reaction he got from stepping one foot into our school, I could just imagine what it would be like when he was walking our halls every day.

How was I going to explain Reed to the entire student body? There'd be all sorts of questions, nothing terribly original, of course, so I'd be repeating the same answers over and over again. It would almost be easier if Mr. Whitney just made an announcement over the loudspeaker—*Vanessa Carlisle just found out she has a brother. And oh, yes, he also happens to be the one and only Reed Vaughn* (cheers and whistles follow, of course—maybe some of Reed's most ardent fans would even stand up and start a wave).

"Hey, Vanessa," a deep voice called down the hall as I made my way to homeroom. I turned and spotted Mike Simpson and Charlie Eubanks coming toward me. Mike and Charlie have been in my class since freshman year, like ninety-nine percent of the senior class.

"Hey," I called back, and waited for them to catch up to me so we could head to homeroom together.

"What's up with you bringing Reed Vaughn to school?" Mike asked, making it sound like I'd decided to display my new brother for show-and-tell.

"Yeah, as if it isn't hard enough to get laid around here, now we have to compete with a TV star?" Charlie stopped in front of the door to homeroom but didn't make a move to open it. "Just make sure you tell your brother that he won't be getting any special treatment around here."

Mike reached for the doorknob and we walked into homeroom. I almost felt sorry for them both. They were right. No girl in her right mind would settle for some twelfth grade Cabot guy when Reed Vaughn was around.

Like I said, the classes at Cabot are small. When I attended Lincoln High School for all of three days, I was one of about five hundred students in my class. Cabot doesn't even have five hundred students in the entire school. Our senior class only had three homerooms, but luckily Taylor was in mine. Thankfully, Reed wasn't.

Sitting there in Ms. Bosworth's science classroom were the usual suspects. Even though you'd think a school as small as Cabot would have one big happy senior class, it wasn't like that. In fact, our annual homecoming weekend was barely a homecoming at all and more like an excuse to mail out solicitations for donations. Even reunions had to include about ten classes to get enough people to fill the University Club dining room.

By senior year we'd all been together for four years and drifted in and out of friendships until we found the ones who fit. It was Cabot's version of natural selection. For the most part I'd already decided who bored me to tears (Charlotte Watson), who was most likely to end up eagerly applying to Arizona State University because it offered both a sorority system *and* the chance to lay by the pool between classes (Ali Parker, Posey Lindstrom, and Ashlee Goldfarb), who was a total bitch with a stick up her ass for no reason at all (the Susans—Sue Plunkett and Sue Stalworth), and who was nice but sort of on the fringe for one reason or another (like Lauren Martin, who, between our sophomore and junior years decided to become an authority on 1980s hair metal bands and now wears a black Guns N' Roses T-shirt under her dress code-compliant button-downs).

So when I sat down in homeroom, I wasn't expecting much. One quick look around produced all the same old faces. And then I noticed one new one.

"Who's that?" I whispered to Taylor while Ms. Bosworth went down the homeroom list, taking attendance.

"Sarah Middleton?" Ms. Bosworth called out before Taylor could answer, and the girl raised her hand.

So her name was Sarah Middleton. But who the hell was that?

After the bell rang and everyone headed off to their first class, I headed to Mr. Whitney's office. I dreaded going there, thinking Reed would still be with him when I arrived. But when I got there, I was relieved to see that the seat across from our headmaster's desk was empty.

Mr. Whitney waved me through the door and asked me to sit down. "Ready for a new year?" he asked, sifting through some papers on his desk.

As ready as I'll ever be, I thought, but just nodded instead.

"Head of the student council, probably another Scholastic Bowl, college applications." He paused and looked up at me. "You have a lot on your plate this year. Are you okay with that?"

I waited for him to mention Reed, but he seemed to be waiting for me to answer.

"I think I can handle it," I told Mr. Whitney, and he nodded. He seemed to understand. He got it. I hadn't been called into the headmaster's office to talk about Reed, I'd been asked to sit here because, unlike my parents and the hordes of fans gathered in front of my house this morning, Mr. Whitney realized how much this was going to change everything for me. Mr. Whitney realized everything wasn't about Reed. Finally!

All of a sudden I appreciated my balding, slightly overweight headmaster like never before. He cared about Vanessa Carlisle, not just Reed's sister.

"It's nice of you to ask," I continued, wondering why I'd never bonded like this with Mr. Whitney before. I was actually feeling a little better. "But I think I'll be okay."

Mr. Whitney waved away my assurance with a thick, stubby hand. "Of course you will. But what I really wanted to talk about was this afternoon's assembly."

I sat forward on my chair, waiting to hear what Mr. Whitney had to say. It was customary for the student council president to say a few words at the assembly. I'd completely forgotten, what with Reed's arrival and all, but I was sure I could come up with something between now and two o'clock.

"What about the assembly?" I asked. Maybe he wanted to give me some pointers.

Mr. Whitney slid his glasses down his nose and looked at me over the faux-tortoise shell rims. "I was thinking at this year's assembly we'd skip the welcome from the student council president."

I slid back in the hard wooden chair and tried not to look disappointed. Even though I hadn't prepared a speech, I also wasn't prepared to have my speech nixed. "Is that all?" I asked. "You don't want me to participate in the assembly?"

"I still want you to participate," he reassured me, and despite myself, I did feel reassured. "But instead of your speech I'd like you to introduce Reed and call him up on stage for a little first-day-of-school welcome. We're all so thrilled to have him at Cabot!"

Fucking Reed. There was just no escaping him.

If I was wondering who the hell Sarah Middleton was, I found out who in my first class. Honors foreign policy and politics. There she was, in the first row. In the seat that I usually picked.

And again in honors physics, only this time she sat near the door.

When I saw her sitting by the window in my AP calculus class, I figured it was time to say something.

"I'm Vanessa," I told her, and sat down at the desk to her right.

"Hi. I'm Sarah."

And that's when I learned her story. She'd just moved from Boston because her mom, a philosophy professor, was teaching for a year at Northwestern University. She was supposed to be her senior class president so it was hard to leave, but at least she'd be back in less than a year, when hopefully she'd be going to Harvard.

I glanced over in Benji's direction to see if he'd heard Sarah's answer. That had to freak him out. I had to admit, it certainly freaked me out. But Benji was too busy punching functions into his new HP 33s calculator.

Shit. The calculator. With everything going on at home, I'd forgotten to buy the required calculator. I'd be screwed for the first class. Of course, I had a ton of good excuses to forget it—my new brother being the main one—but I still couldn't believe it. You can't exactly do calculus on your fingers.

Of course, Sarah's required calculator was sitting right there on the corner of her desk all ready to go. Was it wrong to begrudge someone an HP 33s calculator?

"Harvard?" I repeated.

"Yeah. My mom went there."

Legacy. Hated her.

"And my brother's a junior there, too. He's on the crew team," she added, rubbing salt in the wound. My brother was a spoiled star who probably demanded only green M&Ms in his trailer, and Sarah Middleton's was at Harvard rowing along the Charles River. What next? Her dad was the dean? "What about you? Where are you applying?"

"Yale, and a few others."

"My brother almost went there." Sarah gave me a reassuring smile. "Yale is good, too."

Too? How come she made it sound like I was aspiring to attend Miss Wanda's School of Cosmetology.

The teacher walked in and we turned our attention to the front of the classroom where Ms. Cocheran was already giving us directions.

Even though I nodded my head and passed the course syllabus around the classroom like nothing out of the ordinary was going on, I kept thinking that Sarah Middleton was no set-tutored star, but she was really going to put a crimp in my plans. Because not only was she likely to threaten my number two spot, she was most likely gunning for number one.

Still, Benji sat in the row behind us, not saying a word. There were only six of us in the class, and needless to say, Reed wasn't one of them. In fact, by fourth period I'd had over three Reed-free hours, but I knew it was coming to an end. The entire upper school ate together, which meant that every freshman, sophomore, junior, and senior would be packed into the cafeteria waiting for this year's version of Cabot meatloaf surprise.

But even though I hadn't run into Reed, his presence hung over my head and followed me around like a piece of toilet paper stuck to my shoe—I didn't see it, but everyone around me was whispering about it.

As I expected, every girl I passed in the hall stopped me and asked some insipid question like, What's Reed eat for breakfast. Or, does he sleep in the nude? That little ditty came from Posey Lindstrom, who I don't think quite comprehended the fact that she was asking me if I'd seen my brother naked. I attempted to explain that we shared the same father, therefore half of the same chromosomes, which would make seeing Reed unclothed about as appealing as seeing Benji Coburn in the buff, but she still didn't seem to get it. Which was why her next question was, boxers or briefs?

Thanks for nothing, seemed to be the typical reaction from the guys in my class (no underclassman would have the balls to complain to a senior, even if the girls they thought they might hook up with this year were now drooling over one of *People* magazine's most beautiful people).

But even despite all the comments about Reed, school already felt different from last year. It wasn't just the fact that the halls buzzed with Reed sightings or that, after three years of waiting, I was finally a senior. It was something else. I couldn't quite put my finger on it, but all morning long, everything was a little off.

It wasn't until lunchtime that I realized what was so different. Why everything was so familiar and yet felt so unfamiliar at the same time. Patrick. Or, more accurately, the absence of Patrick.

When I was a junior, I'd always see Patrick between classes and knew his schedule by heart—when he'd be passing from comparative literature to calculus, when he'd stop by his locker to drop off his books, when I could look out the window during French class and see him outside kicking a soccer ball around for gym. It was like he provided a reference point for my day. And now that he wasn't around, it was different.

It wasn't like we ever walked down the halls holding hands or anything. And he never kissed me at school, even if no one was around. Nobody did that at Cabot. It would just be too weird. Still, after lunch when all the guys would hang around the courtyard talking about the Cubs or the Bulls, and Taylor and I would be sitting nearby doing our own thing, Patrick and I would always walk inside together when the bell rang. Every day, like clockwork, I knew what to expect. There he'd be, lingering by the door, waiting for me. And it felt nice.

When Patrick and I started going out, I think everyone at Cabot was a little surprised. Partly it's because Cabot is so small that by the time a guy is a senior, he's pretty much been with everyone he ever wanted to be with. Cabot wasn't big enough to just hook up at a party with someone and then blend into the crowd back in school on Monday morning. Chances were, the girl who provided a needed diversion on Saturday night would be sitting next to you in homeroom, or at the very least, in your class by second period.

For the most part, it seemed like people hooked up with guys and girls from other schools. We all came from different parts of the city, and since Cabot only started with sixth grade, we'd all been somewhere else before coming here. That's one of the reasons Taylor wasn't exactly thrilled when I started going out with Patrick—rumor had it that Patrick had gotten some girl from Lincoln High pregnant the summer before. I asked him about it once, and he said it wasn't true, but Taylor still didn't trust him.

Taylor's never had a boyfriend at Cabot. Not because there wasn't a guy who was interested—for a while Ricky Holden was hot for her but she kept blowing him off—she just wasn't interested. How could anyone compete with Orlando Bloom, Hayden Christensen, or, I can't believe I'm even saying this, Reed Vaughn. No pricey gifts, exotic getaways, or trendy restaurants. So it wasn't like Taylor was jealous of Patrick, she just never thought he was good enough for her best friend.

But when Patrick was here at Cabot , I knew what to expect. We had our routine. Our usual way of doing things. Now it was like starting over in a foreign place. Not only was Patrick gone, but my *brother* was sitting two tables away eating lunch by himself.

"Do you think we should go sit with him?" Taylor asked as we carried our trays to a table near the windows.

Apparently, even though every girl in school was talking *about* him, nobody had actually mustered the courage to talk *to* him.

"I don't want to. Do you?" I asked, testing her.

"No," she answered, passing with flying colors. "He just looks lonely."

I glanced over at Reed, and he was looking anything but lonely. Bored, yes. Self-absorbed, definitely. Grossed out by his plate of meat loaf, absolutely. But lonely? Never.

"He's not lonely. Look." I pointed in Reed's direction. "The new girl, Sarah, just joined him."

And she had. One Sarah Middleton, future Harvard freshman, had placed her lunch tray on the table across from my brother. A future Ivy Leaguer and a guy who probably thought the crimson H on Sarah's notebook stood for Hollywood. I almost wished I was close enough to hear their conversation.

"So what are you going to say about Reed at the assembly?" Taylor asked, cutting the crust off her peanut butter and jelly sandwich. She swore off meat after she learned Natalie Portman was a vegetarian. I remember when we were studying India our freshman year and I'd mentioned to the class that Gandhi was a vegetarian, and Taylor couldn't have cared less. But Natalie's announcement had a much bigger impact than some small Indian guy fasting for world peace.

I shook my head and wished the whole thing would just go away. "I have no idea."

"You really don't like him, do you?"

There were so many things I didn't like about him. I figured I'd sum it up for her in three concise words. "Reed Vaughn sucks."

"So you're telling me that if you found out you had a brother and it was just some guy from Iowa you'd be fine with it?" Taylor asked in the probing voice she usually reserves for when she has her investigative reporter hat on.

I shrugged. "Sure. Why not?"

Taylor knew I was full of shit. She was actually pretty good at getting down to the bottom of things, and I should have known better than to underestimate her. "Oh, please."

"Okay, it wouldn't be fine with me, but it would sure be a hell of a lot easier to deal with," I said.

What I didn't tell Taylor was why it would be easier. Because it was stupid. I knew it was. Still, it didn't change the fact that with Reed here I was constantly reminded of how average I was. Me. Someone who was used to being good at whatever she tried (except anything requiring extraordinary eye-hand coordination, but I could live with that). Someone who never doubted herself or where she stood in the grand scheme of things. But with Reed around it seemed like that's all I did. Reed was a celebrity. He was special. A TV star who got attention everywhere he went. And what had he done to earn it? Pout at a camera and look tortured by the citizens of *Wild Dunes*? Here I'd thought hard work and good grades would get me what I wanted—all Reed had to do was take his shirt off. Reed had raised the bar. With him around, I was just another high school senior—a high school senior who might even be on the verge of losing her class rank to some new girl from Boston.

And there was something else. Until four days ago, when I told her that Reed was my brother, Taylor had loved him. Okay, so I knew she didn't really *love* him, but she was certainly fascinated by him. Bordering on obsessed. It was hard to believe she could just turn those feelings off so easily, and a part of me was afraid that, once Taylor realized the guy on the pages of *People* was actually close enough to date, I'd lose my best friend to my enemy. Now *that* would make a great made-for-TV movie.

I knew we'd have to address it sooner or later. And now was as good a time as any.

"There's something I wanted to talk to you about," I told Taylor. "I just haven't known how to bring it up."

"What? Just say it." She took a bite of her sandwich.

"Please don't sleep with my brother." There. I'd said it.

Taylor stopped chewing her peanut butter and jelly sandwich and just sat there, her cheeks full of sandwich, staring at me.

"It's just that I know how, for some bizarre reason I don't quite get, you used to think he was amazing and all that. But I just couldn't handle it if you made a move for Reed."

"I would never do that!" Taylor blurted out, sending bits of peanut butter and jelly flying. "My God, he's your brother!"

"He's also Reed Vaughn," I reminded her.

"You can't stand him," she added.

"But he's still Reed Vaughn."

"I see where you're going with this," Taylor conceded, realizing she couldn't deny the fact that Reed had consumed an inordinate amount of her time up until now. She wiped her mouth before continuing. "Look, he *was* Reed Vaughn. Now he's your brother. And I'd never, ever even think of doing anything like that."

I couldn't help smiling. "Thanks."

"Boy, the sacrifices we make for our friends," Taylor joked, and then gave me a nudge. "But if Orlando Bloom transfers to Cabot, he's mine, got it?"

I smiled. "Got it."

"Reed Vaughn," a voice suddenly shouted across the cafeteria. Every eye in the room looked toward the entrance, where a small Japanese man was holding up a brown paper bag while reading off a slip of paper. "I have an order for a Reed Vaughn . . ."

Reed raised his hand and flagged the guy over. The entire upper school of Cabot Academy, including a few stunned teachers, watched as my brother handed the delivery man a credit card, took the bag, and proceeded to lay out the contents of three white Styrofoam containers on the lunch table.

"He ordered sushi?" I asked no one in particular.

Taylor just shrugged and went back to her sandwich. "It's his favorite. Probably California rolls and tuna sashimi."

Figures. Cabot meat loaf wasn't good enough for Reed. What next? Would he request special seating in the classrooms, preferably a La-Z-Boy cordoned off by red velvet ropes?

"Hey, Vanessa." Susan Number One put her tray down next to Taylor's and I knew Susan Number Two wouldn't be far behind. "I thought you'd be sitting with your brother."

"He's doing fine by himself," I assured her, and waited for Susan Number Two to arrive, which she did about three seconds later.

"I know. Did you just see that?" Susan Number Two nodded across the room, where Reed was wielding a pair of chopsticks. "So how are things going with you? It must be great having Reed around. I always wanted a brother."

I looked over at Susan Number One, who was smiling at me like we'd been best friends for years. They were both so obvious. Susan Number One and I hadn't sat at the same lunch table since freshman year, and Susan Number Two and I never ate together before, unless we were separated by a bunch of people.

I should probably attempt to differentiate the Susans here, but, quite honestly, it's hardly worth it. Number One is tall Susan, the other shorter. One has long brown hair she likes to twist around her finger when she's thinking (which isn't often), and Two has short brown hair that tends to look all wiry if she lets it grow out beyond her ears. Last year there was some talk of Number One, the taller Susan, getting some modeling work. She's got to be close to six foot tall, so I could see how someone would think it was possible. I never really bought the idea of Susan Number One being a model, so when we found out that her modeling assignment was actually for her mom's Mary Kay makeover party, I felt a little better.

Susan Number One and I were actually friends years ago, at Sharingham. We were in the same sixth grade class, but when she left the next year for Cabot, we didn't stay in touch. When I arrived at Cabot my freshman year, I was sort of expecting us to become friends again. But it was apparent pretty early on that we had nothing in common anymore. Susan Number One isn't the brightest bulb around, and she gives off this holier-than-thou vibe that makes you think she's in the process of coming to some sort of judgment about you. Which she is. She struck me as the kind of person who'd marry her college sweetheart, move to the suburbs, and pop out one kid after another until her days as a Mary Kay makeover model were just a distant memory she brought up at her kids' playgroup. Needless to say, none of those things were on my future to-do list.

So once I met Taylor, Susan Number One and I kind of went our separate ways. The whole experience taught me that friendships have as much to do with timing as they do with anything else. I guess that's the way life is, and that's definitely how it is at Cabot.

I glanced across the cafeteria at Reed and his lunch buddy. They actually seemed to be carrying on a conversation that consisted of more than one-syllable words. Reed had even offered Sarah Middleton a California roll. Great. Sarah liked Reed and she liked him. So my best friend wasn't going to sleep with Reed, but a Harvard-bound Sarah Middleton probably would.

As I watched the two of them talk, part of me almost felt bad for her. Sarah's timing couldn't have been worse. I wouldn't want to show up at a new school for my senior year. But even if one part of me felt bad for her, another part wouldn't let me. I had nothing against Sarah Middleton, she seemed nice enough. But why'd she pick Reed? Why'd she have to be a Harvard legacy? And why was I feeling like she was going to be an even bigger challenge for me than my new brother?

"I sat with your brother at lunch," Sarah told me when we met up again later that day in our senior seminar in women's fiction.

"You know who he is, right?" Taylor asked, taking a seat behind me.

"Yeah, I heard. But we don't have a TV at home, so I haven't really seen the show."

Taylor's eyes bugged out. "You're kidding, right?"

Sarah folded over the cover of her notebook and exposed a fresh piece of paper. "No." She shook her head. "My mom doesn't believe in TV."

That was enough for Taylor. To not believe in God, that was fine. But not believing in TV? Sarah's mother was obviously going to hell.

• • •

At two o'clock the upper and lower schools of Cabot Academy gathered in the auditorium for the first-day-of-school assembly. As always, the senior class was seated in the front row, but this year there was a noticeable difference: a distinct dividing point created by my brother. All the guys were on one side, as if protesting Reed's presence, and all the girls were on the other, gravitating toward him as if he was a magnet and they were incapable of resisting his pull.

"Vanessa, you sit here." Mr. Whitney pointed to the first seat beside the aisle. "And Reed, you sit here." He directed my brother to the seat next to me before taking the stage for his annual welcome address.

I couldn't even look at Reed, who I figured was sitting there smugly preparing for his moment in the spotlight. Instead, I leaned forward and looked down the row of seats until I spotted Taylor. She saw me and gave me an encouraging smile. *Good luck,* she mouthed, and shot me a thumbs-up.

Luck. If the past few days were any indication, my luck had obviously run out. I was about to step onto the stage in front of almost three hundred students, and it wasn't because I was the head of the student council. It wasn't because I had a high GPA or because I busted my ass to do everything just the way people expected me to. No. It was because my brother played a troublemaker on *Wild Dunes.*

My thoughts were interrupted by thunderous clapping, and when I looked up I saw Mr. Whitney staring in my direction, obviously waiting for me to join him on the stage.

"Break a leg," I heard Reed mumble, and barely resisted the urge to give him the finger.

I slowly made my way up the stairs and crossed the polished

wood floor of the stage until I came to the microphone. In a few seconds the entire audience would realize that I hadn't prepared anything to say about my brother. They'd also realize that I pretty much knew nothing about the guy who was living in my house, the person I was supposed to share some genetics with, and who was currently seated in front of me waiting to be praised for his acting achievements and told how glad everyone at Cabot was to be graced by his presence.

Only he wasn't going to get what he came for.

"Normally this is when the head of the student council talks about her plans for the year," I started, speaking slowly as I formed my words and waited for the lingering chatter to die down. "Normally this is when I'd tell you about the student council's efforts to give back to the community, when I'd share some ideas of how Cabot could make this the best year yet for its students." I stopped talking and looked around the auditorium at the faces watching me. No one was talking now. "But why mention canned food drives or collecting winter coats for the homeless—we have a TV star to talk about!" I swallowed hard and continued. "There's no need to discuss community service initiatives when Reed's community service is part of his plea-bargain agreement. Why bring up Cabot's annual fund-raiser when we can talk about Reed Vaughn's cunning display of acting ability? His uncanny ability to pout on cue and channel the demeanor of a screwed-up drifter who stumbles into the fictional, stage set town of *Wild Dunes*?" I looked up to gauge the audience's reaction, and was encouraged. Everyone was listening intently. All eyes were on me, and they seemed to get it. I think they finally got it! I charged on. "Why should I outline my plan to expand opportunities for inter-school social events when I can talk about how Reed looks with his shirt off? And, why even begin to address adding some new after-school programs when I can remind everyone that Reed was nominated for best on-screen kiss at last year's MTV Movie Awards?" I glanced at Taylor and silently thanked her for giving me that little piece of useless Reed trivia. "So, without further ado, I'd like to introduce someone who, until a few days ago, I thought was just another insipid TV actor, and who, now, is someone I could describe with a whole new set of adjectives—my brother, Reed Vaughn."

The auditorium filled up with applause and, for the first time all day, I felt like I had my school back. All of Cabot was cheering for me. In fact, they were now giving me a standing ovation. Or . . . at least the girls were.

Wait a minute.

I scanned the auditorium, row by row, and saw that nobody was watching me as they clapped and cheered. Nobody was smiling at me or giving me a sign that they had any idea what I'd just said. Instead, everyone was watching Reed stand up and walk toward me.

And, as all irony was lost on the crowd I thought I'd had in the palm of my hand, my brother took the stage.

chapter ten

"So how'd it go?" my mom asked, meeting me at the front door.

"Just dandy." I threw my backpack onto the hall bench and started for the kitchen. "There's nothing I like better than getting up on stage in front of the entire school to introduce my illegitimate brother." I thought that pretty much summed it up. There was no reason to regale my mother with stories of how Reed mania had infiltrated the halls of Cabot Academy. How, at the end of the day, I went to meet Reed by the front door and could barely make my way through the throngs of girls hanging around the school's entrance.

Of course, the only girl with enough courage to actually say anything to Reed was Sarah Middleton.

"See you later, Reed. 'Bye, Vanessa," she said to us as we passed her on our way to the bus stop.

Reed waved and flashed her one of the smiles I'd assumed he usually reserved for on-camera close-ups. "Later, Sarah."

It figured. The only friend my brother made the entire day was the same person who threatened to screw up my class ranking.

"He's not illegitimate, Vanessa," my mom corrected me, and looked embarrassed. "Don't say that."

"Fine, how about my *illiterate* brother? And not only did I get to introduce my brother to the entire school during our assembly, I got to watch as he received a standing ovation for having dimples."

"Come on, it couldn't have been that bad," my mom assured me.

"Really? He ordered sushi for lunch. Delivered. While the rest of us were eating meat loaf and sandwiches on stale bread, Reed was catering to his delicate palate and demonstrating his adept knowledge of Japanese cuisine."

"It was only the first day," my mom reminded me, as if that was any consolation.

I turned and headed for the kitchen.

"Where is Reed?" my mom called after me.

"He's coming," I assured her, lest she think I left Reed to fend for himself.

She waited on the front steps until she saw my brother slinking down the sidewalk toward our house, and then followed me into the kitchen.

"I'm going over to Taylor's for a bit, okay?" I told her.

My mom started to say something, but I held my hand up and stopped her. "And before you can even say it, no, I'm not bringing Reed with me."

I couldn't do anything about Reed being my brother, but I didn't have to bring him to Taylor's house with me. I'd done enough sharing for one day.

"Hi, Vanessa." Taylor's little sister answered the door and let me in.

"Hey, Sadie."

Sadie didn't inherit Taylor's love of all things celebrity. Every time I came over, Sadie was immersed in some worn hardcover book she'd checked out from the library with her own card. She reminded me a lot of me when I was her age. In fact, I doubt she'd even know who Reed Vaughn was if Taylor hadn't erected a personal shrine in her bedroom.

"I saw your brother in the hall today. Taylor's right," she said, returning to the armchair in the living room where she'd curled up with a tattered copy of *Little Women*. "He's cute."

Et tu, Sadie? For some reason I thought Sadie would be immune to Reed's good looks. Wasn't she too young to watch *Wild Dunes*? Didn't Taylor's parents install some sort of V-chip to keep them from watching inappropriate material (mostly Taylor's unnatural fixation with *Sex and the City*).

"I guess, if you like that type."

"Do you know Eric Dyson? He's in my class. He'd be my type, if I had one." Sadie pulled her knees up against her chest and wrapped her arms around her legs. "So how is it having him around?"

"Not so good, actually."

Sadie gave me an understanding nod. "That's too bad. I guess that's the thing about your family—you can't choose 'em, but you still have to live with them." She turned back to her book and started reading. I wondered if she was talking about Reed, or Taylor.

"Tough day, huh?" Taylor asked as she shut her bedroom door behind me.

"How much of this am I expected to take? I feel like Reed's taking over every part of my life, like there's nothing left for me," I confided. "Is that stupid?"

Taylor shook her head. "No, it's not stupid."

She must have noticed me cringing at the posters on her wall, because the next thing she did was offer to take them down.

"Would you really do that?" I asked, picturing all the holes and tape marks the posters would leave behind. She'd have to get her entire room repainted.

"Of course I'd do that, if you wanted me to."

I glanced around the room and seriously considered her offer. It was impossible to think that the same guy on these walls was, at this very moment, in my house. He wasn't just some guy posing for pictures. He was real. And a real problem, too. But he was my problem, not Taylor's. She didn't like Reed. She liked the character he played on TV.

"You don't have to do that," I told her. "But thanks anyway."

"You know all the guys are seething, they hate him."

"I doubt Reed cares very much." I laid across Taylor's bed and changed the subject. "So what'd you find out today?"

Although "entertainment editor" was Taylor's official title for the *Cabot Chronicle*, she also dabbled in gossip.

"Let me think." I could see Taylor mentally going through her reporter's notebook. "Charlie Eubanks got busted by his parents for selling pot to his neighbor's au pair this summer. The Susans met two guys from Northwestern at Number One's beach house in Michigan, and Number Two is convinced they're really going to call as soon as they get settled back in their dorms. And, apparently Benji found himself a girlfriend at that science program he went to at U of I."

"Really?" It was hard to believe any girl would find Benji remotely attractive, but if it was going to happen, chances were it would probably be a girl with a Bunsen burner in her hands.

"That's what they're saying." Taylor confirmed. "So how was your first day without Patrick?" Taylor asked.

"It sucked," I admitted. "But only two hundred eighty-three days left, right?"

Taylor gave my shoulder a sympathetic squeeze. "Right. But there are a mere twelve days left until my Emmy party, so take these." She handed me four back copies of *InStyle*. "And let's figure out what I'm going to serve."

With eight pounds of glossy magazine on my lap, I didn't have much choice. For the next hour I helped Taylor go through the magazines and pick out the menu for her annual Emmy party.

"Do you think Reed is going to come to the party?" she asked when we'd finalized the menu.

"I doubt it."

"Mr. Whitney mentioned that he'd like it if I could write a whole Emmy Reed thing for the paper."

I shrugged.

"Maybe you could ask him to come?" she suggested. "It would really be good for the paper."

I didn't want to ask Reed to pass the salt at the dinner table, no less invite him to a party. But it was the least I could do, considering Taylor had been so good about being on my side. And she had more or less gone cold turkey since I told her that Reed was my brother.

"Maybe, but I won't promise anything."

"Good enough for me." She stood up and collected the *InStyle*s strewn across her bed.

Once we put away the magazines, Taylor decided to come with me to get a new calculator.

"I was thinking about getting my belly button pierced," she told me on the elevator ride downstairs.

I didn't even bother asking why. Taylor had probably seen a picture of some starlet with a diamond-studded hoop through her abdomen and decided she just had to have one. I wasn't too worried about her actually doing anything about it. The only thing greater than Taylor's love of all things celebrity is her fear of all things painful. The whole belly button piercing idea would probably go the way of the tattoo she wanted to get on her ankle (a palm tree) and the Brazilian bikini wax fiasco. In the beginning of the summer Taylor had asked me to go with her to the "it" waxing salon in Water Tower Place. I sat in the cramped waiting room while I waited for her to emerge with a bikini line worthy of even the tiniest g-string. Not three minutes later I recognized the shrill screams coming from the second room on the left, and two minutes later Taylor was escorting me out the door.

"What happened?" I'd asked, as she pulled me out of Water Tower Place by my hand.

"That woman had me sprawled out butt naked on the table and then she started slathering this boiling wax on my private parts with a Popsicle stick."

"Well, what did you think they were going to do? Politely coax the hair out?"

"I don't know, but once she started ripping the wax away I thought I was going to die. I told her to stop and got the hell out of there before she could stop me." Taylor had opened her purse to show me the underwear she'd stuffed in there in a rush. "I didn't even have time to put them back on."

"So you didn't let her finish?"

Taylor shook her head at me. "Are you kidding me? No way."

She ended up with a lopsided bikini line for a few weeks, but she never mentioned getting waxed after that. I knew there was no way Taylor could handle someone sticking a needle through her abdomen if she couldn't handle a little warm wax.

"Why don't you just get one of those Kabbalah bracelets or

something," I suggested, when the elevator doors opened and we stepped out into the lobby.

Taylor considered this for a minute. Blood, needles, and a puncture wound in her belly button versus a little red string. Not much of a contest. "You know, that's not a bad idea," she agreed. "I'll have to look into that."

chapter eleven

When I got home from Taylor's, my new HP 33s calculator in hand, I found a note from my mom on the kitchen counter. She was meeting with a client, and my dad wouldn't be home from the theater until 7:00. Reed was nowhere in sight, so I figured he was probably hiding out in his room. I grabbed my backpack and headed upstairs to start my homework.

Before I reached my room, I passed by the bathroom and discovered that Reed wasn't in his room tapping away at his Sidekick. He was kneeling on the bathroom floor going through my stuff.

"I think these are yours." Reed handed me a shrink-wrapped pack of birth control pills.

I snatched the pack from his hand and stuffed it into my pocket. "Just because we have to share a bathroom doesn't mean you can go through all my stuff."

"I wasn't going through your crap. I was trying to make some room in the cabinet for mine. All my boxes arrived today and I have nowhere to put anything."

I glanced down at the toilet, where, in addition to a can of shaving cream and a razor, Reed had placed various tubes of designer hair gel, styling cream, exfoliating scrub, clay mask, moisturizer, and one lone stick of deodorant. In fact, it was the exact same deodorant Patrick used. Musk Speed Stick.

"Look, the way I see it, we have two options," Reed told me, sounding more rational than I'd anticipated. With all of his things on the toilet, and mine neatly stacked under the sink in plastic baskets, I guess he realized he wasn't exactly in a bargaining position. "We can continue to ignore each other or we can try to make this situation bearable."

"And how would we do that?"

"We could start by having you share the bathroom cabinet." He reached for the tube of hair gel. "I realize that there's some sort of organizational rationale for lining everything up according to size, and I figured the fact that all your stuff is alphabetized by product is some sort of indication that you wouldn't want me just tossing my stuff in there haphazardly, so why don't you just tell me how you want it done, and that's what we'll do."

That sounded reasonable enough. And I didn't want him trawling through my baskets messing them up. So if Reed was willing to compromise, I would do the same.

I bent down and pulled out the plastic baskets lining the bottom of the cabinet. "I'll give you one of these for all your stuff," I conceded. "Would that work?"

Reed nodded and I started emptying out my shower gels and lotions. There were a lot of them, and after I'd removed the fifth bottle of body splash (vanilla), yet another jar of body buffer (cucumber melon), a crusty tube of Nair (scent undetermined), and some Body Shop Hemp Foot Protector my mom thought would help cure my cracked heels, I started to think that I should be a lot softer, smoother, and better smelling than I am.

"So, what do you file those under? *P* for pills?" he asked, pointing to the two additional pill packs I was holding in my hand after finding them between a tube of peppermint foot soak and a pumice stone. "Or *B* for birth control?"

I stood up, pill packs in hand, and turned to Reed. "Actually, *N* for none of your damn business."

After the bathroom incident, Reed and I did a better job of tolerating each other. There was still a crowd of girls gathered outside our house every morning, but by the end of the week the number of adoring fans had dwindled down to half of what we saw that first morning. Reed and I had settled into a routine of sorts. He'd go out first and placate the crowd so we could get to the bus stop without being bombarded by screaming girls. Our walks to the bus stop were still devoid of sparkling conversation, and at school I pretty much avoided him while everyone else was still in awe of the *Wild Dunes* star, but we'd both seemed to come to terms with the reality of our situation, and the first week of senior year went by quickly. If it wasn't for the fact that Reed skipped his history class on Wednesday, muttered "*tu maldita madre*" when Señorita Valdez called him to the blackboard in Spanish class on Thursday (he apparently learned to swear while on location in the Dominican Republic with Marnie), and left school during lunch on Friday and never came back, the first week of school would have even been considered uneventful. But even my parents had their breaking point, and being called in to see Mr. Whitney on a Friday afternoon was more than the ever-tolerant Carlisles could put up with.

"Reed," my father screamed, waiting for my mom to pass through the front door before slamming it behind her. "Get down here!"

A few minutes later Reed slunked down the stairs, not even

bothering to mask the look of boredom on his face. "Yeah?" he replied, leaning over the banister.

I stood in the kitchen doorway and waited for my parents to go off on my brother. I wanted to savor every moment.

"Maybe you didn't understand us when we told you the house rules," my dad started, holding up his hands and getting ready to tick off Reed's violations. "You will *not* skip school, you will *not* disrupt your classes, and you will *not*, I repeat, *will not*, order your own lunch delivered to the cafeteria. Do you hear me?"

Reed didn't answer immediately, but when he finally opened his mouth I knew exactly what he was going to say. It was exactly what I'd been thinking. "Hey, you didn't say anything about not ordering lunch," he pointed out, as if the whole misunderstanding was a result of their inability to clearly communicate the rules.

My mom reached for Dad's arm and held onto it, a sign that she'd take it from here. "Reed, we don't want you ordering your own lunch. You can eat the same thing all the other students are eating. Okay?"

Reed shrugged and turned away, but not before catching me surveying the situation from the doorway. And not before seeing the smirk on my lips.

Fuck you, he mouthed.

I did the only thing I could. *No, fuck you,* I mouthed back, but I don't think he saw me. Reed was already on his way up the stairs.

Even though my parents were pissed about Reed's antics, they had noticed that I made room for him in the bathroom and thanked me for my effort. But it wasn't Reed I was thinking about. It was Glenda's comment, and if sharing the bathroom cabinet with Reed improved my chances of going to Europe next summer, then

I could certainly spare a plastic basket and some room in the medicine cabinet.

Even though that state of our relationship had progressed from cold war to a coexistence that, if not exactly peaceful, was at least verging on civil avoidance, I still didn't like the idea that Reed had discovered my pills. I couldn't help wondering if every time Reed was looking at me he was thinking about it, wondering how much sex I was having and with whom.

I'd debated going off the pill while Patrick was away at school and decided against it. Between my upcoming visit, Thanksgiving break, Christmas break, and spring break, I figured we'd be seeing each other about every seven weeks or so, and ditching my pills and relying on condoms for those few weeks hardly seemed worth it. Besides, who needs cramps, bloating, and breakouts?

I was going to New Haven in five weeks for my interview and had already counted the days on my calendar. No period. All systems were go. That was another benefit of being on the pill—you avoided the unexpected arrival of your period at exactly the wrong time.

On Saturday I started working on my Yale application. It was like trying to follow some elaborate recipe, only I didn't have the measurements—was it a dash of volunteer work and a pinch of standardized tests, or equal measures grades and extracurricular activities? And then there was the something extra that couldn't be defined. I'd visited Yale's website so often I could practically recite the ambiguous requirements. It talked about grades and standardized tests, but stressed that there's no hard-and-fast cutoff point (Patrick's acceptance is proof of that). They wanted motivation, curiosity, energy, leadership ability, and distinctive talents. Distinctive talents? Taylor's been working on tying a cherry stem into a knot with her tongue, but I didn't think that was what they were talking about. Curiosity? Last year some guy in the senior class supposedly drilled a hole through the wall between the boys' and girls' locker rooms so he could finally lay to rest the speculation that we all showered together and shared the same loofah. Somehow, I didn't think the Yale admissions committee was looking for that kind of curiosity. So I was completely at a loss and decided to take an "everything but the kitchen sink" approach. If they wouldn't share their exact recipe with me, than I'd give them so many ingredients they couldn't say no.

"What are you doing?" Reed stood in my bedroom doorway watching me.

"Working on my Yale application."

He walked over to my bed and sat down, messing up the color-coordinated index cards I'd organized by subject, main point, and subpoint. "What will happen if you don't get in?" he asked, not even bothering to place the cards back in order. It would have been easy enough for him to do. They were all numbered.

I stopped writing and looked up. "What do you mean?"

Reed had picked up one of my blue index cards and was reading it, his eyebrows knit together like I'd written *War and Peace* on a five-by-seven sheet of paper. "It's never occurred to you that you won't get into Yale?"

Not until now. I reached for the card and took it away from him. "Not really."

"How can you be so sure?" he asked, tossing another blue card into my now haphazardly ordered collection of notes.

"I don't know for sure."

"Then how can you be so confident?"

It wasn't like I was absolutely, one hundred percent confident. I knew there were a million girls like me out there filling out the same applications, applying to the same colleges with the same high grades and test scores. But I did figure I had one advantage, even though I'd never mentioned it to anyone. Not even Taylor. Partly it was that I knew she'd kill me. And partly it was that I knew what I did wasn't exactly right. It wasn't *wrong*, per se, but it was the closest I've ever come to blurring the lines between the two. And that's the reason I wasn't about to explain to Reed why I wasn't more nervous, why I wasn't about to tell him that I'd already written the three essays that Patrick used for his Yale application.

I'd never take credit for Patrick getting in, because I know they look at a lot more than just the essays, and the fact that his parents both went there surely didn't hurt his chances. But a very small part of me would like to think I had something to do with it.

The thing is, I didn't just help Patrick because I wanted him to get in. I helped him because I knew if he got in, then we'd have a better chance at being together after Cabot. Yale was his long shot, and, if rejected, he probably would have ended up at a place like Indiana University or Tulane, where they'd love a midfielder who was the highest-scoring guy in his league. And the thing was, even though Patrick didn't really care where he went to college, I did. And so I knew if Patrick didn't get into Yale, we were pretty much over. And, at the time, I just wasn't prepared to think about that option.

So I helped Patrick with the essays, and the rest, as they say, is history.

"I'm not overconfident, I'm just not going to think about the possibility of not getting in," I told Reed.

"Are you doing early decision and all that?" he asked, leaning back on his elbows.

"No, my parents don't want me to limit my choices."

"Sounds to me like you've already done that."

"Such sage wisdom from someone who could be perplexed by an index card," I pointed out. "I don't suppose you ever considered going to college."

Reed shook his head. "I guess I could do the whole NYU film school thing, but why? To get out and do exactly what I'm already doing? Besides, winter in New York sucks." Reed leaned back on his elbows as he watched me. "So, what's the plan after Yale? I'm sure you have it all figured out."

"Probably either go straight to graduate school or maybe get recruited by one of the big consulting firms or something." I turned my attention back to the application.

"You ever consider taking a year off?" Reed asked.

"A year off from what?"

"School."

"Why would I do that?"

"I guess you wouldn't. It's all part of your grand plan, right, the one you have all figured out for yourself?" He pushed aside a stack of Post-it notes. "Why do you do that? Plan everything?"

"So I know what to expect," I explained, taking the Post-its out of his way. Didn't he see I was busy? Was he so bored that talking to me had become his only viable form of entertainment?

"Don't you like surprises?" the biggest surprise of my life asked me, not even seeing the irony in his question.

"No, I don't."

"What's wrong with surprises?"

"They usually end up being more of a pain in the ass than anything else."

"So you're a control freak."

"No."

"Just a freak?" he asked again, this time smiling at me.

Reed obviously didn't plan on leaving me alone, and I certainly wasn't planning to continue a conversation where I provided Reed with any more ammunition against me, so I decided to change the subject.

"What's going on between you and Sarah Middleton?"

"Nothing, why? Is Taylor going to write something in her column about us?"

"No, I was just asking."

"Sarah doesn't think you like her, you know."

Sarah wasn't stupid. But I didn't *dislike* her. I just didn't know what to make of her. "I like her just fine. I've only known her for four days."

"You've only known me for six days and you already don't like me," he pointed out.

"You've given me more material to work with," I answered.

I waited for a sarcastic comeback, but instead Reed just laughed. And he was laughing *with* me, not at me. At least I think so.

"That's pretty funny," he told me.

"Look, I've still got a lot to do here." I held up the application as proof of the formidable task before me.

"I hope you're not expecting them to admit you based upon your penmanship. It looks like a seven-year-old wrote that."

"This is just my first draft. I photocopied the application so I'd have something to work with. The real application is over there on my desk."

"So that's just sort of a dry run?"

"A rehearsal," I explained, using a term I figured he was familiar with. "Just until I get everything exactly the way I want it."

"Of course." Reed slid off my bed and started for my door. "Good luck with that."

chapter twelve

With four weeks to go until I took the SATs for the last time, I signed up for the equivalent of standardized testing boot camp. I have to admit, I was going to blow it off before I met the latest Harvard-bound member of Cabot's senior class. But what if Sarah decided she wanted to apply to Yale, too? There was no way a college admissions committee would accept two people from Cabot. They would just pick the best one—the one with the highest class rank and better SATs. So I wasn't going to take my chances.

It wasn't like I'd done poorly on the test the first time around, but I figured every little bit helped. So for the next four Saturdays I'd elected to spend my mornings in some basement room in Lincoln Park learning the ins and outs of standardized testing. Taylor thought I was nuts. She wasn't going to get anywhere near a classroom on a Saturday morning.

"Vanessa?"

I looked up at the voice calling my name and saw a guy in a navy blue Sharingham sweatshirt coming toward me.

"Vanessa Carlisle, right?" he asked when he reached my desk.

"Yeah."

"I'm John Larsen. We used to be in the same class at Sharingham."

As soon as he said that, I recognized the brown wavy hair and the big grin. What I didn't recognize were the six inches he'd grown since eighth grade. Or the broad shoulders filling out the navy blue sweatshirt. Usually guys built like that transferred out of Sharingham for high school so they could play sports. Needless to say, Sharingham didn't look favorably upon the blatantly competitive spirit sports required and instead offered activities like team quilt making (all proceeds from the sale of said quilts went to fund some charter school in Guatemala).

"What are you doing here?" I asked.

John laughed. "Same thing you are, probably. Trying to make sure I get into college." He pointed to the desk next to me. "Anyone sitting here?"

I shook my head and John sat down.

"So you're still at Sharingham?"

"Yep. Tried to get my parents to let me transfer after that whole dung beetle incident, but they didn't go for it. They're going to shit when they find out I'm applying early to Dartmouth instead of Reed. They still have their hopes set on raising a future Peace Corp volunteer."

"Or at the very least Teach for America, right?"

John laughed again. "You've obviously met my parents."

Our instructor entered the room and placed a stack of workbooks on the podium at the front of the class.

"Here we go," I told John, and turned to face the instructor. "There's no turning back now."

Four hours later, the instructor reminded us to do the timed practice exam in the workbook and told us we could go.

"It could have been worse, I guess," John commented as we packed up our study materials. "He could have reminded us that competition is so stiff, we have a better chance of getting hit by a bus than getting accepted by our first-choice schools. Or that even though the number of kids applying to colleges has increased, the number of slots available to incoming students has remained the same."

"Okay, enough," I told him. "You're depressing me."

John laughed. He didn't seem too worried. I wished I felt the same way. What I'd told Reed was true. I don't like surprises. And the whole application process was like one big surprise party.

After four years of high school, one ACT test, two SATs, three SAT subject tests, and what felt like at least 978 hours of extracurricular activities, one day I'd log onto Yale's website, type in my password, and *surprise*! There'd be a final decision that would determine where I'd spend the next four years. And whether or not those four years would be spent with my boyfriend. Just one little push of the ENTER key, and my future was decided.

"Want to go grab lunch?" John suggested on our way out.

I was about to say no when my stomach growled.

"Should I take that as a yes?" he asked.

I laid my hand against my stomach and realized I was starving. "I think so."

I followed John out onto the sidewalk and he led the way to Chicago Bagel Authority.

"I love this place," I told him, as we stared up at the funky sandwich names scrawled along the blackboard behind the counter. "I'm going for the Hot Tuna Meltdown. What about you?"

He pointed up to the right-hand corner of the board.

"A Big John?" I asked, laughing. "Really?"

"Absolutely. They named it after me, you know."

I watched John's expression to see if he was kidding, but he kept a straight face.

"Are you serious?" I asked.

John broke out into a grin. "Of course I'm not serious."

I read the description below the Big John—roast beef, special sauce, lettuce, cheese, and pickles on a sesame seed bun. Taylor wouldn't like it. Didn't sound very Natalie Portman–approved to me.

After we placed our orders, John and I found a table and listened for our names to be called.

"I guess I have to ask the question eventually, so here it goes: Where are you applying?" John asked.

"Sizing up the competition?"

"Why? Are you shooting for Dartmouth, too?"

"No. Yale."

John pretended to wipe his forehead with the back of his hand. "Whew! What a relief. For a minute I thought I'd have to embark on some form of sabotage. Maybe pass you a number *three* pencil on the day of the SATs or something to trip you up."

I laughed. "I'll make sure I bring my own pencil. Thanks for the warning."

"Have you been to visit the campus yet?"

"I'm going to New Haven for an interview the weekend after the SATs." For some reason I left off the part about visiting my boyfriend while I'm there. It wasn't that I was trying to hide the fact, but I was having a good time with John. And it would be kind of presumptuous to assume he asked me to have lunch with him because he thought I was interested. Maybe he was just as hungry as I was.

Or maybe John thought I liked him.

My hand reached for the small gold heart charm hanging around my neck. It was still there. I almost expected it to zap my hand or something, like those electronic collars that shock a dog if it ventures beyond its boundaries.

"That's cool." He reached for the napkin dispenser and laid two paper napkins on the table in front of us. "I went to visit Hanover over the summer. It was great."

"John and Vanessa," the guy behind the counter called out, and John stood up. "Stay here, I've got 'em."

I watched John take our sandwiches from the counter and when he turned around and smiled at me, I knew I should say something about Patrick. I had to subtly let John know that we were just having a friendly lunch.

"My boyfriend goes to Yale," I added, when he came back to the table. So much for being subtle. "So I'll be seeing him, too, when I go there."

John gave me another "cool," and started eating his sandwich.

That was it. Cool. Not even a flicker of remorse. No looks that indicated he was the least bit disappointed. No hints that my answer was a huge letdown.

The thing is, I didn't know how to interpret his response.

Was that, "Cool, you have a boyfriend, so I don't have to worry about you thinking I was even remotely interested in you," or, "Cool, thanks for telling me before I made a move and made a complete idiot out of myself"?

It wasn't like I expected him to fall to his knees and proclaim he's been carrying a torch for me since eighth grade, but shouldn't he have said something besides "cool"?

Not that it really mattered. Now John knew about Patrick, so I didn't have to worry that he'd misinterpret anything I said. I could just eat the steaming Hot Tuna Meltdown in front of him.

I took a bite of my sandwich and reached for my napkin.

"So what's going on at old Sharingham?" I asked John, wiping my mouth. "Is everyone from our class still there?"

John started rattling off names, and the rest of our lunch was taken up with stories about people I haven't seen since I was thirteen.

After lunch I was stuffed. John was going to catch a bus back home, and I was going to walk, so I left him at the corner of Armitage and Sheffield.

"My friend Taylor is having some people over to her apartment tomorrow night," I told him before saying good-bye. "You want to come?"

"On a Sunday night? Wow, you Cabot girls really know how to party," he joked.

"Every year she has an Emmy party. It's always on a Sunday night, so it's not a huge bash, but most of our class usually goes."

Even Benji showed up for Taylor's party last year, although he'd probably rather be at home studying than in Taylor's living room listening to Ashlee, Ali, and Posey give us all play-by-plays of the red carpet action.

"Sounds good. Count me in."

I wrote Taylor's address down on a page in his notebook, and told John I'd see him there.

chapter thirteen

$\mathcal{I}$ felt pretty good when I got home, and not just because Reed's posse of fans weren't anywhere in sight—I guess even groupies take the weekend off. No, I felt good because it was nice to talk with someone who didn't go to Cabot, or know Reed, or pretty much have any idea what my life was like right now. And it didn't hurt that I'd aced the practice exam our instructor gave us in class. All in all, there wasn't much that could ruin my mood at that point.

Of course, I never in a million years expected to walk into the kitchen and find Reed fondling my underwear.

"What are you doing?" I screamed.

"I think the word your parents used was 'chores.'" He finished folding the pink bikini bottoms into quarters and then placed them on top of a leaning tower of my underwear.

"Give me those," I snapped, snatching a new pair of bikini bottoms from Reed's grasp.

"What? Your mom told me it was my turn to fold the laundry. Actually, I think she said, 'It's your opportunity to contribute to the fabric of our family,' or something like that."

That sounded like something she'd say, all right.

I turned the laundry basket over onto the table and dumped out the remaining clothes, sifting through the pile until I'd removed every bra, panty, and pair of socks I could find. In addition to my cup size, Reed also didn't need to discover my abnormally large size-nine feet.

"In the future I'd appreciate it if you didn't touch my clothes, thank you very much."

"Fine by me," he answered. "Less for me to fold."

"Fine by me," I repeated, not unaware that I sounded more like his little sister than I'd intended. And then I went to find my mother.

"Did you see this?" I asked my mom when I found her in my dad's office. "Why is Reed fondling my underwear?" I demanded, holding up my pile of undergarments for her to see.

"He wasn't fondling, Vanessa. He was folding."

"Well, I'd appreciate it if next time you didn't ask him to touch the clothes that touch my private parts."

"He's your brother, I seriously doubt he cares."

"It doesn't matter if he cares. I care."

"Your dad and I were starting to think that things were getting better between you two." My mother sighed and stopped typing on her laptop. "We were hoping it wouldn't come to this."

"Come to what?" I demanded.

"Look, Reed's new to our family and he's been getting a lot of attention. We understand what you're going through. It's normal to be jealous."

"Jealous?" I repeated, unable to believe what I was hearing. "Why would I be jealous?"

"Well, you've never had to share your dad and me, or your home, or anything, really."

"I don't care about that."

"It's also normal to be in denial," she continued, ignoring me. "Anyway, Glenda told me about a great therapist she's been seeing. He uses the healing powers of crystals."

"I don't need a therapist. And I definitely don't need a therapist who relies on rocks to heal his patients."

"Crystals, not rocks," my mom corrected.

"I don't care if he has a crystal ball and can pull rabbits from a hat, I don't need to see a therapist. I just need Reed to keep his hands off my underwear!"

I stormed out of the office and up to my room. My parents couldn't be serious. Me, jealous of Reed. Jealous of what? His ability to recite profanities in Spanish? The way he had my parents shut behind closed doors—a Carlisle household no-no—trying to figure out how to deal with Mr. Whitney's pleas for help? There was just no way.

And the one rule Reed chooses to follow is folding laundry? I just didn't get it.

The new house rules didn't allow for going out on a school night, but my parents made an exception for Taylor's party. The Emmys recognized excellence in the television arts, after all, and how could they argue with that? Besides, they loved Taylor. She was a *writer*.

I knew Taylor really wanted Reed to go to her party. It would have been a coup if the entertainment reporter for the *Cabot Chronicle* could actually get a TV star to show up at her Emmy party, but I just couldn't bring myself to invite him. Besides, I was sure Reed would want nothing to do with it.

Everyone kept asking Taylor if Reed would be there and I almost felt bad for her. I didn't feel bad enough to insist Reed come with me, but did feel just bad enough that I thought Reed should feel bad, too.

"You could have been nicer when you told Taylor there was no way you'd go to her party," I told him when I passed through the living room on my way out the door.

Reed glanced up at me, looking like he didn't even feel the slightest twinge of guilt. "Do you even realize that if I was in L.A., I'd actually be *at* the Emmys, not just going to some party to watch it on TV?" he asked me.

Of course I realized that. And I actually enjoyed that fact.

"It's not like you were nominated or anything," I pointed out. "Besides, she takes her job at the *Chronicle* very seriously. And apparently there are other people who think having you around is actually interesting."

Reed laughed at me. "And you're not one of them."

I just smiled back.

"I'll tell you what." Reed stood up and shut off the TV. "I'll go."

"What?"

"I'll go to the party. My tutor's going to be there, and you said yourself, it would make Taylor's year."

"I never said it would make Taylor's year."

Reed grinned at me. "But it would."

God, I hated that self-satisfied smirk on his face. Wait a minute—did he say "tutor"? "You have a tutor?"

"Yeah. Whitney asked Sarah to help me with some classes."

"Sarah? Sarah Middleton is your tutor?"

Reed nodded. "Yep."

What did Sarah Middleton know that I didn't? If anyone was going to tutor Reed, shouldn't it be me? Sarah had been at Cabot for two weeks, I'd been proving myself for three years!

Not that I'd want to tutor Reed, but at least I should have been asked first.

"Well, I'm leaving for Taylor's right now, so I guess I'll just see you there."

Reed stood up and slapped his jean-covered thighs with the palms of his hands. "I'm ready to go right now. Lead the way."

Reed stood there waiting for me to go, so what choice did I have? I led the way.

We walked the six blocks to Taylor's apartment in silence. So silent, in fact, it occurred to me that it had only taken two weeks for the fanfare surrounding Reed's presence in Chicago to die down. No more girls loitering outside our house. No more photographers stealthily squatting in bushes. Without the newsworthy outbursts and tabloid headlines, it seemed Reed was out of sight, out of mind.

Taylor's parents are quite patient with her celebrity obsession. They figured as long as she isn't flunking out of school and doesn't plan to run away to Hollywood instead of going to college, then there really isn't much they can complain about. At least she wasn't pregnant, which was what they feared more than anything. Taylor told them she was still a virgin, but that didn't seem to assuage their fears any. What she didn't tell them was that her sexual status would change as soon as she found a guy who could pass for a Reed Vaughn look-alike. Now she had to either wait for an Orlando Bloom look-alike, or hold out for the real thing. Still, Taylor's parents figured an addiction to *Access Hollywood* was the lesser of all the possible evils that could seduce their eldest daughter.

When Taylor buzzed me into her building I prepared myself for her reaction. I expected her, and everyone else for that matter, to freak out when Reed and I walked through the front door. Instead, the room went silent. Between the girls staring at

Reed and the boys glaring at me, we were both the center of attention.

"Come on in," Taylor told me, maintaining her composure. Bringing Reed wasn't going to earn me any points with the guys in my class, but it would put Taylor forever in my debt. The look on her face could only be described as thrilled, but she was also the hostess, and she wasn't about to let any excitement get the best of her. She was planning to attend an actual Emmy party someday, and this was practice for the real thing.

"Reed, there's food over there on the table." She pointed toward the dining room and then turned to me. "And that guy you invited is already here." She motioned over toward the kitchen, where Sarah Middleton was talking to John.

I felt my stomach tighten as I watched her laugh at something John said. I didn't want John, but I sure as hell didn't want him to want Sarah Middleton.

"Who's that?" Reed asked, following my gaze into the kitchen.

"John."

"John, huh? My sister comes to a party to hook up with another guy." Reed feigned a look of consternation. "What would Pat say?"

"Probably that you're a complete asshole. John's just a friend, Reed." I couldn't resist adding, "And it's *Patrick*."

Taylor saw where this was going, stepped between us, and led me away. "Thanks so much for bringing him," she whispered, and squeezed my arm tight. "I owe you one."

I gave her a look that said she owed me a hell of a lot more than that.

"Okay, I owe you two. Why don't you go over and see John. He's been waiting for you."

Over in the kitchen John was gesturing wildly with his arms as he told Sarah a story that was obviously hilarious. Or at least she thought so. Reed's tutor had a sense of humor, but then again she'd have to if she was expected to turn Reed into a student.

"I think I'll go get something to eat."

I made my way over to the dining room table and reached for one of the tiny burgers with grilled cheddar and ramekins of cornichons Taylor selected out of *InStyle*. She figured everyone liked burgers and the addition of cornichons would make them a little more festive. It turned out cornichons are just little pickled gherkin cucumbers. So much for festive.

"Jesus, hasn't Taylor ever heard of Doritos?" Charlie Eubanks complained, pushing aside the platter of melon balls and prosciutto.

"Or salsa?" Mike Simpson asked, skipping over the mango relish and opting for plain tortilla chips instead.

"What's he here for?" Charlie nodded in Reed's direction.

"Taylor asked him to come," I told him, just in case he thought I was responsible for Reed's presence. Although, in a way, I was.

"Great. Some sort of green dip with red things in it *and* Reed Vaughn. Must be our lucky night." Mike nudged Charlie. "Want to get out of here?"

Charlie didn't even bother answering, and instead, just made a beeline for the door.

"Hey, Vanessa." John waved to me from the kitchen, where he was now standing alone. He pointed to the plate of burgers and nodded his head, which I assumed was a long-distance request for some food.

"You didn't tell me Reed Vaughn was your brother," John said, when I reached him and handed over one of Taylor's miniburgers.

"Why, does it matter?"

"No. But all the girls at Sharingham are talking about him being in the city. According to them, it's a pretty big deal."

I watched Reed basking in the glow of Ashlee, Ali, and Posey's admiration. I swear they were about to genuflect at his feet every time he said something. And Reed was eating it up. He couldn't act his way out of a paper bag, but he sure knew how to work a room.

"It's not, trust me. He lives in his own little Reed Vaughn world, and we're all just expected to be his adoring fans."

"I'm assuming he's the reason I'm one of only three guys left in this whole place?"

I looked around and saw that John was right. Benji had Sarah cornered over by the fireplace, and Reed was on the couch entertaining the six girls who'd perched themselves at his feet like he was the Dalai Lama or something. Other than that, there wasn't another male in sight.

"Reed isn't very well liked among the guys in my class," I explained before taking a bite of my sun-dried tomato-and-goat cheese pinwheel. "What do you think of him?"

I waited for John to side with me, to say that Reed was nothing more than a guy with good looks, a famous mother, and one hell of a publicist. Instead, he stood there watching Reed as if trying to size him up.

"I can't blame them for not appreciating Reed's apparent effect on the opposite sex, but they should give the guy a break. If they were in his position they'd be doing the exact same thing."

Not the answer I was looking for.

"Did you fill this out?" John asked, holding up a paper ballot. "I don't know who most of these people are. Should I be familiar with the writers of variety/music/or comedy specials?"

"I hope not," I told him.

"Good, because for a minute there I was beginning to think I was missing out on the writing genius of Roland Hershberger and

Marty Madison." John crumpled up the ballot and left it on the table. "Thanks for inviting me, by the way."

I had to give him credit. Besides Benji and Reed, he was the only guy left. It was hard not to smile at him. "Well, thanks for coming."

"No problem. I told my parents I was attending a PETA protest. They almost wanted to come with me."

I glanced down at the table where John's ballot lay in a ball, and that's when I noticed it. Tossed on the table next to John's discarded ballot, a close-up of a scowling Reed Vaughn stared up at me from the cover of *Wow!* magazine. His face filled the entire cover, so you couldn't tell where the picture was taken, but I knew. I recognized the scowl. And I recognized the shirt he'd worn on the first day of school.

How was it possible that Reed could scowl and still manage to put his dimples on display? And how could someone who looked so angry also look so damn good-looking?

John must have noticed my eyes lingering a little too long on the photo of Reed.

"Catchy tag line, huh?" he commented, pointing to the large red letters plastered across the bottom of the cover: "Reed Retreats from Hollywood."

Retreats? Please. Revels in attention was more like it.

I checked out the date in the corner and saw that the magazine just came out today, and then flipped it open and thumbed through the pages until I came to what I was looking for—the article, and the photo of Reed getting swarmed by his fans on the sidewalk in front of my house.

Reed had planned it all along. There was a reason he'd gone outside by himself to play the gracious star before taking me out the back so he could play the angry actor forced to leave the spotlight. He'd given *Wow!* exactly what they'd needed—the cover photo of a tortured star needed to sell magazines, and the inside picture that showed he was still the adored by *Wild Dunes* fans. It was all a publicity stunt.

"Everyone, can I have your attention, please." Taylor clapped her hands together and waited for the girls to settle down before addressing the dwindled crowd. "Reed has agreed to be a commentator of sorts for this year's show, which is due to start in one minute. So I thought what you could do is all pull the chairs around so you can face Reed and hear what he has to say about the nominees."

Reed was seated on the couch, but from the self-satisfied look on his face you would have thought it was a throne. Every available chair and pillow in the apartment was picked up and positioned in a semicircle around Reed. Only Sarah was looking at the TV when the orchestra music started and the show's host came out on stage to begin his dialogue. I had to give her credit for that. But nobody else even turned to see the screen. Everyone was watching Reed, waiting at rapt attention to hear what Hollywood pearls of wisdom he'd impart to his audience.

Taylor settled into an armchair and pulled out a spiral notebook. "You can start now, Reed. I'm going to sit over here and take notes."

Leave it to Reed to upstage the Emmys.

"I've got to get out of here," I told John. "Care to join me?"

"I thought you'd never ask." He finished the last bite of his burger and followed me to the front door. "Aren't we going to say good-bye to Taylor?"

Over on the couch, Reed was basking in the glow of his own popularity while poor Benji sat on the floor by himself reading a *National Geographic* he'd found on the coffee table.

Taylor was furiously scribbling on her notepad as she recorded Reed's words.

"Don't worry, she understands. Besides, she owes me one."

John and I started walking toward my house. It was getting cooler out at night now that fall was on the way. I wrapped my arms around me as I walked.

"Cold?" John asked, and reached over to rub the goose bumps that pimpled my arm. His hands were warm and soft and when he pulled them away I was almost disappointed. They'd felt good.

Walking with John was weird but normal at the same time. Weird because, for the past year, anytime I walked with a guy at night it had been Patrick. But normal, too, because walking with John wasn't like walking with a guy.

I thought about what Sadie said—that Eric Dyson would be her type, if she had one. I never really thought about my type before. Reed Vaughn was most definitely *not* my type. I guess Patrick was my type, but even then, there were things that bothered me. Nothing huge. Just the normal things—like how he called his friends "dude," or how he was always grabbing at his crotch when he played lacrosse, as if rearranging himself midfield was perfectly acceptable behavior. Was it really necessary to do that? I didn't have to stick my hands inside my bra and rearrange myself after running, why did he?

I looked over at John and wondered if he rearranged himself. Of course, there were no competitive sports at Sharingham, but still.

"What?" John glanced back at me and I looked away before he could figure out what I was wondering.

"Nothing."

If it weren't for Patrick, I think John would be my type.

"I know he's your brother and all, but why are you the only girl who's immune to Reed's charm?" John asked, sidestepping a parking meter.

I thought about the photo of Reed on the cover of *Wow!* and the ride home from the airport. Maybe I wasn't exactly *immune* to Reed. There were still moments when, for just a split second, I saw what everyone else saw. A star.

"My parents have been taking me to the theater ever since I can remember," I told John.

"I'd think that growing up around it would make you even more into the actor mystique."

"You'd think."

"Never had any desire to get up on stage or anything?"

"God, no. I wanted to get as far away from all that as possible."

"I'd say that a straight-A, Yale-bound student is as far as you could get."

"All their friends and the people they hang around are just so weird, I always wanted to be normal."

"So being normal actually made you different?"

"I'd never thought about it that way before, but yeah, I guess so."

"That makes sense."

How was it possible that in five minutes John was able to make sense of something that nobody else seemed to understand. Sometimes not even me. "Really? You think so?"

John thought about it for a minute before answering. "Sure."

We stopped in front of my house, and I looked up at my parents' window, where there was a bluish glow from the TV. "So, did you walk me home as some grand chivalrous gesture, or are you just afraid to walk alone?"

"I'll never tell." John smiled at me, and for some reason I

couldn't possibly begin to explain, I wanted to kiss him. Apparently he was thinking the same thing, because before I could even get the thought out of my head, John was kissing me.

I was kissing someone who wasn't my boyfriend, and it was nice. Very nice.

And very wrong.

I pulled back and wiped the back of my hand across my lips, removing any trace of what I'd just done. "Hey, I'm sorry. I didn't mean to do that."

John's head was still tipped to the side from our kiss. "Apologizing for kissing me, not exactly what I was going for."

"I'm sorry," I apologized again. "I shouldn't have done that. It's just that . . ." I didn't bother finishing my sentence.

"No problem." John waved his hand away and stepped back until there was a safe distance between us. "We can just forget it ever happened."

"Okay." I took a deep breath. "Well, then, I guess I'll see you on Saturday morning."

"I'll see you then." John started walking away, but then turned around and started walking backward as he talked to me. "You know, I didn't plan that, Vanessa, but I didn't exactly mind, either."

Yeah. Me, neither.

chapter fourteen

My parents always leave their bedroom door open just a crack, as though that extra inch of space would make a difference if some madman broke into our house to murder us all. I pushed the door open, peeked into the darkened room, and told them I was home from Taylor's.

My dad was watching a black-and-white movie on TV, his head propped up on a stack of pillows (filled with all-natural white goose down, of course).

"Is Reed with you?" my mom asked, turning over in bed to look at me. Her hair was spiked up on top of her head and she squinted at me as if I'd woken her up.

"He's still at the party," I told her.

"Is everything okay?"

"It's fine."

"Okay." She laid her head back on her pillow (filled with one hundred percent organic buckwheat hulls, which didn't sound very comfortable to me) and blew me a kiss. "By the way, Patrick called while you were out."

Of course he did. What else would my boyfriend be doing

while I was standing outside on the sidewalk kissing some guy?

"What did he say?" I asked.

"He said he'd try to reach you on Thursday."

I went into my room and closed the door so I wouldn't have to hear Reed when he came home, and then I crawled into bed.

Contrary to what I told my mother, things were most certainly not fine.

"Where'd you and John go last night?" Taylor asked me on Monday morning.

"I couldn't take any more of Reed."

Taylor gave me an understanding squeeze. "Yeah, I kinda figured that."

"Why didn't you tell me about *Wow!*? I saw it on the dining room table."

"I just got it on Saturday and I thought things were bad enough between you two without him landing on the cover of a magazine," she explained. "Did you read it?"

I shook my head. "I didn't, but apparently I'm the only one. The girls were back in full force this morning outside my house."

Taylor leaned up against her locker. "I did get a great article out of the party, I was even thinking of including it as a writing sample for my Boston University application. I couldn't believe Reed predicted the huge upset in the best leading actress in a miniseries category."

"Quite prescient of him," I commended. "Now if he could only harness his power and cure world hunger."

Taylor nudged me. "Come on. Let's forget about Reed. Tell me about John. He seemed nice."

I nodded. "He is."

"Is that, 'he is and I like him,' or 'he is and he'll make someone else a great boyfriend someday'?" Taylor asked, looking for a translation.

Maybe more the first translation than the second, but I didn't want to say so. "Neither. He's just nice."

"I don't know. He seemed pretty anxious for you to arrive last night," she persisted. "Did being with John make you miss Patrick? Are you worried you guys won't make it through his freshman year?"

"We have to," I told her, thinking that, given last night's kiss, it was more likely we wouldn't make it through my senior year.

Taylor frowned. "Why do you have to?"

"Look, forget about it. Everything's fine with Patrick. I guess I'm just nervous about my calculus test."

Like a true friend, Taylor assured me I'd do great. Even though I really wasn't *that* nervous. Sarah Middleton had given me added incentive to study that much harder. Still, at least it got Taylor off the subject of John.

I didn't tell her what had happened with him after we'd left her apartment. I knew she'd start reading all sorts of sordid things into it. Taylor's of the theory that where there's smoke there's fire, which is why she says you can't discount the headlines in tabloids— chances are, if there are rumors of trouble in a relationship, it's only a matter of time until it's the lead story on *Extra*.

But if John could forget our little indiscretion ever happened, then so could I. Or at least I'd die trying. Because, the truth was, I couldn't stop thinking about it. It was just a kiss, and it couldn't have lasted more than a minute—okay, maybe two. So why did I replay it in my head all week?

In the middle of my first calculus test, when I should have been focusing on slopes and asymptotes, I started thinking about it. And the harder I tried to get it out of my mind, the harder it was to forget.

During my senior seminar in women's fiction I tuned out Ms. Blackwell's discussion of *The Bell Jar* and thought about John's lips (so what if it was a story about a depressed woman who kills herself, his lips were so soft). In my honors foreign policy and politics class I avoided answering questions about Latin America in favor of remembering how John's fingers felt when he rubbed my arm. And then there was Taylor's question, which kept repeating in my head when I should have been conjugating French verbs: Why did Patrick and I have to make it through the year? What I should have said was: Because I love him. But what I was thinking was: Because if we don't, I won't know what will happen next year.

By Wednesday morning the Reed Vaughn Fan Club had once again dwindled down to a manageable number of girls, and we were able to leave the house and make it to school on time without spending fifteen minutes placating the masses on my front walk. I headed straight to my locker to meet Taylor, and Reed trailed behind me as usual, in no rush to start the school day. It wasn't until I heard Charlie Eubanks and Mike Simpson grumbling about something that Taylor and I stopped talking and listened to what they were saying. And it wasn't until I heard Mike mutter "fucking Reed Vaughn" that I realized they were talking about my brother.

A few lockers away Reed seemed to be ignoring their comments, which I thought was wise. Charlie and Mike didn't have Reed's chiseled chest and the washboard abs that could only come from personal training sessions, but they were still the two biggest guys on Cabot's football team.

But when Mike and Charlie broke out into loud laughter, Reed had reached his limit. He walked over to them and gave his best Gray snarl. "Why don't you two just shut the fuck up?"

Charlie stepped forward, ready to take Reed on. "I don't think you want us to mess up your pretty face, do you, Hollywood?"

"He won't do anything," Mike chimed in. "Hollywood probably needs a stunt double just to take a piss."

Even if Reed didn't know who he was dealing with, I did. And my brother was way in over his head. Charlie and Mike had everything to prove, and Reed wouldn't stand a chance. This wasn't some fight scene with props, this was two pissed-off defensive linemen.

"Enough, you guys." I turned around to face them. "Just go to homeroom."

"Ooohhhh," said Charlie and Mike simultaneously, wiggling their fingers at me and pretending they were afraid.

"Now you need your sister defending you?" Mike asked Reed. "Do you think she'll kick our ass?"

I actually thought I saw Reed attempt to flex his pecs, and glanced around to see if this was another promotion stunt, another way for Reed to stay in the headlines. But there weren't any photographers lurking in the hallway to capture Reed getting in a fight, there was just a growing crowd of curious Cabot students gathered around us.

I looked over at Reed, and he shook his head at me like I'd done more harm than good.

"I don't need anyone to defend me, least of all *her*," he told them, and gave me a dirty look.

"Hey, she was just trying to help," Taylor cut in, taking a step toward Reed in an effort to stand up for me. She didn't bother saying what was obvious to the rest of us—Charlie and Mike could beat the crap out of Reed.

"I don't need her help," Reed spat back at Taylor. "Or yours. Just mind your own fucking business, okay?"

Taylor stood there a few feet away from Reed, stunned. She looked like she'd been slapped, her face frozen in disbelief that Reed would talk to her like that.

Even the Susans looked shocked, and nobody moved as they waited to see what would happen next.

But Reed had underestimated Taylor. My best friend may be

slightly obsessed with celebrities, but she wasn't an idiot. And she wasn't going to let Reed get away with talking to her like that.

"You know, Reed, you're really not a very attractive person," Taylor announced in a voice that was calm and controlled and no longer impressed with the TV star standing before her. "I mean, you're hot, but it really doesn't change the fact that you're also a total prick."

The hallway was completely silent as Taylor spun around and walked away, her head held high.

"I think Reed just lost that argument," I heard someone in the crowd mutter, just loud enough for Taylor to hear.

She stopped walking and turned to face us. "Reed lost more than that," Taylor declared, her voice carrying down the length of the hallway. "He lost a fan."

Taylor Dennison, entertainment reporter for the *Cabot Chronicle,* had just dissed the star of *Wild Dunes.* None of us knew what to make of it. We all stood there watching Taylor until she turned a corner and disappeared. And it wasn't until I glimpsed Reed's pinched face out of the corner of my eye that I realized my brother understood he'd just made a big mistake.

By the time Patrick called me on Thursday night, I'd decided to put the "incident" with John into perspective. So I'd done something impulsive. I knew it was wrong. I had a boyfriend, someone I shared a history with, a guy who knew my favorite flavor ice cream (chocolate), who understood my irrational fear of the hair that gets stuck in the shower drain, and gave me my favorite flowers for Valentine's day (tulips). My kiss with John was totally unplanned, and telling Patrick about it would only create all sorts of problems. Besides, in the grand scheme of things, I had more important things to tell him. Patrick still didn't know about Reed.

"What do mean, he's your brother?" Patrick repeated, sounding thoroughly confused.

So I told him the whole story about my dad and Marnie. At this point, it didn't even shock me anymore. It had become just another piece of Carlisle family history, like the time I decided to polish Daisy's toenails and she'd dashed across the living room furniture, leaving hot pink streaks on what should have been pure ivory chenille.

"Has he made a move on you or anything?" Patrick wanted to know.

I barely stopped myself from saying "ew." "He's my brother. Of course not."

"Well, he's only your half brother and he probably thinks he can have anyone he wants."

This wasn't exactly the reaction I was expecting. Where was my shoulder to cry on? Where was my sympathetic ear? Where was my *boyfriend*? "He's an asshole, Patrick, and I can't believe you even just said that," I spat, completely dumbfounded. And pissed. I hadn't done anything wrong, at least not as far as he knew, so what was with the attitude?

Patrick paused for a minute and then his voice softened. "I'm sorry. You're right. It's just not that fun hearing your girlfriend tell you that some guy is living with her."

"I guess," I answered, imagining how unsympathetic I'd be if Patrick revealed he was living with some hot girl that ninety-nine percent of the male population wanted to be with.

"Tell me about him."

"Reed's a mess," I told Patrick. "He made a complete idiot out of himself in the hall the other day and now everyone knows what a jerk he is, he's got this new girl tutoring him so he doesn't flunk out of school, and he said 'motherfucker' in Señorita Valdez's class."

"Having him around must be tough," Patrick quickly commented, and I remembered why I loved him.

"It is. Besides, don't you think they should have asked me to tutor Reed instead of some new girl?"

"You don't even take Spanish," Patrick reminded me, which so wasn't the point. "Hey, Vanessa, you'd tell me if something happened with him, wouldn't you?" Patrick asked, taking me back to a topic that truly grossed me out.

"I am not even going to justify that with an answer," I told him, rubbing my temples in anticipation of the throbbing headache this line of conversation would inevitably produce. "It's getting late."

"You're still coming out in three weeks, right?"

"Uh-huh," I answered, my voice straining to remain steady. This hadn't gone the way I thought it would go.

Patrick must have heard my voice change, because he was silent for a minute. "Hey, I shouldn't have said that about Reed," he apologized, the words soft, like he was sharing a secret with me. "It's just hard enough being apart, and now I find out you have some TV guy living with you. This isn't easy—for either of us."

"Yeah, I know," I told him. "I miss you."

"Me, too," he answered, and I knew he meant it.

"Listen, I probably won't be able to talk until next week. Things are starting to get really busy around here."

I didn't say anything, and Patrick must have thought I'd hung up, because he asked, "Vanessa? Are you okay?"

I tried to sound okay, but instead my answer came out sounding something like *mmhumph*.

I heard Patrick take a deep breath. "Look, it's got to get easier, right?"

I nodded, even though he couldn't see me from eight hundred miles away.

"I love you," he told me.

"I love you, too."

Even though it had started out a little rocky, our call ended okay. Still, I couldn't help thinking about Patrick's first reaction to my news. Reed making a move on me. What a dumb thing to say. What a truly, truly dumb thing to say.

On Saturday morning, I decided I should just say something to John. "I didn't mean to give you the wrong idea the other night," I explained, standing next to his desk.

"You didn't give me any ideas. Like I said, let's just forget it ever happened." John pointed to the test he'd been reviewing. "Did you do the practice exam?"

"Yeah." I sat down and opened my book. Not only did I do the practice exam, I completed three of them. Sarah Middleton may be Reed's tutor, but I wasn't going down without a fight. "It wasn't so bad."

"I didn't think so, either."

John wasn't exactly torn up by my rebuff the other night. Maybe I really was just overreacting.

"Hey, can I ask you something?" I closed my book and turned to him so nobody around us could hear. "Did it ever occur to you that Reed would, I don't know, try something . . ." I couldn't even finish the sentence.

"He's your brother," John said matter-of-factly. He obviously understood my incomplete question.

"I know, it's just that someone mentioned something."

John made a face and waved away the idea with his hand. "Well, it's crazy. What kind of person would say something so dumb?"

The kind I was going to visit in three weeks.

chapter fifteen

When I went downstairs on Sunday morning, my mom and dad were huddled over the paper at the kitchen table. I figured it had to be some review of a local art exhibit or an editorial about the state of arts funding in Illinois.

But when they saw me, they both looked up and I knew they were reading about something a lot closer to home than the lack of grants available for performance art.

"What's that?" I asked, attempting to read the headline below the upside-down Entertainment section heading.

"An article."

"Is it about Reed?"

"Yes," my mom answered, slowly moving her elbow to cover the headline.

"Can I see?" I reached for the paper, but my dad pulled it back toward him.

"I'm not sure you want to."

"Why?"

"Apparently someone from Cabot talked to a *Tribune* reporter and she didn't have very nice things to say."

This I had to see. "About Reed?"

Reed and I hadn't talked about the scene in the hallway with Taylor since it happened, but the rest of the day it was the talk of the school. With a few choice words from Taylor, Reed's shiny image had tarnished. Someone probably called the *Tribune* and told them all about how Taylor put Reed in his place.

My mom took the paper and started folding it up. "I think we should all just forget about the article."

"No, I want to read it." Before she could object, I grabbed the paper and opened it to the creased page. And that's when I knew why she wanted us to forget all about the article. Because the article wasn't just about Reed. It was all about me.

"TV Bad Boy Reed Vaughn Creates Drama at Home in Chicago," the headline read. And that was about the kindest line in the entire article.

> *Wild Dunes*'s bad boy Reed Vaughn blew into the Windy City a few weeks ago in hopes of cleaning up his act. After months of trouble in Los Angeles, including numerous drunken episodes, difficulty on the set of his hit TV show, and finally, the car accident that left his brand-new Porsche 911 totaled after driving into a Starbucks on Wilshire Boulevard, Vaughn was sent here to live with his biological father, Bookman Theater artistic director Will Carlisle.
>
> "I don't think it's going so well," says a source close to Carlisle's daughter. "The whole thing was entirely unexpected."
>
> Vaughn is attending Cabot Academy with his half sister, Vanessa Carlisle. But according to the

source, Vanessa isn't exactly thrilled with the idea of having a brother.

"She'd just as soon have him go home tomorrow," says the source, a senior at Cabot Academy. "Maybe she's jealous that her brother is a big star, or maybe she just doesn't like the idea that her parents are so excited for Reed to be here, but either way, Vanessa and Reed aren't getting along."

Vaughn is the son of Academy Award–winning actress Marnie Vaughn and Will Carlisle. The two met while the actress was performing in a Bookman Theater adaption of Ibsen's *A Doll's House* in 1987.

The producers of *Wild Dunes* gave Reed Vaughn an ultimatum—shape up or ship out. Even though the actor is undoubtedly the breakout star of the show, producers feared that his antics would end up hurting the future of *Wild Dunes* if allowed to continue.

"It must be hard for Reed," explains the source. "He's just trying to do what's right so he can go back to work, but between the stress at home with his sister and coming into a new school for his senior year, things aren't that easy."

Time will tell whether or not Vaughn is able to get his act together and return to the set of *Wild Dunes*. In the meantime, it seems as though Reed Vaughn's homecoming isn't so sweet.

"Who'd say this?" I asked, even though I knew they wouldn't have an answer. "Why would they do this to me?"

My mother reached for the newspaper and took it from my hands. "People are going to talk, Vanessa. That's what they do."

"But I haven't done anything to deserve this."

"What's all the commotion about?" Reed asked, walking into the kitchen.

My mom handed him the paper. "There's an article in the Entertainment section about you. And they mention Vanessa."

"Oh yeah?" Reed took the paper and started reading. "Well, they were bound to print something sooner or later. I guess they picked sooner."

Reed placed the paper down on the kitchen table and then looked over at me. "It's just an article, who cares?"

"I care, that's who," I told him, my voice shaking. "I know you don't give a crap about any of us, but we had a life before you showed up, Reed. *I* had a life." I tried not to let him see the tears welling up in my eyes.

Reed stepped back. "Hey, Vanessa, I'm sorry. Really."

He almost did look sorry. Or else he was a better actor than I gave him credit for.

"They really shouldn't have gone after you, too," he continued. "I'm fair game, but they should have left you out of it."

"Reed's right," my dad added. "Getting you involved was totally out of line."

My dad reached for the paper, folded it up, and tossed it in the garbage can. "There. Now we can all forget about it, okay?"

"Forget about it?" I screamed, digging through the garbage until I found the now-soggy paper. "Throwing it in the garbage doesn't mean that everyone who reads that article will *forget about it*." I held up the paper, a brown stain and coffee grounds seeping through the pages. "Everyone's going to read this and talk about me—people I don't even know will be saying I'm some sort of pathetic loser. Forget about it? I don't think so!"

My parents watched my tirade, their eyes darting from my face to the paper and the coffee grounds dripping on the floor.

I smacked the newspaper against the table and then snatched it up and stormed out, but not before I heard Reed ask, "So, is there any orange juice left?"

"Can you believe this?" I tossed the newspaper onto Taylor's bedroom floor. "I'd love to know which pathetic Cabot student told a reporter this. Reed Vaughn's homecoming isn't so *sweet*. She feels *bad* for him. It's such shit."

Instead of looking up at me, Taylor continued organizing her closet. "I'm sure they didn't know it would come out sounding that way," she offered. "Besides, who reads the *Chicago Tribune* Entertainment section on Sundays anyway?"

"Are you kidding me? That article is in the hands of half a million people right now; half a million people thinking my family is screwed-up. Thinking *I'm* screwed-up. Who would do this to me? I bet it was the Susans."

I expected Taylor to defend the reporter's right to free speech, the sanctity of anonymous sources, or at the very least rip into the Susans. But instead she kept her back to me and lined up her shoes.

"You don't think it was Sarah Middleton, do you? Like maybe she did this to throw me off my game or something?"

Taylor kept her head in her closet. "It's not that big a deal. Besides, I'm sure the person never meant to hurt you."

"How can you say that?"

Finally, Taylor turned around to face me. And that's when I knew. Just by the look on her face.

"Oh my God," I practically gasped. "It was you!"

"I'm so sorry," Taylor apologized, and jumped up next to me on the bed. "I swear I didn't make it sound so bad. I don't know why it came out sounding so horrible."

"How could you do this?" I demanded, still in a state of disbelief. My best friend sold me out for Reed Vaughn and an anonymous quote in the *Chicago Tribune*. "How could you do this after the way he treated you the other day?"

"It was weeks ago, I swear, you have to believe me. Some guy was snooping around outside Cabot and I figured it was someone from the press." Taylor spoke quickly, not giving me any time to jump in with more questions. "He looked nice, and I figured they'd get their story anyway, and I thought if they got it from me at least they'd get it right."

"Right?" I jumped up and grabbed the paper off the floor, waving it in her face. "Is this what you think is *right*? Is this what you think of *me*?"

"Of course not. Not at all."

"I can't believe you did this. I can't believe that of all the people who'd screw me over just to get in the paper, you'd be the one to stoop so low."

"I swear it wasn't like that," she insisted, but it was a waste of time. I knew that was *exactly* what it was like.

I jumped off the bed and got the hell out of her room, slamming the bedroom door behind me so hard I heard the sound of shattering glass as a frame fell off the wall. Reed was in pieces on the floor of her bedroom and her best friend was about to walk out the door. At that moment, I really wasn't sure which would bother Taylor more.

When I got home, I went straight to the bathroom, closed the door, and sat there. I wanted Patrick to put his arms around me and tell me it was all going to be okay. I wanted him to sit next to me and hold my hand until I didn't feel like my best friend had just sold me out for a stupid newspaper article. But Patrick was halfway across the country and there was nothing I could do but try to remember what it felt like when we were together.

I got up and reached into the medicine cabinet and let my fingers skim the Musk Speed Stick. I pulled it out and removed the lid. With my eyes squeezed shut, I inhaled the familiar smell of my boyfriend and let it fill my lungs.

And that's when the bathroom door flung open. "What are you doing?" an amused voice asked.

I spun around, but even before I saw him standing there, I knew Reed would be smirking.

My hands flew behind my back, where I dropped the Speed Stick into the sink. "Nothing."

"Nothing?" He walked in and glanced down into the sink. "Looks to me like you're smelling my deodorant."

"Not *your* deodorant," I told him, and then added, "Patrick's." As if that would make it any better.

"Sure. Hey, it's okay. I've had girls do worse. At least it wasn't my underwear."

"I'm not some psycho stalker who wants to know what your armpits smell like," I told him.

"Really?" He opened the medicine cabinet, reached for the Speed Stick in the sink, and placed it back on the shelf. "Then how do you explain your nose getting up close and personal with my antiperspirant?"

"Forget it." I pushed past Reed and rushed toward my room. But I wasn't alone.

Reed followed me.

Despite the fact that nothing I could say would make the scene he encountered in the bathroom seem normal, I still felt the need to explain myself. "Look, Patrick wears the same deodorant, okay?"

Reed shrugged. "Okay."

"And I tried calling him to talk about the article in the *Tribune,* but he wasn't there. So I just wanted to . . ." my voice trailed off as I realized how completely ridiculous I sounded.

"You just wanted to smell him, right?" Reed finished for me. "Sure, I get it."

"No you don't," I told him. "Doesn't it bother you?"

"Doesn't what bother me?"

"The article?"

"Not really. I've had worse than that printed about me. This is tame by comparison."

"But they're lies."

"Are they?"

I didn't answer right away, and so Reed continued talking.

"Your parents have gone out of their way to be nice to me, but it's not like you want me here. Nor does anyone else at Cabot, for that matter."

"The girls are glad you're here," I pointed out, attempting to prove him wrong but only making myself sound lame in the process. Of course the girls were glad he was here—they were *girls.* "At least they *were* glad, until you were a shit to Taylor."

"Yeah, well, I guess Taylor showed me, didn't she?" Reed conceded, looking almost embarrassed as he looked down at his hands.

"She just calls them like she sees them," I told him, which didn't make me feel any better, considering what she'd said about me.

"Anyway, about that reporter, you can't take it so personally. He doesn't know me or you or your parents."

No, he didn't. But the person who gave him all the information did. "I know who told him all those things about us. It was Taylor."

"Really?" Reed asked, his tone a mix of disbelief and amusement. "I didn't think Taylor had it in her. Tell her I'm impressed."

"I'm not talking to her."

"Come on, she didn't know what would happen. Reporters trick people into talking all the time."

"She wasn't tricked, Reed. She betrayed me."

"She didn't betray you, Vanessa. I can't imagine she went out of her way to piss you off. She's your best friend."

"A best friend doesn't tell a reporter that your family is fucked-up. A best friend doesn't make you sound like you're jealous of your brother."

"Don't blame Taylor, Vanessa. If it wasn't her, it would have been somebody else. She actually may have done you a favor. Imagine what the Susans would have said about the situation."

I looked up at Reed. "You know about the Susans?"

"I go to school with you, Vanessa. I see what goes on at Cabot. Contrary to what you believe, I don't live in my own little 'Reed Vaughn world.'"

"You heard that?"

"I'm not deaf, either."

"I didn't think you paid attention to what went on at school."

Reed shrugged. "Yeah, well, Marnie always told me an actor's first job is to observe."

"And here I thought your first job was to annoy." I sat down on my bed and watched Reed laugh at me. "So, what else have you noticed about Cabot?"

"You mean besides the Susans?"

"No. Let's start there. Tell me what you think of them."

Reed actually had some pretty acute observations. And they were funny, too. He saw right through the Susans, thought Ali, Posey, and Ashlee were in danger of starring in a *Girls Gone Wild* video their first year in college, and he even liked Lauren Martin's taste in music.

"What about the guys?" I asked.

"What about them?"

"Does it bother you that they don't like you?"

Reed shrugged. "There really isn't much I can do about it, is there?"

"You could be less of an asshole. You could try to get them to like you," I suggested as an option.

Reed laughed at me. "You can't control everything, Vanessa. I can't make them like me any more than the Susans could make you like them."

He had a point.

"What about Sarah Middleton?" I pressed on. "Do you like her?"

"Sarah's pretty cool, and she's actually not a bad tutor. You'd probably like her, if you ever got to know her."

"So you're not just hanging out with her to annoy me?"

"Does my hanging out with Sarah annoy you?"

"A little. Less than you do, though."

Reed smiled. "I'm sure she'd be happy to hear that. Why am I so much more annoying?"

"Well, without you things would be the way they used to be around here."

"And were they that great before I showed up?"

"That's not the point and you know it. Ever since you came here, everything's different. And Sarah's just one more thing I have to worry about now. Without her I'd be skating through senior year."

"So you mean now you'll actually have to work harder to show your parents you're nothing like them?"

With Reed's amateur Freud impersonation, the conversation had clearly reached its conclusion.

"Look, are we clear about why I had your deodorant?" I wanted to know.

"You mean why you were sniffing my deodorant?"

"Whatever."

"Yeah, we're clear."

"Good, because I only have two more weeks until SATs and I have to study."

Reed glanced at the phone on my night table. "Shouldn't you call Taylor first and tell her you're not still mad?"

I grabbed my SAT workbook off my desk and tossed it on my bed.

"No way."

"Hell hath no fury like a woman scorned," Reed mumbled on his way out of my room, reciting a line I recognized from the play *The Mourning Bride*.

He actually sounded pretty convincing. Maybe he could pull off a Southern accent for my dad's play, after all.

chapter sixteen

For the next two weeks I spent most of my time either in the yearbook office or studying for my SATs. And it sucked. Every minute of it. Taylor called me three times Sunday night and tried to get me to accept her apology, but I just wasn't ready. It would be one thing if she had been tricked into talking to the reporter, like Reed said, but I knew that she'd intentionally told the guy about me. Maybe she even pulled out her *Chronicle* notebook just to make sure she didn't leave anything out.

If I wasn't talking to my best friend there was only one thing to do—everything else. I threw myself into all the extracurricular activities I was putting on my college applications. I made lists. Lots of them. Ideas for new student council events, an outline for every section of the yearbook, research I had to do for an upcoming Model UN program—I organized, prepped, and coordinated. But I didn't step foot into the *Chronicle* office, where I knew my former best friend would be sitting in front of a Mac, laying out her column. And every time I passed Sarah Middleton in the hall or sat next to her in class, I added another item to my list—kick ass on the SATs.

Last year when he was preparing for his SATs, Patrick wasn't nearly as stressed out about increasing his scores. He was pretty much on the bubble as far as scores go, and I think he believed being on the bubble was fine for a lacrosse player. Having three years worth of MVP trophies on the shelf in his bedroom probably helped. The thing about sports was, you couldn't argue with the outcome. There was always a winner and a loser. One team always scored more goals or runs or points than their opponent. You could look at a scorebook and see someone's statistics—how many assists and penalties and goals they were responsible for. So in that respect, I thought Patrick had it easier than I did. Practically everything I did was subjective. There was no competition that determined who got to be the editor of the yearbook. Scholastic Bowl members were selected by the faculty. Sure, votes were cast for student council positions, but there was always speculation over the results. Was the new president really the person with the most votes, or, ultimately, the person the faculty thought would do the best job?

But athletes, they could always look at a scoreboard or the sports page in the paper and see exactly how they stacked up against everyone else. They were supposed to be competitive. Nobody ever thought Patrick was overreacting when he swore and rammed his lacrosse stick into the ground after missing a goal. And nobody was ever *really* appalled if a fight broke out between players after a questionable call from the referee. It was just part of the game.

Now, if I threw Sarah Middleton to the ground after finding out that she got a better grade than me on our physics test, and I thought the teacher made a mistake grading the papers, do you think people would step in and halfheartedly yell, "Break it up, break it up"? No. I'd be suspended and sent for psychological counseling, just like Melanie Carlson, who last year lunged for Carrie Sparks across the lunch table after finding out her boyfriend and Carrie were sleeping together.

On Friday, the night before the test, I called Patrick. I wanted to call Taylor, but we hadn't spoken since I stormed out of her room, and even though I knew she'd make me feel better, I didn't dial her number. I just wasn't ready.

I thought maybe Patrick would be able to give me some advice that would settle my stomach and help me get some sleep before entering standardized testing hell. He was good at storing up his coach's pep talks and pulling them out for moments like this.

I knew Patrick's number by heart, but for a minute I thought I dialed the wrong number.

"Who are you?" I asked, when a girl's voice answered.

"Amory," she told me, sounding offended that I'd even ask. "Who are you?"

The gall! "This is Vanessa, Patrick's girlfriend," I told her, stressing the word "girlfriend" just in case she had any question as to who Vanessa was. But who the hell was Amory, and what was she doing in my boyfriend's room at one o'clock on a Friday night?

"Hold on, he just went into Brent's room for a sec."

I held on and waited for Patrick to return. "Hey, Vanessa, what's up?"

"What's up is that I'm wondering why a girl is answering your phone," I answered, in no mood to play coy girlfriend. I had enough to worry about besides some girl who feels it's okay to serve as my boyfriend's answering service.

"That was just Amory," he told me.

"*Just* Amory?" What did that mean?

"Come on, don't start," he prodded. "I'm glad you called."

"Amory didn't sound so glad," I mumbled.

"She just answered my phone, Vanessa. It's no big deal. So what's really bothering you?"

I rolled over on my side and propped the pillow under my head. "I have my SATs tomorrow and I was hoping you would convince me I'm going to do fine."

"Of course you're going to do fine." He stopped talking for a minute, and it sounded like he was taking a sip of something. "You're going to do great, just like the first time."

"You think so?"

"I know so."

Okay, so he did make me feel a little better, even if he was just saying exactly what I wanted to hear. "I can't wait to be there next weekend."

"I can't wait to have you here."

"I've come up with a list of things I thought we could do," I told him, before turning off my light and crawling under my covers, ready to rattle off the schedule I'd come up with. "First I thought you could show me the residential colleges, and then we could—"

Patrick cut me off before I could finish. "I was actually thinking I could start by showing you my room," he suggested, and I knew exactly what he was implying.

I smiled in the dark. "Yeah, we could do that, too."

"It's late. You should get some sleep, you have a big test tomorrow."

I glanced over at the clock on my desk. "Yeah, you're right. I love you."

Another pause and a sip, and then Patrick said, "Love you, too."

Despite myself, I hoped Amory was close enough to hear him.

How does someone oversleep for a test she's spent countless hours preparing for, a test that will, undoubtedly, help determine her future? Actually, if she's up all night obsessing about someone named Amory (what kind of a name was Amory anyway?), it's quite easy. She tosses and turns about every five minutes, searching for the ever-illusive cool spot on the sheets while attempting various sleeping positions she's sure are going to lull her to sleep. But between curling up into the fetal position, lying flat on her back with her arms above her head, and lying on her stomach with her hands tucked under her hip bones until the one part of her that actually does fall asleep, her left arm, is seething with so many pins and needles she wonders if she's come down with the very same disease she saw on some Lifetime movie her mother was watching last weekend, she completely forgot to set her alarm clock. So even though I didn't manage to get any sleep between 1:30 and 4:30, I did manage to close my eyes just long enough to oversleep.

And so the pins and needles in my arm at 3:00 A.M. were nothing compared to the pain I felt when my eyes opened Saturday morning and I looked over at my clock and saw the time: 7:39 A.M.

Fuck!

I jumped out of bed and screamed, "Mom!"

She came to my door just as I was pulling on my jeans.

"What's wrong?"

"I have fifteen minutes to get to my SATs, that's what's wrong. Why didn't you wake me up?"

"I would have, but I figured you set your alarm." She glanced at the clock on my night table. "You did set your alarm, didn't you?"

"What's going on?" Reed appeared in the hall, rubbing his eyes. "What's all the screaming about?"

"Vanessa forgot to set her alarm for her SATs."

"Can you drive me?" I asked my mom, ignoring Reed. "There's no way I'll make it on time if I take the bus."

"Sure, let me go grab the keys." My mom turned around and headed down the stairs.

"Go ahead and start the car," I called after her, throwing my hair up into a haphazard ponytail. "I'll be down in two seconds, I just have to brush my teeth."

"How the hell do you forget to set your alarm clock?" Reed asked me, as he stood in the doorway to the bathroom watching me brush my teeth. "You of all people?"

"I was preoccupied last night," I told him through a mouthful of toothpaste.

After spitting, rinsing, and grabbing two number two pencils off my desk, I ran downstairs and jumped into our car idling in the alley.

We didn't talk on the way. Thanks to my mom's lead foot, the ride to the testing center took half the time it would have if I'd taken the bus.

When my mom pulled the car up to the curb in front of the building, I barely waited for the car to stop before jumping out.

"Good luck," she called out the window as I tore up the front steps. Despite the sweat forming on my upper lip and the heart pounding in my chest, I was sure everything would be okay. We'd made it in record time.

But it didn't matter. I was too late. It was 8:21 by the time I got to the registration table, and the woman sitting on the folding chair behind a sign labeled A–G wouldn't let me in.

"They're probably just going over the instructions," I told her, trying to appeal to her sense of reason. "And I know the instructions. I've memorized them, I know every word about number two pencils and filling in bubbles."

Still, she shook her head. "Can't do that. It's the rule."

"Look," I told her, putting both of my now clenched fists on the table and leaning over so she knew I wasn't fooling around. I was getting into the auditorium and I was taking that test. And I wasn't going to let some testing Nazi stop me. "I know the rules. I follow the rules. Every single day of my life I live by the rules. I made a mistake and forgot to set my alarm clock, so why don't you just make an exception this one time and let me in?"

"Like I said, I can't do that." She wasn't budging. I felt the sting of tears even before the ache in my chest. This had to be what dying felt like.

"What if I make it worth your while?" I ventured, reaching into my jeans and unrolling a five-dollar bill. This was what it had come to—I was trying to bribe the SAT lady. "Please?" I practically squeaked, thinking maybe she'd take pity on the unshowered, unbrushed girl standing before her in a faded blue T-shirt that read I'M A VIRGIN. Reed must have stuck his T-shirt in my closet by accident.

"I'm sorry," she apologized, but she didn't look sorry at all. She looked like she didn't care. Even if I was proclaiming my virginity.

It was nine o'clock, the test had started, and I had nobody to blame but myself. I had blown it. Big time.

I could have taken the bus home or called my mom and asked her to turn around and come back to get me. But there was no way I could let my parents know I missed the SATs. And there was no way I'd let Reed find out. Instead, I decided to sit on the front steps and wait for the test to be over, to cry by myself on the cold, hard cement steps for three hours until the people smart enough to actually set their alarm for the test started trickling out the front door. For three hours the tears ran down my cheeks as my mind ran down a list of the ramifications of not pushing one little button on a stupid Panasonic alarm clock.

1. First there would be Yale's reaction to my solo SAT score. Obviously they'd think I thought I was too good to take the test a second time. And obviously they wouldn't want some smug girl who thought her first effort was good enough.
2. And neither would any of the other colleges I was applying to.
3. I'd end up at a community college, where I'd have to take a part-time job delivering Domino's pizzas just to kill the time while everyone I knew was away at the college of their choice.
4. Some crazy guy would order an extra-large pepperoni delivered to his remote house on the outskirts of some nature preserve, and then ask me to come in while he got his wallet from the kitchen.
5. When they finally discovered my body buried in a shallow grave next to some overgrown jogging path in a nature preserve, the coroner would ask my mom how this could have happened to such a nice, normal girl, and the only response she'll be able to manage is "she overslept for her SATs."

"What are you doing out here?" John asked when he spotted me on the steps. "And why are your eyes all swollen?"

I stood up, which wasn't easy considering my butt had fallen asleep. "I missed the test."

John didn't say anything. I think he knew there wasn't much he could say.

"Say something!" I demanded, still sniffling.

"Nice shirt."

"Hey, John! Vanessa!" Sarah called out and waved to us through the crowd now gathered on the steps.

"How'd it go?" John yelled back to her.

Sarah shot us a thumbs-up and ran to catch her bus.

John watched me, probably to see if I'd spontaneously combust right there on the steps. "Don't worry. It's fine. You did great the first time."

"That's not the point. Maybe I would have done better this time."

"Or maybe you would have done worse."

"You're just saying that because you're hoping your score went up and you beat me." John's first score was sixty points lower than mine.

"Yeah, maybe." He smiled at me. "Look, it's not the end of the world. Repeat after me, *This is not the end of the world.*"

Reluctantly I obeyed between postcry hiccups. "This is not the end of the world."

"There. Now just keep saying that until you believe it."

I repeated it to myself the entire way home, but not once did I ever start to believe it.

chapter seventeen

"Where is everyone?" I asked my mom when I found her in the living room outlining the windows with a tape measure. You'd think after installing a vast array of balloon curtains, valances, pleated shades, vertical blinds, and plantation shutters, she'd know the dimensions by heart by now.

"Reed and your dad went over to the theater."

So my dad had finally suckered Reed into going to work with him. "Are they going to be home soon?"

"Probably not for a while. Your dad's still trying to get Reed to take a look at the script for *Running Out*. I think your dad really wants to direct him this spring."

"I thought *Running Out* was just some little experimental play in the studio theater."

"It is."

"And I thought it was about a gay couple."

"That's the one."

"A gay couple that is run out of some hick town in the South."

"Like I said, that's the one."

"So who's Reed going to play?" I couldn't picture Reed playing either a small-town Southern boy or one half of a homosexual couple.

"Look, Vanessa, I don't know. You can ask them when they get home." She stepped back and appraised the window, holding her hands up and framing the space with her fingers. "Now I need your opinion and I want you to be brutally honest. What do you think about taking down the drapes and hanging some jeweled beads from the rod so they create a prismlike effect when they catch the light?"

Was this 1971 and were we living in a VW van?

"Like a laser light show in our living room?" I asked, even though I've learned from past experience that when my mom says she wants you to be brutally honest that's not exactly what she means. "Won't it be a little hard to see if you're sitting on the couch doing something and you've got shards of light blinding you?"

My mom considered this for a minute. "You're right. Maybe if we moved the couch against the other wall . . ."

I left her alone to figure it all out.

I couldn't imagine Reed letting my dad direct him, no less in a play in the little studio theater. It didn't compare to the seven-hundred-seat main stage where the larger productions were held. Besides, what the hell did Reed know about stage acting? It wasn't exactly like the Skippy peanut butter commercials Reed did as a kid, and it couldn't be further from *Wild Dunes*. Thanks to Taylor, I'd seen *Wild Dunes* under duress, and I've got to be honest, if he wasn't Marnie Vaughn's son and didn't look so good, I doubt Reed would be acting anywhere, no less at the Bookman Theater.

Besides, Reed had never done theater before, so he didn't even have his Equity card, which meant the Bookman would have to buy him one. Seemed like a lot of trouble to go to for some guy who was used to his own custom-designed trailer, not sharing a dressing room with four other performers.

My dad and Reed came home around six o'clock and brought dinner with them. It was the kind of pizza I hate, some gourmet version of what should just be mozzarella cheese, tomato sauce, and a plain white crust. Instead I ate something that included Japanese eggplant, goat cheese, and sun-dried tomatoes on whole wheat dough. By the time I was through picking off all the ingredients, it was barely worth eating. Not that anyone would have noticed. My dad was too busy telling my mom about the play and how he wanted to cast Reed in the role of the adopted son of one of the gay men. How Reed was ever going to pass for some Southern-fried teenager, no less the son of a gay man, was beyond me.

"Your dad and I had an idea we'd like to talk to you about," my mom told me when she and my dad came into my room later on that night. "We thought it would be nice if Reed went to New Haven with you this weekend."

"Why?"

"We thought that maybe if he saw a college campus, what other kids your age are doing, it might be good for him."

"He doesn't care about college," I told them, just in case the fact slipped their minds. "He barely cares about high school."

"Still." My mother looked to my dad.

"Look, it's just one weekend."

Sure, to them it was just one weekend. To me it was the first time I'd see Patrick since he left for school. Besides, how was I going to explain to Patrick that Reed would be tagging along?

"No," I told them, and crossed my arms to show them I was standing my ground. "Absolutely not."

"What do you mean, *no*?" my mom asked, as if she didn't understand the word. "It's not like you to be so difficult."

"I'm difficult?" I pointed upstairs. "Have you seen the guy living in the guest room?"

My dad frowned. "Come on, Vanessa. Is it really such a big deal?"

"Yes, it's a big deal!" I threw my hands up in the air in disbelief. Of course it was a big deal! "Patrick and I haven't seen each other in almost two months, we need time to . . ." I hesitated, trying to think of the right word, even though the word that kept coming to mind was *fuck*. And that wouldn't work. "We need time to reconnect. What am I supposed to tell Patrick?" I asked them.

"You're a smart girl," my dad answered. "You'll figure it out."

Was he kidding me? "No, I will not figure it out. I'm tired of figuring everything out. The only thing I should be figuring out is what to pack for my trip—not how to include my brother in my plans."

My dad shot me a look that said that was exactly what I'd have to do. Reed was coming to Yale with me. And there was nothing I could say to change that.

I couldn't even remember to set an alarm clock, and now I was supposed to explain to my boyfriend why my brother was hanging around? Didn't it even occur to them that I'd want to be alone with my boyfriend? That I'd want to do all the things parents fear their kids are doing when they're not around? How did they know I wasn't planning to get drunk at a keg party and dance on a pool table? Maybe my parents were starting to overestimate me.

"I hear we're going on a little road trip," Reed said to me as we walked to the bus stop on Monday morning.

I was already dreading school. Another week avoiding Taylor.

Four days until my Yale interview, where I'd have to explain why I *decided* not to take the SATs a second time. And then a weekend trying to ditch Reed so I could spend time with Patrick. The only consolation was Reed's waning popularity and the fact that our front sidewalk had remained empty for six days straight.

"I heard the same thing."

"Do you plan on sleeping with Pat while we're there?" Reed asked.

"That's really none of your business," I answered, adding, "and it's *Patrick*."

"Believe me, I don't care about your sex life—or lack thereof. I was just wondering if you'd be sleeping in your room or his."

"Why, do you plan on having company and need an extra bed?"

"No. Your dad asked me to keep an eye on you, and if he calls looking for my sister I'd like to be able to know that I'm telling him the truth when I say you're doing fine."

"He actually asked you to look after me?"

"Yeah."

I laughed. That was perfect. Rehab Reed was supposed to keep an eye on me. Forget to set one alarm clock and you're labeled irresponsible. My parents hadn't overestimated me. I'd underestimated them.

chapter eighteen

"I suppose you're not used to flying coach." I maneuvered my knees between the seatback tray and the magazine pocket, trying to get comfortable.

Reed shifted in his seat. "I told your dad I'd pay to go first class, but he said no."

"He probably thinks sitting back here builds character or something."

Reed laughed. "The only thing sitting back here builds is a stiff neck and claustrophobia," he told me, and pointed toward the front of the plane, where a navy blue curtain separated us pretzel-eating economy classers from the elite. "Right now we'd be up there feasting on fresh fruit and warm chocolate-chip cookies."

We? As in Reed and me? *I* could be behind the curtain being waited on hand and foot?

"Not to mention the fact that our feet would be propped up on a footrest instead of stuffed under the seats in front of us," Reed added.

"You offered to pay for me, too?"

"Well, yeah."

That was pretty nice of him, I had to admit. And a little out of character. Why didn't my dad tell me Reed offered to buy us both first-class tickets? If he wanted me to get along with Reed, letting my brother buy me a seat in first class would have been a good way to start. Then again, my dad probably kept it to himself because he knew no matter how much I hated the idea of Reed, there was also no way I'd turn down a seat in the first-class cabin.

"It's only a two-hour flight. We'll survive."

"Ever had those chocolate-chip cookies?" Reed reached for the *SkyMall* magazine and reclined his seatback, trying to get comfortable. "You have no idea what you're missing."

My dad had reserved seats for us on the 11:05 Connecticut Limo from Bradley Airport, which would drop us off on campus at 12:18 and give me just under an hour to get settled into the hotel and ready for my interview.

I pointed to an overhead sign and headed toward the sliding doors. "This way," I called to Reed.

Contrary to its name, Connecticut Limo wasn't a limo at all. It was a big, white van with a large, blue Connecticut Limo logo down its side.

"Here it comes, hurry up," I called to Reed, who was taking his time making his way across the crosswalk.

When the van stopped in front of the terminal, I let a few passengers on while I waited for Reed.

"Come on!" I yelled again, and then asked the driver to wait a minute.

When he reached me, Reed slipped a twenty-dollar bill out of his jeans pocket, handed it to the driver through the passenger window, and then leaned in and whispered something to him. After a minute, the driver nodded, waved to me, and pulled away.

Our ride to New Haven was leaving without us!

"What the hell did you just do? I've got an interview in less than two hours!" I glanced at my watch. It was already 11:15.

"That's not our limo," Reed told me, and then pointed across the street to where a shiny black stretch limousine waited for its passengers. "That is."

"That's our ride," I repeated, taking in the long body of the limousine.

"Yep," Reed confirmed, and looked both ways before crossing the road to our ride. "I called Connecticut Limo, ordered a *real* limousine, and put the remaining balance on my credit card," he explained as the driver opened the rear door and waved us inside the cool interior. "As far as your father knows, right now we're on a van with fifteen other people headed to New Haven."

I was pretty impressed that Reed could come up with this all on his own. Even without the assistance of his personal manager or agent or publicist, or whoever it was who usually handled these sorts of things for him.

Reed reached for the platter of Danishes and muffins resting on the side console. "So what do you think?" he asked me.

I stretched my legs out, leaned back into the slippery leather seats, and reached for the ice bucket, where a carafe of fresh-squeezed orange juice sat chilling in a mound of crushed ice. I think I could get used to the star treatment.

As we rode toward New Haven, I stared out the tinted window the entire way, checking out the scenery. Hopefully I'd be taking this ride a lot during the next four years and I wanted to memorize every sign and landmark along the way.

Reed held the remote control in his hands and flipped through the radio stations trying to find a song he liked.

"You know everything about this place. Any idea where I'd find a decent station?" he asked me.

I shook my head. "Sorry, no such luck."

"I would have thought you'd done extensive research on the selection of music available in the greater New Haven area." Reed stopped on what sounded like classic rock.

"And I thought after seeing your *Wild Dunes* performances my dad would have given up on you by now."

Reed put aside the remote control and reached for another muffin. "Marnie did a lot of theater before she got her first film role. She said it was the best preparation for an acting career."

"You mean as opposed to spreading some Skippy on a piece of white bread before taking a bite?"

"It was Jiff, not Skippy," Reed corrected me. "And that commercial paid for my first car, I'll have you know."

"So are you really going to do my dad's play this spring?"

"I'm seriously considering it."

"And you don't care that you'd be playing a supporting role?"

"It will be weird, but it might also be nice for a change," Reed admitted.

And you know what? I actually believed he meant it.

When the car pulled off the highway, I knew we'd arrived. Somewhere on the beautiful campus in front of us, my boyfriend was waiting for me. We'd been talking about this weekend for so long it almost didn't seem real. I reached for the small silver button on the door and watched as the tinted glass window slid down, giving me a view of the campus I'd only ever seen in college catalog photographs. As I watched the Gothic buildings get closer and closer, a small shiver crept up my spine. It was finally happening. Just like we'd planned.

The top of the cathedral-like library rose above the campus, and the gables of the residential colleges angled toward one another. For some reason it made me think of that scene in *Mary Poppins,* where the chimney sweeps dance from rooftop to rooftop. The leaves had started to change color and stood like vivid little sunbursts next to the gray stone of the buildings. It was amazing. Not that the leaves don't change color in Chicago, it's just that the trees are usually planted in small two-foot-by-two-foot squares of dirt in the sidewalk and have signs warning that not cleaning up after your animal carries a fine of up to one hundred dollars.

"Wow."

Reed sat forward and looked out the window next to me. "So you think you're going to like it here?"

"Like it? I love it."

"What time is your interview?" Reed asked as we carried our bags to our adjoining hotel rooms.

"One o'clock," I told him.

"Well, good luck." He slipped the card key into its slot and stepped into his room.

"Don't you mean break a leg?"

Reed popped his head out into the hall again. "I thought you weren't into acting."

"I'm not, but I'll take any luck I can get at this point."

"Okay. In that case, break a leg."

Once inside my room I unpacked my makeup bag and gave myself a little touch-up.

Subtle blush and lip gloss—check.

I brushed my teeth and breathed into my cupped hand.

Minty fresh breath—check.

I checked out my image in the full-length mirror on the back of the closet door.

Wrinkle-free pants and shirt—check.

It was time. Everything up to now had just been practice for this moment. And I was ready. By the time I walked out of that admissions office they'd want me on the cover of next year's catalog.

Okay, maybe not. But still, I was all set to go.

I wound my way along the stone sidewalks cutting across the grassy lawns until I found what I was looking for. The admissions office.

I checked in at the front desk and sat down in the reception area with four other students who I assumed were also waiting for their interview. It was obvious we were all sizing one another up, but nobody said a word or even looked at anybody else. Instead, we all pretended to read the information booklets and course catalogs on the side tables—as if we all hadn't already committed their content to memory months ago.

I looked around the small room and tried to guess who was there, what niche they were all hoping to fill. The quarterback for the state championship football team. The ballerina. The artist. The musician. The environmentalist.

Each time I glanced up, someone quickly diverted his or her eyes away from me. I couldn't help but wonder what they saw when they looked at me. Were they trying to figure out what my niche was? Were they sizing me up, trying to figure out if I was their competition? It was hard to believe that anyone sitting in the admissions office would feel threatened by me. At Cabot I was special, but around here, girls like me were a dime a dozen, which is why I'd been practicing my answers for my interview for weeks now.

All of a sudden statistics ran through my head—applicant numbers, admission percentages, incoming class demographics. And that's when my hands got moist, my mouth went dry, and I realized that everything hinged on this moment. The next four years, my relationship with Patrick, getting into the school I couldn't imagine *not* getting into—it all depended on this interview.

I glanced across the room at a set of eyes fixed on my knee, which was nervously bouncing up and down and, from the dirty look I was getting, quite annoyingly. I attempted an apologetic look, and stopped my runaway knee tapping.

"Vanessa Carlisle," the woman behind the desk called out.

I stood up, smoothed the front of my pants with my damp hands, and went to meet the student waiting for me by the door.

It was showtime.

My interviewer was Becky, a junior and biology major from Atlanta. She seemed nice enough, but then again, that was her job.

Becky didn't throw me any unexpected curveballs, and I started to relax. Maybe I'd gotten all worked up over nothing. I thought I was doing a pretty stellar job of addressing her questions. I made sure my responses answered her questions and revealed a little bit about myself to set me apart from every other private school girl applying to Yale.

So when she asked, "What's been the most difficult thing about your senior year so far?" I was a little stumped. I hadn't prepared for that one. "Tell me about your extracurricular activities, what subject do you enjoy the most, how do you see yourself contributing to the Yale community?", those answers I had down pat.

But the most difficult thing about my senior year? I had to think about that one for a second.

"Actually, it hasn't been very difficult so far," I finally told her.

"Cabot has prepared me well for a rigorous course of study this year."

I thought my answer would satisfy her, so I sat there and waited for her follow-up question, which I figured would be about my course load or something to that effect.

Instead, Becky just smiled at me and looked down at my information sheet. "I can see that. But what I meant was, is there anything that you've found personally challenging about this year? Honestly?"

Personally challenging? Honestly?

Like having Sarah Middleton show up with her 4.0 grade point average and Harvard notebooks? Like having my boyfriend go to college halfway across the country? Like finding out my best friend screwed me over? Like finding out I had a brother?

"There is one thing that I didn't exactly anticipate," I ventured slowly, not really knowing how to put a good spin on this answer.

"And what's that?"

"I'm an only child and right before school started my parents told me I have a half brother."

I guess she was expecting some boring "pressures of being a senior" answer or "fear of leaving home for the first time" response, because all of a sudden she seemed to perk up.

"Really?" She jotted down a note on my information sheet and sat forward on her seat. "That had to be a bit of a shock for you. Can you tell me more about that?"

I debated how much I should tell her. I didn't want my *honest* answer to make me sound like the girl described in the *Tribune* article. But the truth wasn't some rosy picture of discovering a brother who ended up becoming my new best friend, either.

Then again, she was pretty excited to hear my answer.

Maybe this was an opportunity to *really* set myself apart from all the other private school girls sitting out there in the waiting room. Maybe Reed was my ticket into Yale. The clincher. Maybe when the admissions committee was sifting through tens of thousands of applications from valedictorians and captains of the lacrosse team and concert pianists who saved exotic animals from near extinction, someone would reach into the pile, pull my application out, and say, "Now here's someone with an interesting story, what do you say we make her a member of our incoming freshman class?"

I mean, come on, how many other applicants could claim to discover they had a TV star for a brother?

"Well, my parents are in the theater and years ago, before I was born, they separated and my father had a relationship with one of the actresses in his show."

Becky sat forward, waiting for the punch line. But I was just warming up.

"A few days before school started we found out he was coming to live with us."

"That had to be a huge surprise." She sat back, thinking my story was finished. It wasn't. The best was yet to come.

"Oh, it was. It changed everything."

She nodded. "I imagine it did."

"But even more surprising than discovering I had a brother was finding out that my brother was Reed Vaughn."

This time she didn't nod. And she didn't move in her seat, either. She just sat there trying to figure out what to say to me. All the training the admissions office had provided didn't prepare her for my answer.

"Your brother is Reed Vaughn?"

Now it was my turn to nod. Mission accomplished. "Yes, he is."

"Wow."

"So, in addition to the *normal*," I stressed the word to make sure she knew my situation was anything but ordinary, "challenges the other students you're interviewing are facing during senior year, I've also had to deal with the unexpected news that Reed was coming to live with us."

She scribbled something down on the paper in her lap and I had a feeling I knew exactly what she was writing in the comments section on my interview sheet: Admit this girl. *Now.*

I'd aced my admissions interview, and in less than two hours I was going to meet my boyfriend in his dorm room for a well-needed reunion. Needless to say, I had a smile on my face the entire way back to the hotel. The irony of using Reed's celebrity to get Becky's attention wasn't lost on me. With a little dramatic timing I'd managed to play the Reed card to my advantage for once.

He must have heard me come in, because a few minutes later Reed was knocking at the door adjoining our rooms.

"How'd it go?" he asked me when I let him in.

"I think it went really well." There was no reason to tell him *why* it went so well. It wasn't like he needed an ego boost.

"What are your plans now?"

It was just after two o'clock and I was meeting Patrick back in his suite after his last class.

"I'm meeting Patrick at four."

Reed nodded, and just stood there straddling the space between our two rooms. It was probably just my imagination, but he seemed to be waiting for me to say something. Like maybe invite him to come with me or something. And that definitely wasn't going to happen.

"What are you going to do?" I finally asked, because I didn't know what else to say at this point.

"I'll probably just watch some TV and go get a bite to eat or something."

"Sounds good." I was not going to ask him to come with me. There was no way. I'd waited almost two months, and I wasn't going to share Patrick with Reed. I'd already shared enough.

"I'm going to get changed," I told Reed, and made a point of reaching into my suitcase to grab a pair of jeans. "So I'll see you tomorrow?"

He got my hint and backed up into his room. "Okay, see you tomorrow."

I didn't run to meet Patrick, but at the pace I was going, it was pretty damn close. When I got to Old Campus, where all the freshman live, I was fifteen minutes early. I didn't want to seem too anxious, so I hung out in the quadrangle of Victorian Gothic dormitories and tried to imagine living there. As I walked across the lawn, I could absolutely picture it—sitting out on the lawn in the fall, trudging through snow in the winter, playing Frisbee in the quad in the spring. This was exactly where I was meant to be. I just knew it.

I was imagining what it would be like to be able to meet Patrick between classes and hang out studying together at night, when I spotted him coming toward me.

I'd know his walk anywhere. If Patrick's midfield shuffling of his private parts annoyed the hell out of me, he made up for it with that walk.

"Vanessa!" Patrick called out and waved at me when he spotted me across the lawn.

I didn't even bother replying. Sure, I could have walked to meet him, I could have acted like it was no big deal, like I was too cool to get this excited. But screw it, I'd waited way too long to be with Patrick, and I wasn't waiting another minute.

I ran to him, threw my arms around his neck, and buried my face against Patrick's skin. "I've missed you," I told him over and over again until even I thought I was sounding ridiculous.

"I'm finally here," I told Patrick, pulling back to look at him. He laughed at me. "I can see that."

We leaned in, our lips meeting for a kiss, and for a split second I almost thought we forgot how. But after a little maneuvering, everything fell into place. And it was exactly how I remembered it.

Patrick took my hand and led me to his dorm while I gushed about my interview with Becky and how amazing the campus was in real life. The words just tumbled out, and, if it wasn't for the fact that we met up with some of his friends before we got to Patrick's suite, I don't think I would have stopped talking at all.

"This is Vanessa," he said, letting go of my hand and introducing me to a group standing around the entryway. "And, Vanessa, this is Grant, Brent, Kelly, and Amory."

The idea of really being here with Patrick was still so overwhelming, all the faces blurred together. But when I heard him say "Amory," I snapped to attention and took in the tall, thin brunette with hair that spilled over her shoulders and all the way down her back.

"Hi," I said, and everyone said hello back. I looked for a barbell-speared tongue when Amory opened her mouth, and was almost relieved when I didn't see one. But for some reason, maybe it was the cool way she eyed me up and down when I reached for Patrick's hand, I got the feeling she was giving me the once-over, as well.

"We'd better get going," Patrick told them, and I followed him upstairs.

"This is nice," I told him when we got to his suite. "Your room is actually better than I expected."

The navy blue comforter on Patrick's bed was similar to the one he had at home, and I recognized the throw rug next to his bed. Other than that, everything looked new.

"Mind if I join you?" he asked me, dropping his books on the desk and coming over to the bed where I was sitting.

I barely had time to say "not at all," before we were under the comforter.

In bed with him, the familiar feel of his skin, how his fingertips felt smooth as he ran them along my waist just light enough to tickle a little, it all felt absolutely right.

The room was silent as we kissed, but I could hear the faint hum as the red digital numbers on Patrick's alarm clock changed. Already, the weekend was going too fast. *Stop!* I wanted to yell. I wanted to make time stand still so I could savor every minute with Patrick, I wanted to take the seven weeks we'd been apart and put every missed moment into this weekend.

"God, I've missed you," I whispered in his ear as he lay on top of me.

"I almost forgot how amazing you feel," he replied, brushing the hair out of my eyes. "You didn't go off the pill, did you?"

I shook my head and felt him growing hard against me.

And we lay there together in Patrick's room, everything else—my interview, my brother, my class rank—faded into the background. I was exactly where I was supposed to be, and nothing else seemed to matter.

chapter nineteen

"Did you have fun with Patrick last night?" Reed asked when I got back to the hotel around four o'clock the next day.

The effort he made to use my boyfriend's preferred name did not go unnoticed by me.

"Yeah," I told him, not even trying to hide my smile. "I did."

"Well, the least you can do is tell me about it considering I just sat around here watching reruns of *Three's Company* on TV Land."

Taylor was the person I wanted to talk to. I could tell her the same thing ten times six different ways and she'd still be excited. Reed wasn't even in the same league as a best friend, but I told him about meeting Patrick's friends, eating in the dining hall, and hanging out in his suite, and I have to admit, it was nice to tell someone. Of course, when I talked to Reed I left out the part about spending the night with Patrick. Reed wasn't my real brother, but still, it would just be too weird.

"If it was so great, why are you here right now instead of hanging out with him?"

"Patrick wanted to go to the library and get some studying done before tonight. I'm meeting him at seven back at his room." I flopped on the bed and reached for the remote control.

"So what are you going to do until then? Hang out here watching TV?"

"I'm relaxing." I picked up the cable guide and started flipping through the pages, looking for something to watch.

Reed came over to the bed and sat down. "Marnie went to Yale, you know."

No, I did not know. But it figured. Here I was busting my ass to get in and Reed Vaughn was a legacy who, with some studying and decent SATs and his Hollywood halo, could get in without much effort. For a minute I wondered if I could claim Marnie on my application but I didn't exactly know how to describe our relationship—mother of half brother? Woman my dad slept with while separated from my mom?

"She did?"

Reed nodded. "I know that must crush you, some dumb actress attending your revered Yale."

"I never said Marnie was dumb."

"No, but I know you think we're all dumb, don't you?" He didn't bother waiting for me to answer. "Anyway, Marnie went to the drama school and asked me to stop by and say hi to an old friend who still teaches here. Want to come with me?" Reed offered.

"I'm meeting Patrick at seven," I told him.

"So what are you going to do? Sit around here for three hours watching TV and doodling on the hotel notepad?" he asked.

I put my pen down and stopped doodling. "I'm fine."

Reed waved his hand at me and got up. "Whatever. If that's what you want to do. Far be it from me to argue with the girl who knows everything."

I didn't really want to sit around watching TV. Nor did the idea of staring at the walls of my hotel room thrill me.

"Fine, I'll come." I slid off the bed and grabbed my purse. "Do you know where we're going?"

Reed held the door open and waited for me. "I'm sure we can find our way there."

"I have a campus map in my bag," I told him, and started for my suitcase.

Reed reached for my arm and stopped me. "We don't need a campus map, and we don't need to plot out the most efficient route to take," he said, pulling me through the door behind him. "I think two intelligent people can get where they're going without a map."

Two intelligent people? What kind of math was Reed doing?

Reed did a pretty decent job navigating his way to the theater, which was over on Chapel Street in a converted Baptist church.

It was weird, being in another theater. Growing up I was something of a staple around the Bookman. My dad would take me to the theater with him when my mom was out with clients or needed me out of the house so she could work. I used to have fun hanging out in the costume shop storage room trying on old-fashioned hoop skirts or making myself a long, curly-haired brunette with a little help from the wig room.

Yale Repertory Theater was way older than the new Bookman space in downtown Chicago, but it reminded me of when my dad would take me to the old space over by the Art Institute.

Reed told the woman behind the ticket counter that we were there to see someone named Jeffrey, and she pointed us to a door leading to the back of the house.

"Who's Jeffrey?" I asked Reed as we followed her directions and passed things I recognized—the cast board, the call board, a sign indicating the prop room.

"He's the floor manager. He was around when my mom was here."

It was the first time I'd heard Reed call Marnie his mom. It almost made him seem normal for a minute.

"There he is." Reed pointed toward a balding man seated in front of a TV screen perched just offstage.

We went over to Jeffrey, who was busy watching the actors run through a scene onstage.

"Jeffrey?" Reed asked hesitantly, standing a few feet away.

Jeffrey turned around and immediately grinned. He obviously knew exactly who he was looking at. "Reed Vaughn."

There was a lot of hugging as Jeffrey greeted Reed and started gushing about Marnie and how he knew she'd always be a star. The whole time I stood behind Reed waiting for someone to remember I was there. Finally, Reed turned to me.

"Jeffrey, this is Vansesa Carlisle."

"You're not Will Carlisle's daughter, are you?" Jeffrey asked, squinting at me as if trying to figure out why I looked vaguely familiar.

I nodded. "That's me."

Jeffrey came over and shook my hand. "Will's doing some great things over at the Bookman. Tell him I send my best."

"I will."

"Hey, Rachel," Jeffrey called out, and then pulled Reed toward a woman who looked like she was an actress. "Look who I have." He pushed Reed ahead of him and waited for Rachel to answer.

"Well, let's see." Rachel stepped forward and scratched her chin, pretending to inspect Reed. "I recognize the cheekbones, but I can't quite figure out where Marnie Vaughn's son got gray-green eyes."

I waited for the announcement that they came from my father, but neither Reed nor I volunteered the information.

"Hi, Reed, I'm Rachel McPhee, your mother and I go way back."

Jeffrey reached for my hand and pulled me forward, too. "And this is Vanessa Carlisle. Will's daughter."

"Will Carlisle's daughter? God, that's a name from my old days in Chicago." She stepped back and looked at us. "You're both making me feel so old."

"Are you two staying for the show?" Jeffrey asked. "It starts in an hour, we could try to get you some seats or you could watch from here."

"Oh, I'm not staying. In fact," I looked over at the clock on the back wall. "I should get going."

I thanked Jeffrey and Rachel, and told Reed I'd see him tomorrow morning.

"Who was that?" I caught Rachel ask Reed as I walked away. "Your girlfriend?"

I thought I heard Reed stifle a laugh, before answering, "No. That was my sister."

Patrick wasn't in his room when I got to his dorm, and so I wandered the halls until I found him in the common room hanging out with Brent and Kelly and Amory.

Amory and Patrick were sitting on the couch huddled together, laughing about something they were reading in the *Yale Daily News*.

When Brent noticed me, he went over to Patrick and nudged him.

"Hey, what's up?" Patrick asked, getting up from the sofa and coming over to me. "I thought you were coming over at eight."

"Seven," I reminded him. "What are you doing?"

He turned around and glanced over at Brent and Kelly and

Amory. "Just killing time." Patrick waved to them and led me upstairs to his suite.

Once we were alone, it was just like last night except this time I was more relaxed than Patrick. Although it wasn't anything he did or said, I could tell something was bothering him. We'd had a ton of things to talk about last night, about Reed and school and what his first few weeks at college had been like. But tonight it felt almost like we'd run out of things to talk about. I knew that was impossible, but, still, the idea made me uneasy.

"What's wrong?" I asked him as we lay on the bed together.

"Nothing. Why?"

"I don't know, you just seem preoccupied tonight."

"It's nothing. I just have a lot to do for my classes on Monday. They're more work than I thought they'd be," he finally admitted.

"If you're so concerned about classes, maybe you should be studying instead of hanging out laughing over some newspaper article." I didn't mention Amory's name, but I knew he got the hint. "Isn't your tutor helping?" I asked.

"My tutor is fine," he answered, his tone short.

I rolled away from him feeling a little dejected. Okay, a lot dejected. There was no reason for him to be angry with me. I wasn't the one making his classes more difficult. I was just hanging out in his bed.

"Hey, I'm sorry." Patrick wrapped an arm around my waist and pulled me back next to him.

"How sorry?" I asked, half joking.

Patrick started kissing my neck. "Well, why don't I show you?"

Afterward I nestled my head against Patrick's shoulder, and I must have fallen asleep, because when I woke up it was 11:30 and he was gone. Looking around the room, seeing the place where Patrick would be spending his year without me, I soaked it in. There were still the things I recognized; his worn Cubs baseball cap hanging from his closet doorknob, his CD player perched on the windowsill, a faded navy blue polo shirt bunched up in the corner by his sneakers. For some reason seeing the same old things he had in his room at home, even though they were in a foreign place, made me feel better. Like if they belonged here, then I could belong here, too.

I pulled the rumpled sheet up around me and waited for Patrick to return. But after twenty minutes he was still a no-show. My jeans were crumpled on the floor beside the bed, so I gave up my attempt to appear seductive, got up, and got myself dressed.

I thought maybe Patrick was in Brent's room, but the entire suite was empty.

I went out into the hallway, still no Patrick.

A burst of laughter erupted down the hall and I followed the noise until I found its source.

"Have any of you seen Patrick?" I asked four guys sitting around their suite drinking beer.

"I saw Pat downstairs, I think," one of them told me, and pointed toward the stairwell.

I went down to the first floor and heard what I thought sounded like the TV on in the common room. But when I walked into the room I realized it wasn't the TV I'd heard. In fact, the TV was off. I'd overheard a conversation between two people who were now kissing in front of the fireplace.

When she heard me in the doorway, the girl pulled away and turned to look at me. And that's when I saw that the guy she'd been kissing was wearing the same green flannel shirt my boyfriend had been wearing just a few hours ago. And I realized that I'd found Patrick, and he'd just been kissing Amory.

chapter twenty

$\mathcal{I}$n the dark it must have looked like I was running away from some crazed lunatic, but what I was really doing was getting far away from Patrick. I ran as fast as I could down the stairs and across the lawn, the entire time clutching my stomach as if I'd been kicked. Watching Patrick pull away from kissing Amory had taken my breath away.

Unfortunately, lacrosse requires better aerobic conditioning than scoring in the top two percentile on your SATs, so it didn't take long for Patrick to catch up to me.

"Come on, Vanessa," he pleaded, not even breaking a sweat as he followed me to the hotel. "It was stupid. It was nothing, I swear."

I couldn't turn around. I couldn't face him without picturing him kissing her. *Just Amory,* my ass. I ignored him while I recited the square roots of factors of nine in my head.

Eventually Patrick stopped asking me to stop and listen to him. Instead, he followed me through the hotel and up to my room in silence.

"This is ridiculous, Vanessa," he told me as I slipped my card key in the door. "Say something."

Even square roots can only help so much, and when I turned to face him, I finally lost it.

"What can I say?" I screamed, my shrill voice echoing down the empty hallway. "That I'm glad you at least had the courtesy to run after me? You were kissing her, Patrick," I couldn't even bring myself to say her name. "And I was upstairs in your fucking bed!"

I wanted to reach out and smack the shit out of him, I wanted to hurt him, make him feel the pain I was feeling.

"I'm sorry, Vanessa, really." Patrick reached for my arm, but I ripped it out of his grasp.

"You want me to say something, Patrick, here it is: You're a fucking prick and I never want to see you again," I yelled, before pushing my door open.

I hated him. I hated that he could do this to me. And I hated that I wanted him to grab me and tell me he loved me, that it had all been one huge mistake he never planned on repeating. How was it possible to hate him so much and still need him so much at the same time?

"What the hell is going on?" Reed demanded, appearing in his doorway wearing only a pair of boxers and a Lakers T-shirt.

Patrick looked over and saw Reed watching him. "It's nothing, man. Just go back in your room."

"Nothing? Are you kidding me?" I spat, before pushing past Patrick and heading for the bed. I just wanted to go to sleep and forget this entire trip ever happened. I wanted to wake up and discover it had all been a bad dream.

But Patrick still didn't get the message. Instead of taking off, he came inside and sat on the bed next to me. What now, was he trying to earn points for persistence?

Reed stood there watching us, not making a move to leave. "Is everything okay, Vanessa? Do you want me to stay?"

"Look, it's fine." Patrick placed a hand on my knee.

I reached for his hand, the same hand that I'd been holding just a few hours before, the same hand that I'd let run up and down my body in bed, and slapped it off. "No, it's not fine." I got up and walked over to Reed, who, by this point, had stepped inside the room. I stood next to Reed and we both faced Patrick. "Get out."

Patrick stood up and came toward us, but stayed just far enough away to be out of Reed's reach. "You're overreacting, Vanessa. She's just my tutor."

"Your tutor?" I practically choked. "She's the one you've been spending so much time with?"

"She's just a friend, Vanessa," Patrick insisted. "I swear."

"And are you fucking this friend?" I demanded.

He didn't answer, and in the silence that fell around us I thought I felt my heart stop.

"Oh my God," I cried, and smacked my hand against my head. "I am so stupid!"

"She said get out," Reed reminded Patrick, and then stepped aside so he wasn't blocking the way through the door.

Patrick watched me. "Vanessa, please?"

I looked down at the faded burgundy rug, noticing for the first time there was a diamond pattern dotting the dingy matted pile. There was no feng shui energy here. Just a cheating boyfriend. And a girlfriend who needed to decide what to do with him.

I glanced up at Reed, who was waiting for me to answer. He looked at me and seemed to be willing me to show him how strong I was, to stand up to Patrick. There was no way I wanted Reed to see that I felt like melting into a puddle right there on the tacky burgundy carpet.

"Just leave, Patrick," I told him. Reed nodded at me, giving me his vote of confidence. And I took it an ran.

My hand reached for the thin gold chain around my neck and gripped it. "Just leave," I yelled, and threw the necklace at Patrick, where it landed, broken and tangled, at his feet.

"What an asshole," Reed said for the twenty-sixth time since Patrick walked out.

We were both sprawled out across my bed staring at the stucco ceiling, a position that I hoped kept Reed from seeing my face, which at this point was not only unattractively tear-stained, but painfully swollen, as well. About an hour ago I'd started trying to count the number of concentric circles in the plaster pattern, but instead of taking my mind off the vision of Patrick and Amory, it just reminded me that geometry was never one of my favorite classes. "I don't want to talk about it anymore, okay, Reed?"

I also didn't want to cry about it, but the words caught in my throat. I couldn't stop thinking about it. For the last hour that's all I'd been doing. Thinking about Patrick kissing someone else. Thinking about Patrick living just one floor above Amory for the past seven weeks. Thinking about how many times he'd kissed her before tonight. And thinking about how, in one seemingly short moment, everything I thought I knew about us had changed. Everything I thought I knew for sure had disappeared.

Reed didn't press the issue, and instead got up and went into his room.

"Think this might help?" he asked when he came back, a fat joint held between his fingers.

"Didn't they teach you anything at that place in Malibu? I thought you weren't supposed to smoke anymore."

"I'm not. I don't," he added. "I just bought this off some guy at the theater tonight, for old time's sake."

He sat on the edge of the bed and held the joint out for me.

"Are you trying to corrupt your little sister?" I asked, punctuating the question with one long sniffle.

"I thought my little sister was incorruptible."

"Do you have a lighter?" I asked, propping myself up on my elbows.

Reed produced a yellow Bic from his other hand. "Right here."

I took the joint from Reed. "Light it up, big brother."

I've given up on being the type of person for whom pot has any sort of earth-shattering effect. I don't wax philosophic about the wonders of the universe. It doesn't give me any sort of insight into the human condition. Half the time I can't even focus on any one thing long enough to carry on a conversation. Mostly I just get sleepy and end up wanting to crawl into bed and pass out.

"How are you feeling now? Any better?" Reed asked. He was lying on the bed next to me flipping through the room service menu.

"Not at all," I admitted. Even stoned it was hard to forget the scene I'd walked in on. I just hoped Patrick was as miserable as I was right now. No, I hoped he was *more* miserable. "I was so stupid! What was I thinking? Of course he was going to find someone else."

"You weren't stupid, he was. I know guys, Vanessa, and they're schmucks. Take your brother, for example." Reed thumped his chest and waited for me to laugh. But I couldn't. I didn't feel like I'd laugh ever again.

"That's not good enough, Reed. That doesn't excuse what he did."

"Look, forget about Rat or Dick or whatever it is you want me to call him."

Now he made me smile. Reed was trying so hard to play the role of big brother dispensing advice. "Either one of those names will do just fine."

"Okay. So forget about him. You can do better than Rat."

It wasn't worth arguing about. I didn't want to do better than Patrick. I just wanted Patrick. Or at least I used to.

"It's not like you were planning to marry the guy or anything, right?"

I didn't answer.

Reed turned on his side and faced me. "Right?"

"Of course not."

"Then what's the problem?"

The problem is that now everything was fucked-up. The problem was I still loved him. There. I'd admitted it. I still loved him. Unfortunately, finding Patrick with Amory didn't change the fact that he was the one I wanted to be with.

"The problem is that I was supposed to go to Yale and be with my boyfriend and now all I'll ever remember about this entire trip is seeing them together."

"Come on, it's not that bad. You can still go to Yale. You're definitely going to get in." Reed patted my hand in what I was sure he thought was a brotherly way. "I know you will."

Although I appreciated Reed's vote of confidence, I wasn't sure I wanted to get in anymore. All of a sudden Yale didn't seem like the perfect place I thought it was.

Or maybe that was just the pot playing games with my mind.

"I wrote the essays for Patrick's application, you know."

"No." Reed spoke slowly, stretching out the word until it almost sounded like two syllables. "I did not know that."

"Well, I did."

"Why the hell would you go to all the trouble of writing his essays?"

"I don't know, at the time it sounded like a good idea. I thought he needed my help."

"Are you saying he's too dumb to write his own?"

"No. I just thought, maybe, if he had some help, they'd be better."

"By 'better' I'm assuming you mean good enough to get him into Yale."

I shrugged and licked my lips. My mouth was feeling awfully dry all of a sudden.

"You really are a control freak, aren't you?" Reed continued. "You'd go to all that trouble, risk getting caught and thrown out of school or something, just so he'd go where you wanted him to go?"

"That's not the way it was," I insisted. "He wanted to go, too, sort of."

Reed frowned. "Come on."

"Besides, I wouldn't have gotten thrown out of school. Maybe disciplined or something, but not thrown out."

"So you'd rather jeopardize your own chances of getting in than let him roll the dice? Are you really that afraid of taking chances?"

I shook my head. "That's not it at all."

Reed wasn't buying it. "I don't know who you think you're kidding, but you're not fooling me."

I wasn't doing a very good job of pleading my case. And Reed seemed so normal, like he wasn't even stoned. Maybe that's what happens to you when you get baked all the time. You learn how to pull it off.

Taylor gets all weird when she gets stoned, saying whatever it is she's thinking at every moment no matter how ridiculous she sounds. The last time we smoked a joint, on Fourth of July with Patrick and his friends, she just sat there and asked me the same questions over and over again.

What do you think Justin and Cameron are doing right now? Where do you think Julia Roberts is? Her ranch in New Mexico? Do you think Paris Hilton is, at this very minute, filming herself having sex?

I hadn't bothered answering. I'd been having enough trouble staying awake as it was. Thinking about Justin and Cameron would have surely given me added incentive to knock off altogether.

Then Taylor occupied herself by repeating odd names like she was some sort of linguistics professor. Charlize. Char-leeze. Shar-leese. Demi. Dem-e. Deh-mee. That kept her occupied for at least an hour.

"Ever meet Demi Moore?" I asked Reed.

"Once," he answered, skimming the menu one last time, but still not exactly thrilled with his late-night options.

This time I turned to face him. I hadn't expected him to say yes. "Really?"

"Yeah. We were at the same party." Reed closed the menu and tossed it across the room, where it landed on the desk. "This menu sucks. Want to order some pizza?"

At the mere mention of pizza, I wanted it more than I'd wanted anything else in my entire life.

I reached for my cellphone sitting on the night table and handed it to Reed.

"Make it an extra-large."

Thirty minutes later Reed and I were eating pizza on my bed.

"This is so good," I told him, my mouth so full it came out sounding like I was speaking a foreign language.

Reed was too busy stuffing the last of his slice into his mouth to answer. I was sitting on a hotel bed with Reed Vaughn, shoveling pizza into my mouth like it was my last meal before the electric chair, and he didn't look anything like the TV star plastered up on Taylor's walls. Or even the character he played on *Wild Dunes*. He looked like any other seventeen-year-old with a bad case of the munchies.

He hadn't mentioned Patrick since I told him I didn't want to talk about it. Instead he kept asking me questions about myself, steering the conversation away from anything remotely resembling Patrick.

"You've been to Europe, right?" I asked Reed as I reached for another—my third—slice.

"Marnie took me everywhere with her when she shot on location."

"Taylor and I wanted to go to Europe this summer," I told him, and then remembered that I still wasn't talking to Taylor. All of a sudden I felt sad again. My best friend and my boyfriend, both gone. And all I had for a stand-in was Reed.

"Speaking of Taylor, when are you going to get over it and accept her apology?" Reed wanted to know. "She made a mistake. That's what people do. Nobody's perfect."

Reed was right. I wanted my best friend back, not because I'd just lost my boyfriend, but because I missed her.

"Besides, it's going to be awfully lonely in Europe all by yourself," Reed added.

"It doesn't matter. My parents won't let me go."

Reed wrinkled up his nose, like the pizza tasted funny. "That's weird. They don't seem like the type to keep you from experiencing something new. I would have thought they'd taken you to Europe themselves by now."

How weird. Reed was talking about my parents as if he knew them well enough to predict what they'd do.

"Didn't you ever wonder who your dad was?" I asked him between bites.

He thought about my question for a minute. Or at least I thought Reed was thinking about it. Maybe he was just trying to finish the gob of cheese in his mouth so he didn't end up choking.

"I guess I did, sometimes. But it wasn't like I'd come home from school every day and wonder where my dad was. Marnie and I traveled a lot when I was younger and she was shooting on location all over the world. We didn't exactly sit down at the dinner table and stare at the empty seat at the head of the table."

"Didn't you ever ask who he was?" I couldn't imagine not at least *asking* about the guy who was partly responsible for bringing me into the world.

"I knew he was someone Marnie met doing a play. I knew he was in the business. But other than that, I guess I figured he probably didn't want some strange kid showing up on his doorstep."

I smiled. Neither did his daughter. "So what do you think of him?"

"Your dad?" he asked.

"*Our* dad," I reminded Reed.

"He seems nice enough. Your mom is cool, too. But does she always go around rearranging stuff? I swear, every morning I get up and things are all in different places."

"I know. You can't get too used to anything, and every season the entire décor changes. Last spring she went on a white kick—everything was white, the area rugs, the slipcovers, the walls, the drapes. Daisy would go outside and roll around in the yard and then come in and leave her paw prints all over the place; she made a huge mess. Needless to say, the white phase didn't last very long."

"I don't think my mom even picked out the colors in our house. We just came home one day and her decorator had completely re-done the place."

"So our home lives aren't so different after all, are they?" I laughed and Reed smiled at me.

"I've never done a play before, you know," Reed said, out of the blue. "I've never even done any live stage work, period, but it was pretty cool tonight watching from backstage with Jeffrey."

I put down my half-eaten pizza crust and studied Reed for a minute. I would probably regret doing this, but I was going to do it anyway. "Want my opinion?"

"Could I actually stop you from giving it to me?"

"I think you should do my dad's play. It would really mean a lot to him." I noticed how serious my tone had become, and tried to make light of it. "Besides, once he sees that you have no idea what the hell you're doing, he'll drop the idea once and for all."

"How can you be so sure I'd have no idea what the hell I was doing?"

"I've seen *Wild Dunes*."

"You've seen *Wild Dunes*? Vanessa Carlisle has deigned to watch some silly little show about silly kids in a silly place?" Reed clutched his chest. "I'm flattered."

"Don't be." I tried not to smile, but he looked so funny, his hand across his chest like he was being all chivalrous or something. "Taylor made me."

"Well, still. If the great Vanessa Carlisle has seen *Wild Dunes,* maybe there's hope for me yet."

I removed my fourth piece of pizza from the box and took a bite.

"So what did you really think when you found out about me?" Reed asked, pointing to the liter of Sprite next to me.

"Pretty obvious, isn't it?" I passed him the Sprite. "What about you? What'd you think when you found out about me?"

"Pretty obvious, isn't it?" he echoed back.

"You know, I wasn't going to tell you this, but you actually came in handy today during my interview."

"How was that?"

I told Reed about my interviewer's unexpected question and her reaction to my answer.

"See, finally you found a use for me."

"Well, it's about time," I joked. "I know Chicago isn't exactly L.A. Do you miss it?"

"Not really. The show is shot on location in Oregon, so I'm used to being away."

"Did you always want to be an actor?" I asked.

"I don't know. I guess after spending so much time on the set with Marnie it just seemed like the thing to do. I never really gave it much thought."

"And now?"

Reed shrugged. "What about you? Did you always want to go to Yale?"

"Before this weekend I couldn't imagine going anywhere else."

"And now?"

This time it was my turn to shrug.

Reed tossed the last crust into the pizza box and laid his hands on his stomach. "I'm stuffed. And tired." He dragged his legs off the bed and stood up. "I'm going to bed. Are you going to be okay?"

Reed's question brought back the vision of Patrick and Amory. I couldn't imagine ever being okay again. "I need to sleep," I told him.

Reed grabbed the empty pizza box, carried it over to my dresser, and set it down before going to the door.

"You're not going to tell my parents what happened with Patrick, are you?" I asked, before he closed the door behind him.

"No way. I'm not the kind of brother who tattletales on his little sister." Reed winked at me. "Good night, Vanessa."

I winked back. "Good night, Reed."

I didn't even bother changing my clothes. I just closed my eyes and went to sleep, wondering just what kind of brother Reed was after all.

chapter twenty-one

The first thing I did when I got home was toss all my pills in the garbage (I wrapped them in tissues and put them inside an old Walgreens bag, just in case anyone decided to go rummaging through our trash). The funny thing was, as I pushed the Walgreens bag to the bottom of the garbage can, I wasn't just mad at Patrick anymore. I was mad at myself. I'd been so convinced that I had all these good reasons for staying on the pill after Patrick left for college, reasons that had nothing to do with him and everything to do with me. But as I looked at the seven yellow pills remaining in my current pack, I had to admit that he was the only real reason I'd renewed my prescription. And I hated it. I hated that I'd been so stupid. I hated that I'd trusted him. But most of all, I hated that I was a stereotype—the girl who waited back home while her boyfriend was off doing whatever, or whoever, he wanted. And, apparently, what Patrick wanted was Amory.

He was the first, and now it was over. And I felt completely alone.

• • •

"So how was your trip?" Taylor asked when I saw her at school on Monday. We were the only two people in the hallway and she loitered beside my locker while I dropped my books off before heading to lunch. "Did your Yale interview go well?"

"I think so."

"Look." Taylor put a hand on my locker and caught the door just as I was about to slam it shut. "I'm sorry. I never would have talked to that guy from the *Tribune* if I thought it would hurt you."

"But you did."

"I know. And it was stupid. And I've said I'm sorry a million times. I even tried calling the reporter back to ask him to print a retraction, or at least another article that said what I really meant. Doesn't that count for something?"

It counted a lot. Taylor looked so repentant standing there, waiting for me to say something, how could I possible stay angry at her? "I'm sorry, too. I shouldn't have stayed mad for so long."

"I mailed in my application last week. I wish you would have read my essay before I sent it." Taylor was applying early decision to Boston University, her first choice.

"I'm sure it was fine."

Taylor shrugged. "Still."

"Let's just forget about the article, okay?" I suggested, and moved her hand away so I could close my locker.

She gave me a tentative smile. "Really?"

"Really. It's over. Just don't go around talking to any more reporters. I don't care how nice they look."

Taylor nodded, and mouthed the words *I swear* before crossing her heart with her index finger. "So tell me about your weekend."

"It sucked," I confessed, ready to tell her every horrible, sordid detail.

Taylor fell into step next to me as we walked toward the cafeteria. "So your interview didn't really go well?"

"No, my interview was fine. Great. It was catching Patrick kissing another girl that sucked."

Taylor grabbed my arm. "Oh my God. That's horrible."

"It *was* horrible. It was the worst weekend ever." The familiar lump in my throat was back, making it harder and harder to speak each word. Taylor gave me an encouraging smile and I knew she could tell.

"Who was she?"

"She lives in his dorm, and she's his tutor. Her name is Amory."

Taylor wrinkled up her nose. "What kind of name is Amory?" she asked.

"Exactly." I didn't have to explain. Taylor immediately understood. God, it was nice to have her back.

As we walked to lunch it all came tumbling out. I told Taylor about New Haven, about finding Patrick and Amory in the common room, and how he followed me back to the hotel trying to explain what happened.

"But Reed wouldn't let him," I added. "I actually think Patrick was a little afraid of him."

"Reed could kick Patrick's scrawny ass," she piped in, obviously trying to make up for talking to the *Tribune* reporter. My six-foot-two lacrosse-playing boyfriend was hardly scrawny. Although I did kind of like the idea of Reed kicking Patrick's ass. I almost wished he had.

"Oh my God." Taylor pointed to my unadorned neck. "You're not wearing the necklace."

"Nope."

"So this is it? It's over?" Taylor wanted to know. She even looked mildly hopeful.

I didn't answer her. I didn't know what to say. Was it really over? Was I going to give up on someone I'd spent so much time with?

"I don't know," I finally answered. "I really don't know."

"Have you talked to him since you got home?" Taylor asked.

I nodded. "He wouldn't stop calling last night."

I made it sound like it was easy not returning his calls, but it was hard. Every time the phone rang, Reed would give me a look and wait to see if I answered. It was obvious when it was Patrick, his cell number popped up on caller ID. Late last night I finally caved in and picked up the phone when I saw it was him. Reed wasn't around to stop me, and I really just wanted to talk to Patrick. I knew he was a prick, but a part of me wanted to hear what he'd say, to hear him say how sorry he really was that he'd screwed up. I wanted groveling for forgiveness and pledges of undying love. As dumb as I knew it was, I wanted him to fight for me, to prove that I hadn't made a mistake by believing in him. Or us.

As soon as Patrick heard me say hello, he did start apologizing. I listened but didn't offer my forgiveness. That would be just way too easy for him. Patrick had to suffer like I had. He had to feel like shit a little longer. So instead of accepting his apologies I told him we'd get together when he came back in November and see where we stood.

"So what's going to happen?"

I started walking toward the cafeteria. "He'll probably be here for Alumni Day, so I guess I'll see him then and we'll decide where we stand."

"*We'll* decide?" Taylor repeated, noticing the cracks in my façade.

"*I'll* decide," I corrected myself.

Every fall, Cabot hosts an Alumni Day for recent graduates who come back home for their first semester break. Mostly it's so last year's graduates can talk about their colleges, let us know whether or not they were well prepared for their courses, or even if, in hindsight, they think they made the right choices in where they ended up. Usually only recent graduates come back, or maybe the ones who graduated two years before. After that, they lose interest.

For the most part the alumni walk around and say hi to their former teachers and all the students. They'll sit in on classes and join us for lunch. This year Alumni Day coincided with Patrick's fall break, so I figured he'd definitely come back. Patrick was the type who'd enjoy hanging out with his former teammates, rehashing each and every game from last season.

"Does Reed still want to kill him?" Taylor asked.

"Let's just say he's not one of Patrick's biggest fans."

Taylor nodded as if she understood. And she did. Taylor wasn't exactly heading up the Patrick Ramsey fan club, either.

"So you and Reed are getting along now?"

"It's more like a tentative peace treaty. I wouldn't say we're best friends."

"Your parents must be happy about that."

"Are you kidding me?" I held open the cafeteria door and let Taylor enter first. "They're practically planning our first family trip to Disney World."

Taylor and I made our way through the lunch line and then went to find a table. Reed was already sitting in his regular spot with Sarah, and a few weeks ago—actually, a few days ago—I would have walked right past his table without even acknowledging him. But after Reed was so willing to keep me company after Patrick left the hotel, it seemed kind of an ungrateful thing to do.

To sit with Reed or not to sit with Reed, that was the question.

"Hey." I nodded to Reed as I passed him.

"Hi, Vanessa," he replied, but didn't ask me to sit down or anything. And that was fine with me. I think Reed and I had found our comfort zone and it was somewhere between coexistence and friendship. It had only taken seven weeks, a weekend in New Haven, and one cheating boyfriend to make it happen.

chapter twenty-two

$\mathcal{I}$ was right. Patrick did show up for Alumni Day. When I got to school that Thursday, there he was by the lockers, talking to a few guys on the lacrosse team. And he looked good. Even better than I remembered, in jeans and his green flannel shirt. Alumni don't have to follow the dress code, and seeing him dressed just like he was that night I found him with Amory made my stomach turn. I couldn't tell if Patrick was completely oblivious of the blatant reminder of that night, or if he was trying to send me some sort of subtle message that he had repented. At least this time we hadn't just had sex.

In the three weeks since my trip to New Haven, Patrick had e-mailed me every few days. The messages were never long, but after the first week I found myself waiting for them to arrive each night in my in-box. At first I told Taylor about the e-mails and even let her read a few of the first ones just to see if she could decipher any more meaning in them than I'd been able to. But after the first week I stopped offering her a sneak peek and kept them to myself. She would have just told me that he was still a prick, no matter how often his e-mails arrived. So I couldn't show her any more because they were getting to me. And I didn't want to be reminded that I should stop reading, and start pushing the delete button instead.

I shouldn't have been surprised to see him. Like I said, I figured Patrick would come back. But seeing him there in the hall, just like I saw him all last year, it kind of threw me off.

I still hadn't made up my mind whether or not I'd go over and say hello when he caught me staring and waved.

I could see Taylor bristle. "Don't do it," she whispered from beside my locker. "Be strong."

I opened my locker door and stood behind it so he couldn't see me. "What am I supposed to do? Hide behind things all day?"

"I wish you could, but obviously that's not really an option. Just act cold toward him."

He looked good over there talking to his former teammates, so good it brought back the familiar pangs. The same ones I'd get when I'd see him in the halls last year. The same ones I'd had when I went to see him at Yale.

"He's coming over," Taylor warned me, glancing over her shoulder as my self-appointed lookout. "Want me to stay with you?"

"No. I can handle it." I shook my head and hoped I sounded convincing.

"Okay." She patted my arm. "But if you need reinforcements, just yell."

I turned my back to Patrick and watched Taylor walk away, the entire time trying to muster all the strength I had to just not cave in the minute he said something to me.

"Hey, Vanessa." I turned around and there they were, the same brown eyes I used to see every day last year.

"Hello, Patrick." I was the very picture of cold. I was an ice princess. Taylor would be proud.

"You look great," he told me, looking down appraisingly. I saw the Susans out of the corner of my eye and knew they were watching us.

"Thanks."

"Maybe we can talk later," he suggested. "I'd really like a chance to explain."

"I don't know if that's such a good idea."

"Come on. You, me, Starbucks, just like it used to be?" he coaxed, glancing over at his lacrosse buddies. "Don't make me look like an idiot, Vanessa."

"I didn't make you look like an idiot. You did."

"So let me make it up to you. Maybe?"

I hesitated, and in that hesitation I knew I'd given him an opening. "Maybe."

I wanted to look away, to act like I couldn't care less that his face, and his lips, were about five inches away from mine. But this ice princess was melting, and before I could get myself together Patrick leaned in and kissed me. Either out of habit, or, more likely because I wanted to, I found myself kissing him back.

"I'll see you later," he told me, pulling away.

I started to say something, but Patrick was already on his way back to the lacrosse guys.

So much for being cold. I'd heated up pretty quickly.

"What's going on?" Reed asked me, coming down the hall.

For a minute I thought he was asking about the kiss, but then he glanced down the hall and seemed to notice Patrick for the first time.

"Why's he here?" Reed tipped his head toward Patrick and frowned.

"It's just some alumni thing today," I halfheartedly explained.

"I hope you told him to fuck off."

Not exactly. "Don't worry. I took care of it."

"I'm not worried," Reed assured me, his voice losing its edge. "I know you wouldn't do anything stupid."

I could take care of myself. And that's why, when I saw Patrick waiting for me by my locker at the end of the day, I figured there was no harm in accepting his offer to grab a coffee at Starbucks.

Before we left school I braced myself for another attempted kiss or some hand holding, but Patrick didn't try to do anything. Instead we walked side by side and didn't say much.

"So what do you have to say for yourself?" I asked when we reached Starbucks.

"I don't want to fight, Vanessa. I just want to talk."

"What I don't understand is why you'd say you wanted to stay together if you really wanted to be with other people."

"I didn't plan on being with anyone else. And I didn't sleep with Amory, if that's what you're wondering about."

Wondering, obsessing, what was the difference when you were picturing your boyfriend with another girl?

I really wanted to believe him. It would make it so much easier. Besides, it wasn't like I'd been entirely faithful. I'd kissed John. Maybe there was some kind of universal karma at work or something. Maybe now we were even.

When we got to Starbucks, Patrick held the door open for me and sat down at the first empty table we passed, which just happened to be the same table we always sat at. There was no way he could have planned that, but still, maybe it was some sort of sign.

"Aren't we going to order first?" I asked.

"Let's talk first."

Once I was seated across from him at the same exact table we used to sit at last year, with the exact same guy with the dragon tattoo behind the counter making drinks, I knew I was in trouble. I could hear Reed's voice in my head, how sure he was that I wouldn't do anything stupid, and I hoped he was right.

Patrick waited for me to take my coat off, and then started explaining. "Look, I know what I did was shitty . . ."

"Shitty, mean, selfish, cruel, insensitive—there are more adjectives, should I go on?"

"Okay, all of the above," he offered.

"Then why'd you do it?"

"I don't know." Patrick shook his head and looked down at the black tabletop, wiping a few stray crumbs onto the floor while he talked.

"I was in your bed, Patrick." The girl behind the register looked over at us and I lowered my voice. "We'd just had sex!"

"I was at school, and you were back home, and Amory and I were spending a lot of time together." Patrick looked up at me. "It's not like I planned it or anything, but all of a sudden you were there and she was there and it was a little confusing, to say the least."

I thought about John and our kiss. "Confusion I can understand, sticking your tongue down her throat while I'm upstairs in your bed, that's a little more difficult to comprehend."

"I know, it's a bad excuse, but school's been harder than I thought it would be. My classes are tougher, and it sucks because everyone else seems to know what they're doing. The only reason Amory and I ever got together in the first place is because I was falling behind in econ after the first two weeks." Patrick almost looked upset as he reached his hand across the table and touched his fingertips to mine. "Being back at Cabot today was so great, seeing you, and everyone from the team and the same teachers, it was like I knew where I stood again. It's not like that at Yale. There, I don't know shit."

"So what are you saying?" I asked, watching Patrick's fingertips creep up the palm of my hand until they settled there, intertwined with mine.

"What I'm saying is that I screwed up. I'm sorry. And I want to give us another shot."

I didn't quite know how to take what Patrick said. Did he want to get back together just because I reminded him of home? Because I was his safe choice? Or did coming back for Alumni Day really remind him of what he was giving up—namely, me? I wanted to believe it was the latter, and it was just so nice being there with him, I wanted to believe that the night in the common room didn't overshadow twelve months together.

Maybe if I'd had more time to stay mad, or to start getting over him, it would have been different. But when he brought me my Strawberries & Cream Frappuccino exactly the way I liked it, with skim milk and whipped cream, without even having to ask what I wanted, it was like no time had passed at all. And when he reached into his pocket and dangled the gold necklace from his finger, the clasp fixed and the charm hanging exactly where it had been the night he gave it to me, I was a goner.

Reed was waiting for me when I got home. "Where have you been?"

"I went out after school," I told him, keeping my answer purposely vague.

"Not with Taylor, you didn't. I saw her on my way to the bus stop. So who were you with?"

Reed's unexpected interrogation put me on the defense. And that's exactly how I was feeling—defensive. Because Reed had been convinced I could take care of myself, that I wouldn't let Patrick get to me, and I'd proven him wrong. And while proving him wrong would have made me do the happy dance a few months ago, now it just made me look stupid.

"While I appreciate the brotherly concern, I don't have to keep you informed of my comings and goings now, do I? Because being my big brother for all of two months doesn't exactly give you much credibility in the role model department."

"Forget it. I know who you were with." Reed shook his head and went to watch TV.

I followed him into the living room. "Look, Patrick knows he screwed up," I explained. I didn't need to justify my decision to Reed, but I really wanted him to understand. I don't know why, but all of a sudden, I cared whether or not Reed liked Patrick. "If I can forgive him, I'd think that you could."

"Funny, you weren't feeling so forgiving when you were crying in your hotel room."

"Look, he made a mistake. It's not like I've been the perfect girl-friend since he's been away."

"Oh, yeah." He didn't even try to hide the sarcasm. "You've been so out of control."

"I kissed John after Taylor's party."

"And it didn't even occur to you that maybe something wasn't right with you and your boyfriend if you're kissing someone else?"

"It was a one-time thing. For both of us." I wanted Reed to understand, but it didn't sound like that was going to happen.

"Right. And it has nothing to do with the fact that you're afraid of letting go of this idea you have of Pat greeting you at Yale with open arms."

"That's not it," I insisted. "You don't know what it was like before he went away."

"Maybe not, but I know what it's like now that he's away. You're so afraid of not following this master plan you have laid out for yourself that you're willing to let your boyfriend treat you like shit. Isn't it about time you faced the fact that you can't predict the future?"

Reed waited for me to deny his accusation, but I didn't. Who was he to be talking to me about facing facts? "That's awfully big advice coming from some washed-up boy toy who won't get up on stage because he's afraid everyone will find out he's not much more than a pretty face," I snapped, and was instantly filled with regret.

Reed stood there silently, his lips pressed together tightly in a flat line as he took in the words that now hung in the air. There was no returned insult, no escalating name calling, just my brother who looked like he'd received a mortal blow.

"I know you're just trying to help, but I don't need it," I told him, but Reed didn't want to hear my explanation. He just held up a hand telling me to stop.

"So are you two back together?" he asked, emotionless.

I nodded.

"You know, Vanessa, for someone who likes to think she's so smart, you can do some pretty dumb things sometimes." He turned up the TV volume so he didn't have to hear my reply, but it wasn't necessary.

I didn't have one.

chapter twenty-three

The peace treaty that Reed and I had brokered in New Haven pretty much unraveled after Alumni Day. Patrick and I spent the weekend together, and then said good-bye until Thanksgiving. I thought maybe Reed would see that everything was back to normal between Patrick and me, but instead he was still pissed that I forgave my "cheating asshole of a boyfriend," as Reed referred to him whenever he saw me on the phone with Patrick.

Reed just didn't get it. He wasn't around last year to see what we were like before Patrick went away to school. Just when things seemed to be verging on normal, and Reed and I had figured out how to go from strangers to pseudo-siblings, he decided to take some sort of moral high ground.

"Can't we just agree to disagree?" I finally asked him, after getting the silent treatment for a week.

"We can agree that your taste in boyfriends sucks," he told me.

"You're not being fair to me. You hardly even know him."

"I know what he did to you when you visited him. And I know how shitty he made you feel."

"And that's enough?"

Reed nodded his head and seemed sure of his answer. "Enough for me."

And with those three words, the peace treaty was broken.

That's why I guess I wasn't too surprised that the next day Reed told my dad he wanted to be in the play. Reed knew I thought he'd be horrible, and I figured he was doing it to prove me wrong. But even if I wasn't surprised he did a reading for my dad, I was completely shocked that my father thought my brother did a good job. In fact, a job good enough to be cast in *Running Out*.

I couldn't believe that Reed was even a fraction as good as my dad made him out to be. It wasn't like there was an acting gene he could inherit from Marnie. It had to be random luck. Reed just probably had a lucky day, and the fact that his own father was the judge, well, there had to be a little nepotism at play, as well. Of course, that theory was shot to hell when my mom went to the theater one night to watch Reed work with my dad.

"I have to say, I was pretty surprised," she told me, taking off her coat and laying it on the couch next to me.

"That bad, huh?" I asked, just a little satisfied that someone was finally going to get honest about Reed's acting abilities.

"No, that good," she told me, looking a little surprised herself. "If he keeps working this hard, by the time the show opens he'll be phenomenal in the role."

Phenomenal? Reed? Now I knew she had to be exaggerating. Not to mention delusional.

My mom took her coat off the couch and started for the foyer closet. "I think I'm going to help out with the production, work on some scenery," she told me, her voice fading as she left the room. "The whole family working together, it'll be fun."

The whole family? As in, all of us? "You don't expect me to do anything, do you?" I called back, ready to argue that I had enough going on at school without having to help out at the theater.

"No," she assured me, coming back into the living room. "You've made it clear how you feel about the theater."

Oh. Then wasn't the *whole family* missing one of its members?

"We had a great idea," my dad announced at Thanksgiving dinner. "We're going to California with Reed for Christmas."

"Christmas in California? What are we going to do, decorate a palm tree? What about snow and cold weather and all the things that make it Christmas?" I asked, and turned to my mom. "Besides, we always have Glenda over for Christmas."

"Hey, don't worry about me." Glenda reached for the whole-grain stuffing. "I'll be fine. After all the holiday craziness I'd love to just sit around and do nothing for a few days."

"Glenda will survive without us," my dad agreed.

I swirled my fork in my lump of mashed potatoes and watched gravy pool in the reservoir I'd created. Christmas in California, there was just no way. As it was, with his relatives visiting and all the studying he was doing to catch up with his classes, I'd only seen Patrick for all of four hours. Besides, it was Christmas, and you were supposed to spend Christmas at home.

"I'm not going," I told them, slicing a hole in the side of my mashed potato reservoir and watching the gravy spill out. "There's no way."

My dad looked to my mom for help, but she was probably planning a new color palette for the dining room as he spoke.

"Come on, Vanessa. It will be fun," my dad continued, trying to convince me. "We've never spent the holidays away from home before."

"There's a reason," I reminded them. "It's the holidays, you're supposed to stay home! That's why they call it 'home for the holidays' and not 'staying in some stranger's house for the holidays.'"

In fact, I knew lots of kids from Cabot who went away for the two weeks we were off. They went skiing in Colorado, or went to Florida or the Bahamas. But we'd always stayed home. The windows at Marshall Field's, Zoo Lights at Lincoln Park Zoo, the garland strung along Michigan Avenue. *That* was Christmas, not some strange house with a Jacuzzi.

"Forget it. I'm not going. I'll stay with Glenda," I announced, and turned to her for reinforcement.

"Maybe?" Glenda glimpsed at my mom over the cornucopia in the center of the table and waited for a reaction.

The shaking head and puckered brows weren't exactly the response I was looking for.

"Then again, maybe I'll head somewhere warm, too, like Mexico," Glenda backpedaled, and avoided my gaze by reaching for the salad. So much for coming to my aid.

Glenda passed the salad to my mom, who placed some leafy greens on her plate. "Well, it's already planned," my mom said, taking the salad bowl from Glenda. "We're all flying there together on the twentieth."

"First class," Reed chimed in, with a little grin.

"Marnie insisted," my mom explained. "Her gift to us."

The twentieth. The same day Patrick was due back from school. I wouldn't even get to see him.

"I can't believe Marnie even *wants* us to visit. Haven't you told her what it's been like around here?" I avoided looking at Reed, who I was sure was rolling his eyes at my Thanksgiving day performance. But I didn't care. "Now we're taking this circus on the road?"

"Marnie wants to see your parents again," Reed answered, putting his fork down. "And meet you."

"Now why would she want to do that?" I demanded.

Reed shrugged and went back to cutting his Tofurky. "Beats me. I guess because you're my sister."

Taylor was driving me crazy waiting to hear from BU (she started sleeping with her BU sweatshirt under her pillow for good luck). SATs were over and done with, if not exactly taken. I'd heard all about Sarah's *fabulous* Harvard interview in calculus class. Reed was giving me the cold shoulder between silent treatments. Patrick and I were back together, even if that meant we only talked on the phone once a week while he got ready for his final exams. And in a few weeks it would be Christmas and I'd be surrounded by palm trees instead of evergreens.

When John called and asked if I wanted to meet him and go to the Sharingham Holiday Bazaar (the Sharingham Bizarre, we used to call it), I jumped at his offer. Finally, an afternoon with someone who was removed from everything else that was going on in my life. I didn't tell anyone where I was going, not because I thought I was doing something wrong, but it felt slightly hypocritical. Would I want Patrick spending the afternoon with Amory at some holiday bazaar? Absolutely not. But John was just a friend, not someone trying to lure me away from my boyfriend. Besides, I was unlureable.

Every December, Sharingham has a holiday bazaar with products from around the world. Hand-woven Dhaka shawls, beaded jewelry, and nettle caps are just a few of the scratchy, oddly colored, and musty-smelling things available.

"So what do you think?" John asked, showing me around the school on our way to the cafeteria.

"The halls are a different color, they knocked down the wall between the meditation room and the library, and the greenhouse is new."

"It started out as an experiment in hydroponics, but instead of plants all we were able to grow was mold."

I laughed. "The more things change, the more they stay the same, right?"

Instead of agreeing with me, John shook his head. "Not really. I never understood what that was supposed to mean. The more things change, the more they just change."

John led the way, and in a few minutes we were standing in line to enter the bazaar. The cafeteria was filled with long rows of tables, each displaying wares from countries I could hardly pronounce. The aisles were filled with students and parents and what looked like people who just wandered in off the street looking to get out of the cold.

"So how are things going with your brother?" John asked, as we slowly walked up and down the aisles, stopping sporadically to pick something up and try to figure out what it was.

"He's mad at me for getting back together with Patrick, so not very good."

John put down a rattan basket that looked a lot like the garbage can in my dad's den. "I didn't know you broke up. I thought you were going to see him when you went to visit Yale."

"It's a long story."

John stopped walking. "In other words, you want me to butt out."

I didn't want John to butt out, I just didn't want to talk about Patrick. It made me feel disloyal, which is odd considering he'd made out with Amory while I was two floors away and obviously didn't have any pangs of disloyalty. At least when I kissed John, Patrick was halfway across the country. For some reason, I thought that made it less offensive.

But that wasn't my point. I didn't want to talk about Patrick because I was having fun. I liked spending time with John. When I was with him, I didn't have to think about anything but just being with him. As my dingbat brother was going around the house saying, I was "in the moment" (that was some ridiculous acting advice that had become his new mantra as he prepared for the play). Talking about Patrick defeated the entire purpose.

"I'd just rather not talk about it," I told him, and picked up a card. "Weren't you looking for an elephant dung greeting card to help support conservation in Zambia?"

"I was, but my mom got me one for my birthday. Here's that African mask you wanted." He held up a carved wooden mask and looked at me through two small round eyeholes. "What do you think? Are you going to put it on your Christmas list?"

I took the mask away from him and placed it back on the table. "Maybe next year."

"Isn't it hard, with him away at Yale and you here?" John asked, starting to walk down the aisle. He was obviously thinking I didn't want to talk about the long story, not the boyfriend topic in general.

"It's not easy," I admitted.

"Is it really worth it?"

"It will be."

John tuned to me. "When?"

I picked up a small ceramic Aztec god figurine and held it in my hand, avoiding his gaze. Next September, I wanted to tell him, but all of a sudden it seemed so far away. Too far away to know anything about it, not the least of which was whether or not it would be worth the waiting. And I felt ridiculous for even thinking it would be.

When I first started counting the days until the end of school it didn't seem like an eternity. Every day I could cross off a square on my calendar and know there was one less day to go. It seemed manageable. Even, somehow, controllable. But in the ninety-eight days since I first found out about Reed, so much had already happened. So much had already changed. Like the fact that I was spending the afternoon with John, and the little seed of doubt that seemed to be growing ever since Reed planted it a few weeks ago.

I handed the figurine to John and asked, "Can we talk about something more pleasant, please?"

He examined the god. "Who is this?" John asked the woman behind the table.

"Tezcatlipoca," she told us. "He's associated with the notion of destiny."

"Have you finished all your college applications yet?" John asked, turning to me.

"Almost. Two to go."

He looked down at the god in his hand for a minute and then declared, "I'll take it. How much?"

"What are you going to do with an Aztec god?" I wanted to know, watching John pull a ten-dollar bill out of his pocket.

"Give it to you. Sort of an early Christmas present."

"But why?"

"If anyone is banking on the notion of destiny, it's you." John took his change from the woman and gave me the figurine.

"Thanks. But you really didn't have to do that."

"I know. But I wanted to."

We left the table with the Aztec figurine displays and continued browsing. It wasn't until we'd walked down the last aisle that I realized I'd been holding the god in one hand while fingering the necklace around my neck with the other.

I knew I didn't have to like John just because he bought me some odd little ceramic god with a stripe of black across his face and a mirror in place of one of his feet. And I certainly didn't have to spend the rest of the afternoon with him.

But I wanted to.

chapter twenty-four

"What is this?" I practically stuttered, walking into the living room.

My mom whipped around to face me. "Ta-da!" she cried. "What do you think?"

I looked around the room and didn't know what to think. The couch was covered with some sort of Mexican blanket, and not exactly one that looked all that new. The coffee table had been replaced by a plank of particle board straddling two milk crates, and the windows were now draped with what looked like bed sheets. All the pictures on the walls were gone and a Jack Daniel's fluorescent sign blinked over the fireplace, which had been turned into some sort of barbecue pit.

"What am I supposed to think?" I asked back.

"Think trailer park. Think all-American poverty. Think oppression."

All I was thinking was, What the hell is she talking about?

"Your mom did a great job, didn't she?" my dad asked me, coming into the room. Reed trailed behind him holding a glass of water.

"I'm trying out a few things here before coming up with some final set ideas," my mom explained.

"So we're supposed to live like this?" I asked, watching Reed out of the corner of my eye. He didn't seem too bothered by the change in décor. And why should he? He was the reason I was standing in a living room with a rug crocheted with a NASCAR logo.

"This way your dad and Reed can rehearse at home until theater rehearsals start after the holiday."

"As a matter of fact, we were just about to run through a scene," my dad told me, flipping through a script he picked up off the couch.

I waited for him to ask me if I wanted to play Daisy Duke, but instead he walked over to Reed and started discussing the scene. My mom arranged some empty glass whiskey jugs on the coffee table, and nobody seemed to expect me to stick around.

Was it that impossible to picture me in a pair of short shorts and cowboy boots?

The doorbell rang and my mom asked me to get the door. She was too busy looking for her old Lynyrd Skynyrd albums.

"You won't believe what's going on in the living room," I told Taylor when I found her standing on our doorstep. She had her reporter's notebook clutched under her arm and a look that told me this wasn't a social call.

"Oh, I know," she told me. "Reed's going to let me watch rehearsals and write a series of columns about his first play. I'm going to call them 'The Making of a Theater Star.' "

"But the rehearsals are in my living room, Taylor." Still, she didn't seem fazed. "And my living room has been turned into a trailer park."

She just shrugged. "All the better, it's freezing outside, and now I don't have to take the el downtown. And I was hoping to interview your mom about the set design anyway."

Taylor left me standing in our foyer while she walked toward the opening chords of "Sweet Home Alabama" coming from the living room. "I'll come upstairs and see you when I'm done," she told me, and disappeared into my family's makeshift trailer.

The whole thing was unbelievable. And there was only one person who would appreciate the scene in my living room and manage to make it something I could laugh about. I looked down at the small figurine I'd had clutched in the palm of my hand and went upstairs to call John.

While Reed was in his room packing for California, I was in my room putting the finishing touches on my college applications. I could have used the common application, but I decided to complete each college's own individual application. The essays were similar enough that it didn't create that much more work, and I thought, just maybe, it would give me an advantage over other students.

"All set for Los Angeles?" my mom asked, appearing in my doorway.

"I guess. I'm almost done here."

Instead of leaving, she came in and stood next to my bed, peering over my shoulder at my applications. "I know you're not that thrilled to be leaving for Christmas, but it will be fun, right?"

I glanced up from the page I was working on and saw that she actually expected me to answer her question. "I still think we should be staying home, but I guess what I think doesn't matter."

My mom moved the applications aside and sat down next to me. "It matters. It's just that this is something we have to do." She almost made it sound like an obligation.

"It's his mom, it's something Reed has to do, not us."

"Let's try to make this pleasant for everyone, okay? Are you packed?"

I nodded.

"Good." She stood up to leave, but didn't. "Do you think that brown sleeveless dress makes my arms look flabby?" she asked, out of the blue.

My mother doesn't have an ounce of fat on her, and she wasn't one to ask me, someone who hasn't worn a skirt since seventh grade, for fashion advice. "I don't think so, why?"

"It's nothing. I just want to make sure I bring the right clothes." She shook her head and walked to the door. "Forget it. I'm just being ridiculous."

But I knew she wasn't being ridiculous. She was trying to figure out what to wear when she met Marnie.

The morning we left for California, it was so cold I was almost glad to be getting out of Chicago. Not so glad that I was rushing out the door, but glad enough to pack a bathing suit and suntan lotion. After I called Patrick and said my final good-byes, I took all five application envelopes, double-checked that they were sealed and the postage was securely affixed, and went downstairs to make the drop.

"Come on, Vanessa. We're going to miss the plane," my mom called from the street, where she and Reed and my dad were waiting in a cab.

I placed the envelopes in the wrought-iron mailbox and closed the lid. Then I lifted it again and peeked in, just to make sure they were still there. Of course they were.

"Vanessa," my mother screamed again, "we're going to miss the plane!"

From this point on, both literally and figuratively, it was out of my hands.

I knocked on the shingles for luck and headed down the steps toward the taxi. "Coming."

•   •   •

Marnie's house wasn't exactly what I'd imagined. Yes, it was beautiful. Yes, there were immaculately manicured flowers and gardens dotting the driveway leading to the house. Yes, it looked like something out of a magazine my mother would use as inspiration. But it wasn't huge, and there wasn't a guard shack out front manned by a security patrol hired to protect the award-winning actress (although there was an electronic gate that Reed had to punch a code into to open up and let us in). But instead of being some modern glass-and-steel marvel or a castle worthy of royalty, Marnie's house looked like a comfortable stone cottage that just happened to land smack dab in the middle of the Hollywood Hills.

"Welcome," Marnie cried out when she saw our car pulling up to the house. She'd been waiting on the front steps, which I wasn't expecting. I kind of thought that Reed's mom would be inside watching reels of herself in the screening room or something. But she was just sitting on the stone steps in a pair of white capris and a bright pink tank top, looking like any other mother who also happens to have a gold statue from the Academy of Motion Picture Arts and Sciences on her fireplace mantel.

Reed was the first one out of the car and Marnie ran to give him a hug, just like any other normal mother would do.

"You must be Vanessa," she said to me, once I'd climbed out of the car and stretched my legs. "I'm so glad to meet you. Reed's told me all about his sister."

I didn't know whether or not that was true, but I decided to believe her. She was either genuinely excited to meet me or acting, and because she was so good at what she did, I knew I wouldn't be able to tell the difference.

My parents emerged from the limo and another round of hugs ensued. We were just one big happy family.

Reed headed for the house and I followed him. "Pretty nice digs," I observed as he showed me around. "But, what, no screening room?" I whispered, pretending to be horrified.

"This is just the beginning."

I take back what I said. The house *was* huge. We went down flagstone hallways, through glass-encased atriums, and must have passed at least three different slate patios just outside pairs of French doors until we came to the pool.

"It's probably too cold for a swim, but you can go see if you want," Reed offered when we were outside on the largest terrace overlooking the pool. The view from Marnie's backyard was amazing.

"You can see forever from up here."

"Enjoy it," Reed told me. "Half the time it's too hazy to see much."

After my tour, I went inside and changed into shorts and a T-shirt. Reed was right. It wasn't exactly summer outside, but it had to be at least forty degrees warmer than it was that morning in Chicago.

I grabbed a towel out of the linen closet in my bathroom and staked out a spot on one of the lounge chairs scattered around the pool. Reed was sitting on the terrace closest to the house, calling people on his cellphone to announce his arrival.

I laid down on the lounge chair and closed my eyes, inhaling the fragrance of flowers and sunshine and freshly cut grass.

I must have fallen asleep, because when I woke up, Reed was gone. As a matter of fact, it seemed like *everyone* was gone.

I wandered the halls of Marnie's house, peeking into empty bedrooms and nooks that must have had some purpose, even if I couldn't figure out what they were. Finally I came to what I assumed was Marnie's bedroom.

"Hello," I called out, stepping one of my bare feet into the room and feeling the thick white carpet cushion my feet.

"Out here," a voice called back, and I followed it until I spotted Marnie sitting outside on yet another stone terrace, a book open on her lap.

"Where is everybody?" I asked her.

"Reed took your parents for a drive to show them around." Marnie pushed her chair back and placed the book open-faced onto the table next to her.

"I can leave you alone if you'd like to read," I offered, not really wanting to go away. It was weird to see Marnie Vaughn doing something normal. When she was in Taylor's magazines or being interviewed on TV, she was always doing something *actressy*—munching on a Cobb salad during an interview, sitting in a director's chair on set, or wearing some sparkly gown as she stepped up to a podium to make a speech or accept an award.

"No, stay." She patted the chair next to her and motioned for me to sit down. "Reed and your parents tell me that you're hoping to attend Yale in the fall."

I crossed my fingers and held them up to show her. "If all goes well."

"I remember when I got into Yale. Even though it was grad school, I waited for weeks, running to the mailbox every day, looking for the acceptance letter. When the envelope came, I completely lost it, went around waving the letter in the air. My parents didn't know what the heck I was doing. They thought we'd won the Publishers Clearing House sweepstakes or something."

"You don't have to wait for the letter anymore. Now you can check online."

"Really? That sounds like kind of a letdown, doesn't it? Takes away the element of surprise, the moments of complete panic when you're holding the unopened envelope in your hands wondering what it says." Marnie looked down at her empty hands and smiled, as if envisioning her own acceptance letter.

"I never thought about it like that."

"Your parents are really proud of you, you know."

"I guess so." It had never really occurred to me that my parents would actually be proud if I got into Yale. I always thought they'd be more impressed if I adopted a village full of kids from Save the Children or something. "In some ways I think they pictured their kid turning out more like Reed than me."

Marnie laughed. "That's funny. I always pictured my kid turning out more like you."

"Really?" Now I laughed. "Why?"

"I'm from Connecticut originally, and all this," Marnie swept her hand through the air toward the green hills surrounding us, "is vastly different from where I was raised. I thought Reed would grow up like I did."

"Like you did?" I asked, trying to figure out what she meant.

"Normal," she clarified. "But obviously that didn't happen."

"He's better now than he was when he left here," I told her, feeling for some reason that I needed to defend Reed. "All our Starbucks are still in tact."

Marnie smiled. "That's good to hear. Still, he'll be coming back here in a few months and I don't know what will happen then. I worry about him."

"Why?"

"Because everything's always come so easy for Reed. Did you know that he didn't even try out for his first commercial? A casting director saw Reed one day when I dragged him to a set with me, and the next thing I knew he was pitching Kool-Aid on TV. And he hated Kool-Aid."

I made a note to tell that story to Taylor. She'd love it.

"Even with *Wild Dunes,* they wanted him before he auditioned," Marnie continued, telling me more about Reed's life in ten minutes than he'd shared in all the months he'd been living with us in Chicago. "That's one of the reasons I'm glad he's going to be working with your dad at the theater this spring. Maybe it will remind him that everything isn't supposed to be so easy."

"My dad's looking forward to working with Reed."

"I know. Did you ever do anything at the Bookman with your mom or dad?"

I shook my head. "Not unless you count volunteering as an usher. And, actually, my volunteering wasn't exactly voluntary. Once I got older, I never really liked hanging around."

"That's too bad for them. As crazy as our lives always were, I enjoyed having Reed at work with me."

"Maybe having Reed around the theater will make up for me."

Marnie made a *tsk, tsk* sound. "I'm sure it won't."

She was so easy to talk to, I almost forgot I was talking to a famous actress. There were probably reporters and gossip columnists who'd give their first born to have a private audience with Marnie Vaughn. And I knew one.

"Would you consider doing me a favor?" I asked.

Marnie was quick to agree. "Sure."

I told Marnie my idea and she handed me the cordless phone resting on the arm of her chair. I dialed and waited for an answer.

"There's an early Christmas present here for you," I told Taylor when she picked up. "Somebody wants to say hi."

Marnie took the phone and held it to her ear. "Hello, Taylor? This is Marnie Vaughn."

The shrill screaming on the other end of the phone made me smile. For the first time in my life, I think I knew how it felt to be Santa Claus.

chapter twenty-five

"I'm heading out to meet some friends," Reed announced, coming into the great room where Marnie and I were both relaxing and flipping through her stack of magazines.

"Why don't you go out with Reed," Marnie encouraged, looking over at me. "You'd like that, wouldn't you, Reed?"

We'd been shopping all day and I was really quite content to sit on the couch reading. The idea of going to some loud dance club, or whatever it was Reed was planning, didn't thrill me. Besides, it was Christmas Eve. And call me traditional or whatever, but I still thought Christmas Eve was for sitting around the house listening to Christmas carols and eating food that was bad for you. Marnie had even filled the refrigerator with two-gallon containers of egg nog after I told her how much I loved it.

"That's okay. I'm fine, really," I told Marnie, and went back to reading my magazine.

"Vanessa, can you come here a sec?" my mom called from the dining room table, where she and my dad were wrapping last-minute gifts. There aren't a lot of walls in Marnie's house, mostly wide-open rooms separated by steps or half walls or giant sculptures. So I knew my parents had been listening to our conversation.

I got up off the couch and followed my mom into the kitchen.

"Marnie would really like it if you went with Reed," she told me once the swinging door closed behind us.

"I'm fine hanging out here. She doesn't need to feel bad."

"That's not it," my mom explained, pulling out a stool at the breakfast bar and sitting down. "It will be the first time he's been with his friends since he came to live with us and Marnie's afraid that Reed might fall into his old habits."

"So I'm supposed to baby-sit him?"

"Not baby-sit. Just be there in case he needs you. Please," she added. "For me?"

"Okay, I'll go," I announced, joining Marnie and Reed back in the great room.

Marnie smiled and mouthed *thank you*.

"I'll wait here." Reed gave my gym shorts and Cabot T-shirt the once-over. "You might want to go and change."

"Do you always go out on Christmas Eve?" I asked Reed, as he drove down the winding road toward the valley. Marnie was letting us use her Mercedes for the night, and it still had that new-car smell.

It was odd having Reed drive. He'd never driven our car in Chicago, and I was so used to seeing him on the bus or in the backseat of a cab that watching him behind the wheel of Marnie's Mercedes made him almost seem like a different person. Back home I was the one who told him how to get places, which way to go. But here I was the one in the passenger's seat, and Reed was in control. And I wasn't sure I liked it.

Reed sped around a curve and I was thrown against my door. "Don't worry, we'll be home in time for you to have visions of sugar plums dancing in your head."

• • •

Reed took me to Gecko, a name I recognized from Taylor. It was *the* place to see and be seen among Hollywood's younger crowd. Probably all of Reed's friends would be there, or at least everyone who ran in his circle. I wasn't sure he had friends, at least not the kind that I had. Mostly they seemed to be people he'd worked with, costars who all met up at the same clubs and hotel rooftop bars.

And that's exactly what Gecko was, an open-air, ivy-covered pavilion on top of some boutique hotel in West Hollywood. It wasn't exactly lavish. And it wasn't even a bar, really. At least not the kind of bars we had in Chicago. Gecko had a simple tin roof, rustic log beams, and plain wood furniture. But it did have the most amazing views of Los Angeles.

"Wow."

"I know what you're thinking," Reed told me, making his way toward the bar.

I followed behind, my head swiveling from side to side as I took in the scenery around me. "What am I thinking?"

"Taylor would love this."

Reed was right. That was exactly what I was thinking.

I spotted a familiar stick-thin blonde, who on the cover of last week's *Star* had been a brunette. "Is that . . ."

Reed didn't even wait for me to finish. "Yep."

"And that's . . ." I nodded over toward a corner of the roof, where a pair of silicon spheres were practically bursting out of a silver tank top, like they were trying to break free and make a run for it.

Reed nodded. "Right again."

"Oh my God, they're even thinner in real life. And does anyone have real boobs around here, or are they all man-made?"

"What do you think? Some industries require hard hats and tool belts, out here they require big tits and blond hair. It's an occupational requirement."

Sounded more like an occupational hazard.

"What do you want to drink?" Reed asked when we made it to the bar.

"I don't know. Something good."

Not a minute later I was holding a funky martini glass filled with a light green liquid. "What's this?" I asked, taking a sip.

"An appletini. Like it?"

"It tastes like a sour apple lollipop," I told him, taking another sip.

"That's the idea." Reed was holding a short, squat glass with something clear over ice. I had a feeling it wasn't water.

"Are you sure you should be drinking that?" I asked, assuming it was vodka or gin or something equally prohibited in rehab.

"I'll be fine," he assured me.

"Don't they card around here?" I looked toward the door, where the bouncer had just let us waltz right in.

"Are you kidding me? Underage celebrities are good for business."

"So who are we meeting?" I asked.

"Them." Reed pointed across the rooftop to where a posse of impossibly good-looking people were laughing at someone's story. I recognized most of them, including the former farmstand-shopping Rebecca Stewart.

Reed walked me over to the group, who stopped laughing long enough to gush over Reed, and then listen as he introduced me. They showered me with perfunctory smiles and obligatory hellos, and then went back to their conversation. Reed was immediately enveloped into their circle, but somehow they managed to keep me on the fringe with a few strategically placed elbows and stiletto heels that I didn't dare get near for fear of losing one of my big toes to an accidental stomping.

At home Reed barely mentioned any of his friends back in L.A. Even now I had a hard time believing this collection of eye candy was really his friends. At least not the type of friends I had, like Taylor and John. They seemed more like, I didn't know what the word was. Associates? Contacts? It was hard to believe that Reed had gone from this crew to befriending Sarah Middleton. He'd definitely upgraded.

Reed's friends reminded me a little of the Susans, although of course these girls were in an entirely different league. It was the way the girls said something that sounded like a compliment but also managed to include an insult, as well ("She's got a fantastic body, if you don't mind the lipo scars").

But while the girls at Cabot were enamored with Reed from day one, I seemed to have the opposite effect on his friends. Nobody was asking if I slept in the nude. I seriously doubted they even took the effort to remember my name.

Even Reed didn't seem to quite fit in like I expected him to. He didn't stand on the outskirts of the group like I did, but he didn't exactly look comfortable, either. When a photographer asked the group to stand together for a picture, Reed stepped forward, then hung back, like he couldn't decide if he wanted to be included or not. And when someone told a joke, the look on his face almost reminded me of Benji's at Taylor's Emmy party. First he laughed when they laughed, but I wasn't sure he got the jokes, or, if he did, whether he actually thought they were funny.

"I'm going to get another drink," Reed told me, holding up a glass that now only contained melting ice. "Want one?"

I'd been so busy dissecting the insipid conversation and overly dramatic hand gestures that I'd only made a dent in about half of my appletini.

The idea of standing on the periphery of the posse didn't make me want to stay by myself. I so obviously did not belong to their club. I was merely a guest of one of their members. "No, but I'll go with you."

"So what do you think of them?" Reed asked me while we waited for the bartender to pour him another drink.

"They're interesting," I answered, choosing the most innocuous response possible.

"I knew you wouldn't like them."

"And you do?"

Reed took a few minutes to look across the crowd at his friends before giving me a noncommittal shrug.

The bartender handed Reed his drink and my brother started to walk back to the group. "You coming?"

I shook my head. "I think I'm going to walk around."

Reed gave me a look that said "suit yourself," and left me standing there alone.

So I walked around and soaked it all up. The designer outfits and perfectly highlighted hair, the false laughter and "call me's" shouted across the bar while people held up their thumbs and pinkies like phones. It was so different. So stereotypical. So Hollywood.

Taylor would have been in her glory.

I almost wished she was here to see this. But even more than Taylor, who'd be mesmerized at the mere sight of half the people in Gecko, it was John I really wanted there with me. He'd see right through all the phoniness, and we'd have some good laughs making fun of all the glamorous people.

"Having fun?" a voice asked, coming up behind me. I turned and came face-to-face with Rebecca Stewart. Her hair was redder than it was when Taylor pointed out her picture in the magazine a few months ago. I had to remember to tell Taylor espresso was out, cranberry was in.

"It's pretty here," I told Rebecca, whose only reply was, "I guess."

"I'm going to get myself and Reed another drink." She held up two empty glasses.

"Do you really think that's such a good idea?" I eyed the empty glasses, but Rebecca just stared blankly at me.

"Given all his problems," I went on, hoping she'd get the point. "He doesn't exactly need another trip to rehab."

"Rehab?" Rebecca laughed as she said the word. "Reed didn't go to rehab. He needed a break. 'Rehab' just sounds a lot better in print."

"Rehab" sounded better? "Better than what?" I asked.

"Cracking up?" Rebecca told me, like I was a complete idiot for even asking. I almost expected her to add a "duh" at the end of her answer. "Reed was having some problems, you know, that whole James Dean syndrome—live fast, die young, and leave a good-looking corpse, or whatever the saying is."

"Are you telling me . . ." I left my question open-ended, not even wanting to say it out loud. It was too unbelievable.

"Telling you . . ." Rebecca repeated, having no clue what the hell I was saying.

"Are you telling me that Reed was trying to kill himself when he crashed into that Starbucks?"

This cracked Rebecca up. "God no. The only thing worse for your career than getting cancelled midseason is dying. Reed didn't want to die. He was just having a little trouble figuring out where Gray stopped and Reed started. Besides, he has the looks, but let's be honest, he's not the greatest actor in the world. It's normal. Happens all the time with guys who play the bad boy. Sometimes you see it with the girls, too." Rebecca went on, as if well schooled in the psychological profile of young actors. "But mostly they're just really hos. It's the guys who can't handle it."

Rebecca left me standing there digesting the information that my brother had been on the verge of "cracking up," to use her term. For some reason, I found the news even more disturbing than the idea of Reed in rehab.

The rest of the night Reed didn't even make an effort to talk to me, so after watching him make several more trips to the bar, I went over to my brother and told him I was ready to go.

He rolled his eyes at his friends before conceding, "It *is* Christmas Eve, I guess."

"Give me the keys," I told him once we were downstairs on our way to the car. I was pretty sure Marnie wanted her new Mercedes back in one piece. I knew *I* wanted to make it home in one piece.

Reed squinted at me as if trying to comprehend what I'd just asked him. "Why?"

"Forget it." I reached into his front pocket for the keys, but Reed grabbed my hand and stopped me.

"I can drive," he insisted, and pushed my hand away.

I pried the keys from his fingers and held them behind my back. "No you can't."

"What the hell is your problem?" he yelled, following me to the car.

"My problem is that you're back here for a whopping four days and already you're the same old asshole you were when I first met you. You're ridiculous."

I pushed the button on the key chain and automatically unlocked the car doors.

"I'm ridiculous?" Reed turned around and threw his hands up in the air as he walked away from the car. "She says *I'm* ridiculous," he mumbled to himself, then came back toward the car. "What's ridiculous is someone who thinks that life has to fit into this perfect little picture she has in her head of the way things are supposed to be."

"Get in the car."

"You think that doing well in school and having everything all mapped out makes you better than me? Better than my friends?"

"Who are you kidding? They're not your friends, Reed," I told him, my voice rising.

"How the hell would you know? Who are you to decide what friends are? You can't even keep your boyfriend from fucking somebody else while he's away from you."

His words sliced through me, and I placed my hands on my stomach, almost expecting to feel a wound.

But Reed wasn't done. He was just getting started.

"And then, like an idiot, you take him back, just because you don't want to admit you were wrong about your little plan to be together. God forbid you don't know what's in store for you. God forbid everything doesn't work out exactly like you want. You can't even admit that you like somebody else, even after you end up kissing the guy!"

I closed my eyes and inhaled the warm night air. "Shut up, Reed. You're drunk."

"Yes, Vanessa, I'm drunk. In real life people get drunk. And this is real life, not the perfect little world you're hell-bent on creating for yourself."

"Get in the car, Reed," I ordered.

Reed didn't move.

"Get in the fucking car right now or I'm leaving without you. And when I get back to Marnie's I'm going to tell them why I left you here, and you'll be back in the looney bin so fast, living with me will seem like Disneyland compared to what you'll be in for." Once I'd said it I couldn't believe the words were out of my mouth. And from the look on Reed's face, neither could he. I walked around to the passenger side of the car and opened the door. "So, like I said. Get in the car, Reed. Now."

This time he listened. And we drove home in silence.

chapter twenty-six

$\mathcal{I}$ didn't tell Marnie or my mom and dad about what happened in the parking lot outside Gecko. I wanted to. I wanted to send Reed as far away from me as possible. The things he'd said to me were horrible, but what I'd said to him was almost worse. And even if we were never going to be like a real brother and sister, especially after that night, I still felt like we owed each other something. And that something was keeping what was said to ourselves. Because as ugly as the truth is, it's even uglier when someone says out loud what you've been thinking to yourself.

The ride home from Gecko seemed to take forever, and by the time we got to Marnie's house everyone was asleep. All the rooms were dark, but the Christmas tree in the corner of the great room was still lit. The small lights cast a yellow glow that illuminated the piles of presents scattered around the tree.

"Merry fucking Christmas, sis," Reed mumbled, and then headed down the hall to his bedroom.

• • •

Reed and I didn't say a word to each other for the rest of the trip unless it was absolutely necessary. My parents and Marnie noticed something was wrong, but every time they asked me about it, I just told them to forget it.

The weeks after we got back to Chicago were pretty bad. It was already dark by the time I got home after school, and every day was bitterly cold. It didn't snow, which would at least make the cold weather worth suffering through. Instead there was only the kind of wind that seemed to slap against you, stinging your skin no matter how many layers of clothes you wore.

As soon as we returned from California, our living room was returned to normal, and my dad and Reed went to work on the play, so they were gone until at least eight o'clock every night. Patrick was already back at school for his second semester. Taylor got into Boston University, so she was more or less just biding her time until graduation. And all my applications were in the mail, so I didn't have much to do except read books, watch TV, and wait.

John was in Grenada for all of January, fulfilling Sharingham's mandatory one-month "residency" in a third world country. He had sporadic access to e-mail and I started looking forward to his random messages in my in-box. Although the idea of living in a place where people carried machetes around everywhere they went (John said it was for cracking open coconuts and chopping things, not for attacking people in the middle of the night—nobody even had locks on their doors), I figured he could do a lot worse than the Caribbean. When I was in eighth grade, the seniors went to Uganda and half of them got sick from the malaria shots.

The first week of February I was sick for most of the week. I hadn't been sick for that long—about five days—in more than two years. I was usually pretty healthy, which is why I won the attendance award three years running in elementary school. The certificates were probably still in a box in my closet, buried under years of report cards and math awards and newspaper articles covering various competitions I'd won.

If January verged on depressing, staying home sick in February was as close to insanity as I've ever come. I was alone all day long while Reed went to school and my parents were working. My mom came home every day at lunchtime to make me some soup or toast, but I was never very hungry.

Reed must have felt bad for me, because even he went out of his way to be nicer. He brought home my assignments and sat on my bed and told me a few funny stories about the Susans. I wouldn't laugh, though, until he left my bedroom and closed my door behind him. And I never said thank you for going around to my teachers and asking for the day's assignments.

I knew what he was trying to do, and it wasn't going to work. Bringing me homework and Tuesday's issue of the *Cabot Chronicle* wasn't going to make up for what he'd said to me in California.

Patrick called a few times that week to see how I was doing, but it wasn't the same. We hadn't seen each other since Thanksgiving, and every time we talked we had less and less to say to each other until it almost became easier not to talk to him than it was to talk to him. Here I'd more or less spent two months fighting with Reed over Patrick, and now I was beginning to wonder if it had been worth it. I'd dreaded going to California for Christmas because I wanted to spend time with Patrick, but what happened between me and Reed was way worse than being apart from my boyfriend.

Mostly I spent that week alone, either sleeping or thinking. The thinking usually just made me wish I'd chosen to sleep instead. It was the same thought spiral every time:

Think about how lucky Taylor was to know where she'd be in September.

Think about how not knowing where *I'd* be really sucked.

Wonder what the admissions committee at Yale was doing at that very moment, and whether or not they had reviewed my application.

Wonder what Patrick was doing at that very moment, and who he was doing it with.

Imagine what it would be like to get into Yale and be able to spend every day with Patrick.

Imagine what it would be like *not* to get into Yale and *not* be able to spend every day with him.

Consider the pros and cons of going somewhere else, like Smith or Williams.

Question why, all of a sudden, going somewhere else actually seems like an option.

Question why, all of a sudden, I'm actually starting to want options.

Later that week John surprised me and came over after school to see how I was doing. I hardly recognized him, he was so tan. And his hair had thin coppery highlights in it. He looked great.

I, on the other hand, looked like I'd spent the week in bed with barely enough energy to change my underwear.

"I brought you a Hot Tuna Meltdown," he told me, handing over the tin foil–covered bagel. "I don't know if it's still warm, but I figured you could always pop it in the microwave."

"Thanks." I took the bagel and led him to the living room. He hadn't seen me since December and I wasn't looking too great in my gray sweatpants and sweatshirt. I wished he'd given me some warning, at least I could have brushed my hair. Thank God I'd brushed my teeth.

"So you must be psyched these days," I said, taking a seat on the couch.

"Why?"

"No more wondering where you'll be next year. Taylor got into BU and she says it's a huge relief."

John sat down in the armchair across from me. "I didn't get into Dartmouth, Vanessa. They deferred me to regular admission."

"Oh my God, you must be freaking out."

"No, not really. I was bummed for a while, but then I got over it. Swinging a machete will do that to you."

"Don't tell me you're joining the Peace Corps or something."

"Nah, but I'm thinking maybe I'll go somewhere else. I'll have to see where I get in."

I watched John to see if he was just saying that just to make himself feel better, but he really seemed to mean it.

"So where'd you end up applying?" he asked me.

I counted the six schools off on my fingers. "Williams, Smith, Swarthmore, Wellesley, Amherst, and, of course, Yale."

"Of course, *Yale*," John mimicked me and laughed. "Not a whole lot of safety schools in that bunch," John pointed out.

"Why, do you think I'll need a safety?"

"I was just saying. Even I've added a few safeties."

"Even you?" I teased. "Well, it's too late now. Deadlines have passed and it's out of my hands."

"That sounds pretty cavalier for someone who practically had the Yale admissions office on speed dial."

Yeah, it was. "I guess that's what puking your guts out all week will do to you."

• • •

That night I was finally feeling a little better, so I decided to re-heat John's Hot Tuna Meltdown and give it a try. My parents were out to dinner with Glenda, so if it didn't stay down, at least my mom wouldn't force me to drink apple cider vinegar, a cure she insists will replenish my low levels of potassium and magnesium.

I sat at the kitchen table and slowly ate the bagel sandwich. It wasn't quite as good as it would have been if it hadn't been languishing in the refrigerator for three hours, but I managed to almost eat the entire thing.

Just as I was debating whether or not to take one last bite, Reed came into the kitchen looking for something to eat.

"How are you feeling?" he asked me, his head stuck inside the refrigerator as he debated his options.

"Better."

"Your mom said John came over to see you today." He decided on a leftover three-bean salad and sat across the table from me.

"Yep." If Reed expected anything more than one-word answers from me, he wasn't going to get them.

After attempting a few more conversation starters that didn't lead anywhere, I think he finally realized that.

"Look, I'm sorry about that scene at Gecko," he told me, taking a break from the three-bean salad.

"You were an asshole."

"I know I was," he admitted. "I was in no shape to drive. You were right."

"I'm sorry." I leaned my ear toward Reed and pretended I didn't hear what he said. "What was that?"

"I said you were right. You were right. Okay?"

"No, it's not okay. You could have killed both of us, not to mention the fact that if our parents found out—all three of them—your ass would have been back in rehab so fast you'd be begging me to have Glenda bake you a cake and slip a key in there so you could escape."

"It's not like jail, Vanessa. You don't *escape* from rehab," he told me, taking a forkful of three-bean salad and holding it up to his mouth. "Besides, I think we both know I wasn't in rehab."

"Why didn't you tell me?" I asked.

"What was I going to say? You already thought I was a fuckup, why would I tell you the show thought I should take a break from being Gray?"

"Because you're not Gray. You're Reed."

"Ah, therein lies the problem, right? Who is Reed? A month in some beachside retreat was supposed to help me figure that out."

I was starting to think that a few months in Chicago was supposed to help him figure that out.

"You know what pissed me off so much that night? The fact that you were right," he admitted.

"Again? I must be on a roll. What was I right about?"

"Rebecca and everyone. I stood there with them, listening to them talk, posing for pictures, and all I could do was see them through your eyes, and it made me mad."

"You never cared what I thought before," I reminded him. "Why start now?"

"Because when I looked at them I realized how you saw me—and I didn't fit in with them anymore."

"I'd think that was a good thing, considering."

Reed shrugged. "Maybe."

It took a lot of energy to be mad at someone for so long. Especially when he lived in the same house. I wanted us to go back to the way it was after New Haven, after I'd gotten used to having Reed around. Used to having what some would consider a brother. "Okay," I conceded, ready to forgive him.

"Okay, you forgive me, or okay, I'm still a dick?"

"Do I have to decide right now?" I asked, and cracked a smile. "Tell me about what went on at school all week."

Reed filled me in on what I'd missed, which wasn't much. Still, I felt like I'd been gone for weeks. I could only imagine what it was like for Reed to go home after being away for months.

"So do you think you'll hang out with the same friends when you get back to California?" I asked him as he polished off the three-bean salad.

He shrugged. "I don't know. I kinda had to try and remember what we had in common in the first place. It reminded me of how Daisy runs to meet her friends at Bark Park and then cautiously sniffs their asses for a while as she decides whether or not she still wants to play with them."

Not quite the analogy I'd use, but I knew exactly what he was talking about. "It's sort of like that with Patrick and me," I told him.

Reed frowned. "Do we really want to talk about Patrick? Shouldn't the topic of your boyfriend be off-limits for us?"

"No. I want to talk about it. I've been thinking about him a lot this week."

"Thinking about how you'll be together next year?"

"Or not," I told him.

"That's breaking news. Go on." Reed seemed interested in hearing the rest of what I had to say.

But how did I explain what I was thinking without making it sound like I was doubting my relationship with Patrick?

"It's just like you said. When we're not together I can't wait to see him or talk to him, but when I finally do, it doesn't measure up to what I expected."

"Maybe you expect too much."

"So I'm supposed to lower my standards just so I'm not disappointed?"

"You do tend to set the bar very high," Reed pointed out. "Maybe you just need to be a little more flexible."

"You mean less of a control freak."

"I didn't say it, you did." Reed pushed his chair back and got up from the table. "Hey, did your mom tell you the news?"

"What news?"

"Everyone loves the sets for *Running Out*." Reed turned on the faucet and started washing his dishes.

"Really?"

"Yeah. She keeps saying this play is turning into a real family affair."

"Not exactly," I told him. "I'm not doing anything."

"Well, sure." Reed turned off the faucet and reached for a dish towel. "But it's not like you want to, so I figured you didn't count. I didn't mean anything *bad* by it. Don't take it personally."

"I'm not," I assured him, not exactly convinced I believed what I was saying.

chapter twenty-seven

Usually when my parents go away they ask Glenda to stay with me. It's not that they don't trust me, they say, they just want someone else around in case the house bursts into flames or something equally unlikely happens. I've never minded in the past. Glenda wakes up at the crack of dawn to go to the bakery, so she's usually gone by the time I get up anyway. And after spending all day in the kitchen at work, she never rushes back here to cook me dinner. So I usually end up fending for myself most of the time, which, as an only child, I was used to.

This time my parents were going away for the week that just happened to be my spring break. My dad was a volunteer for the National Endowment for the Arts, and they'd asked him to go on a site visit to some regional theater in Atlanta. They decided that, as long as Reed was there to help me put out any errant fires, we'd be okay without Glenda.

But then Reed decided to go back to L.A. to visit Marnie for spring break, and my mom wasn't so sure I should spend the week alone.

"We can still ask Glenda to come over, if you want," my mother offered when Reed sprung the news on us that he'd decided to go to L.A.

"I'll be fine," I assured them. Taylor and her family were going to visit her grandmother in Arizona, so it wasn't looking like I'd have the most exciting week of my life. There would be plenty of time to identify and extinguish any unexpected fires.

On Saturday morning my parents and Reed left for the airport and my mom made me promise, one more time, to call Glenda if I was feeling like I wanted some company.

Saturday night I decided to go see a movie. Most of my class was away for the week, but I knew one person who was still around. Sarah Middleton.

I dialed her number and she was all too happy to meet me over at the theater on Clybourn. We decided to see some romantic comedy that she'd heard was pretty good. Afterward we got some hot chocolate at the Starbucks across the street to warm up.

"Why didn't you go to California with Reed?" Sarah asked me, once we were sitting down with our drinks.

"My parents thought he should have some time alone with his mom," I explained, even though I'd sort of wished an invitation had been extended. It was a lot warmer in California than it was in Chicago.

"He's really nervous about the play he's doing with your dad," Sarah told me, blowing on her hot chocolate to cool it off.

"Really?" I wouldn't think a little regional play could make a TV star nervous. "Why?"

"He doesn't want to let your dad down, and he knows everyone's going to be watching him, just waiting for him to screw up."

I waited for her to say that Reed knew *I* was waiting for him to screw up, but she didn't.

"Are you nervous about hearing from schools?" I asked, stirring my whipped cream into my hot chocolate.

Sarah stopped blowing on her drink. "Are you kidding me? I'm terrified."

She was? I didn't expect her to say that, even if she really was terrified. "Aren't you pretty much a shoo-in?"

"Not when there are twenty thousand applications vying for two thousand spots. Nobody's a shoo-in. I was just thankful you and Benji weren't applying there, too. When I saw you got an A on the last calc exam, I almost felt sick."

"Why?"

"I got an A minus."

"Ohhh, an A minus, I can't believe I'm even sitting here with such a slacker," I joked.

She laughed. "I know, I'm a huge letdown. Just don't tell anyone on the Harvard admissions committee."

Sarah took a sip of her cocoa, and I realized for the first time that we were more alike than I thought. I could see why Reed liked Sarah. And he was right. Once I got to know her, I did like her.

The weathermen had predicted the weather would be decent all week, in the mid-thirties. But on Monday morning I awoke to four inches of snow. And by Tuesday I was bored out of my mind. It was amazing how seventeen years of being an only child can give way to the constant chaos of a new brother. I tried calling Sarah, but her mom told me she'd gone sledding in the park. When I dialed John's number, I really wasn't expecting him to be home, Sharingham has a different vacation schedule than we do— but he answered on the second ring. There was some sort of teacher training program going on and they had the day off.

"Want to come over?" I asked, before realizing that John and I would be alone in my house.

John said he'd be over in an hour.

I had an hour to figure out what I wanted to happen. And I'd need every minute.

I went upstairs to my room and opened up my jewelry box.

There it was, the small gold heart that Patrick had given me last summer for my birthday. Last June, when he gave me the necklace, I thought I'd never take it off. I couldn't even pinpoint exactly when I stopped wearing it. After Christmas? When I got sick? Once I realized that, no matter how much I wanted everything to work out the way I planned, things change?

In June I couldn't have imagined what I'd be doing in March. I certainly couldn't have imagined that in a few weeks my dad's play was going to open, and my brother would be in it, and I'd be receiving my acceptance letters, and school would almost be over. There were only . . . I'd actually stopped counting the days until I was finished with senior year. If I had to guess I'd say there were probably around eighty days left. Eighty days to go and I wasn't any closer to a summer in Europe. That was just about the only thing that hadn't changed this year. My parents still weren't going to let me go to Europe with Taylor.

It seemed like Patrick gave me the necklace ages ago. Everything was so different. I thought, I'd hoped, this year would be exactly like last year, only without Patrick. But instead of being short one boyfriend I'd actually gained a brother, lost a best friend, lost a boyfriend, gotten them both back, and now . . . now I didn't know what I had. I had a necklace and a guy I spoke to on the phone once every other week. A guy who knew the Vanessa I was last year, not the person I'd become while he was away. Patrick and I had so little to talk about anymore, so little of our lives intersected, and when they did, they relied too much on the past.

If you had asked me that day, the day Patrick gave me the necklace for my birthday, I would have said I'd be visiting Patrick for my spring break. But when he extended the obligatory invitation, the answer wasn't so easy.

Maybe I should have gone to visit Patrick. Maybe I was giving up too easily.

Just as I was about to reach for the necklace, the doorbell rang. And instead of taking the necklace out and fastening it around my neck, I didn't make a move for it. Instead, I closed the top of the jewelry box and headed downstairs.

"So your parents let you stay home alone while they're away?" John took the bowl of microwave popcorn and followed me into the living room. We were going to see if there was anything on TV worth watching.

"Not usually," I told John. "Their friend Glenda would have stayed with me, but I convinced them I'd be fine."

"And they wouldn't care that you're having some strange guy over?"

"Are you strange?"

"You know what I mean."

"Not really. They trust me."

I wasn't so sure *I* trusted me. Maybe having John come over wasn't such a great idea after all.

John and I sat on the couch and flipped through the channels.

"Hey, there's your brother." John pointed to the TV, where a rerun of *Wild Dunes* was playing.

"Want to watch this?" I asked.

"Sure," John agreed.

We watched the show, but I couldn't tell you what it was about. My mind was somewhere else.

I had a boyfriend. Supposedly. But that wasn't what was going through my mind. Instead I kept thinking, Why hasn't John tried to make a move on me?

Here I was the one who'd laid down the law, who'd set all the parameters around our relationship. And now I was the one who wanted to change that.

I reached for the bowl of popcorn sitting on the cushion between us and placed it on the coffee table. If I was going to do this, I wasn't going to worry about getting butter-flavored oil on the slipcover. It was going to require all of my attention.

I leaned against John's shoulder and when he didn't back away, and instead pulled me into him, I decided to do it. Maybe I just needed to get it out my system once and for all.

I leaned in toward John and closed my eyes, preparing to kiss someone who, until now, had been just a nice guy. And who was now the guy I was making out with.

It was good. It was really good.

"What was that all about?" John asked, as we pulled apart and caught our breath.

"I really don't know."

"Are you sure you want to do this?"

I nodded. "I'm sure."

We were alone in my house and there was no school tomorrow.

John leaned me down against the cushions and started kissing me again. This time I wasn't as nervous. And it was even better. John was an amazing kisser.

"Did you hear that?" John asked, stopping midkiss.

"It was probably just Daisy," I told him, and pulled him toward me again. Now that I'd started, I didn't want to stop.

But John didn't make a move to kiss me. "It sounded like the front door."

"It couldn't be." But then I heard them, too. Footsteps. And they were coming toward the living room.

"Vanessa?" a voice asked, the footsteps stopping as soon as the person saw us lying on the couch. "Am I interrupting something?"

chapter twenty-eight

"What are you doing here?" I asked, jumping up from the couch.

"I came back early," Reed answered, placing his bag down on the floor. "Hey, John."

"Hey, Reed." John stood up and looked at his watch. "Vanessa, I should probably get going."

I walked John to the front door and waited for Reed to leave us alone. Instead he stood there watching us, a slightly amused look on his face, like he was enjoying my discomfort.

"It wasn't what it looked like," I explained to Reed, once I saw John head down our front walk.

"It looked like you and John were making out on the couch while you watched *Wild Dunes.*"

Okay, so it was what it looked like. "I wasn't expecting you to walk in," I told him, as if that was the only problem. That I'd been interrupted. Not that I was cheating on my boyfriend. Not that I'd been thinking about how close we were to my bedroom.

"Why'd you come back early? You're not supposed to be home until Sunday."

"The play starts in four weeks. I want to be ready."

"So you came home to rehearse? Wouldn't it have made more sense to stay in L.A. and practice with Marnie?"

"I tried that, but she was freaking me out. The more she tried to help, the worse I did. It was too much pressure."

"If acting in front of Marnie was too much pressure, you're in for a huge treat when you step on stage in front of hundreds of Bookman patrons."

Reed gave me a little wave. "Hey, thanks a lot. That really helps the situation."

"Sorry."

Reed didn't seem like he was in any rush to unpack. He sat down in one of the leather armchairs and swung his legs up over its arm. My mom hated it when I did that. I walked over to the other chair and sat the same way.

"I thought maybe you'd be lonely by now and I'd come home and keep you company. But I guess you already had company." Reed looked like he was waiting for me to say something.

"What?" I asked.

"Is there something you want to tell me? Like why John was here?"

"I invited him over."

The next morning Reed was at the kitchen table, his script open in front of him.

"Frosted Flakes? What are you, six?"

"Old habits die hard. I went out this morning and picked up a box," he told me, tipping his cereal bowl on its side and taking one last spoonful of Frosted Flakes. "There's only so much Muslix a person can suffer through." He got up to put his bowl in the sink. "I'm going to call Sarah and see if she wants to run through my lines with me."

"I could help you," I offered.

Reed turned around and looked at me like he was trying to figure out if he'd heard me right. "You?"

"Yeah. I know I'm not a real actor," I conceded.

Reed didn't even hesistate. "According to you, neither am I."

I managed to keep a straight face until I saw Reed start to smile. Then we both couldn't help but laugh. I reached for the box of Frosted Flakes he'd left on the table.

"So do you want me to help or not?" I asked, pouring myself a bowl.

"Sure. At least I know you'll be honest with me if I suck." Reed checked the clock on the microwave. "We're leaving here in an hour."

"Where are we going?"

"The theater."

"Do we really have to go all the way down there?" I complained. "Can't we just do it here?"

"No way. I want it to be just like the real thing."

"Fine," I agreed. "I'll be ready in an hour."

Reed started to leave the kitchen, but before he left, there was one more thing I needed to know.

"You didn't also happen to pick up real milk, did you? Soy milk just doesn't seem to go with Frosted Flakes."

He pointed to the refrigerator. "Top shelf, next to the orange juice. And there's a bag of Doritos in the pantry."

Our house hadn't seen Doritos since my mom banned all artificially colored snack chips in 1997. I guess there were some good reasons to have a brother, after all.

Going to the Bookman with Reed was strange. I didn't have the same giddy excitement I felt when I was younger and my dad would let me watch the cast prepare for a production, but I didn't dread the sight of the familiar marquee, either. It was the first time I'd gone to the theater without my parents. And the first time I'd gone with my brother.

Reed led me through the front of the theater and through the doors that were reserved for employees and performers. Even though I knew my way around, I let him show me the way. He pointed out the dressing room he shared with other members of the cast and didn't even seem to mind the idea. We walked past the entry to the main stage and kept on walking until we reached the door to the smaller studio.

"Here it is," Reed announced, and then opened the door as if it were the grandest place in the world.

For the most part, the room was dark, but a few canned lights were pointed at the stage and provided enough light for us to read from the scripts we each had in our hands.

We stepped out onto the wooden stage and Reed pulled up two stools that were standing against the wall.

"One for you, one for me," he singsonged, and if I didn't know better I would have thought it was Reed's turn to be giddy. He was acting just like I used to. My brother looked completely comfortable on stage, even if all the seats in the theater were empty and there was no one there to give him the adulation and praise he could find on the set of *Wild Dunes*.

I took my place on the stool and laid the script on my lap while Reed took his script and flipped through some pages. Once he found the page he was looking for, he sat there silently until he was ready. I could almost see him change, even though he was still the same guy sitting on the stool. But somehow he wasn't Reed any longer. And he wasn't Gray. His facial expression, the way he held his shoulders, he was a poor Southern teenager about to explain to his friend why he was leaving the only home he'd ever known to be with his father.

When Reed spoke it wasn't like he was reciting lines, it was like he was feeling them.

"Your turn," he pointed out, looking up. "The next line is yours."

"That guy is nothing like Gray," I told him, also thinking that Reed was nothing like Gray, either.

Reed almost seemed embarrassed. "Thanks."

"You've really been working hard on this, haven't you?" I asked.

"Well, yeah."

"Why?"

Reed closed his script and tipped his head to the side while he tried to figure out how to explain it to me. "You've always looked forward to the first day of school, right?" he finally began.

I nodded, although I didn't quite get where he was going with this.

"You can't wait to see who your teachers are, whether or not you'll like them, or even if they'll like you."

"They always like me," I told Reed, and he smiled.

"Anyway, you're starting something new, something unknown. It may be a little familiar, I mean, you've been to school before, but now you have all new subjects, new things to learn, people to meet, things to challenge you. And it's scary, and you don't know what to expect, but it's also exciting. Because you already learned what you were supposed to learn last year. So you've just gotta take your chances and hope you're prepared."

I must not have looked like I understood because Reed's expression changed. "That didn't make any sense, did it?" he asked, frowning.

"No, it did," I reassured him. "Really, I think I get it."

"I guess what I meant was that I know how to be on a TV show. I know how to play Gray. Shit, I could play him in my sleep. And the show will probably take me back for next season and extend my contract, and I could go on playing Gray until *Wild Dunes* is retired to syndication. But that's not what it's all about. I want more than that, even if I have to take my chances."

"I really do get it," I repeated, and I meant it.

In that moment when I found Patrick and Amory, it was like everything I thought I knew just blew away. I wouldn't say my life flashed before my eyes (melodrama is more for Reed than me, even if my midnight dash across campus might sound otherwise), but I would say that everything shifted a little until it looked like nothing I recognized. It was horrible, and miserable, and I didn't know anymore what would happen. But, after going through several cases of Kleenex, I survived. I wasn't the same person who arrived at Yale with a schedule in hand and a sure idea of where she was headed.

Even though it had taken me almost five months to get there, I knew that I was ready to take my chances, too.

Patrick wasn't surprised. And he wasn't mad. I think it was more like a mixture of relief and maybe a little nostalgia. When I called him that night, he sounded a lot like I felt, like we'd had a good run but it was time to see what came next.

"It will be weird seeing you on campus next year," he told me right before we hung up. "You're going to get in, you know."

I had a feeling I'd get in, too, but it didn't matter so much anymore. There were four other colleges considering my applications and I wasn't ready to eliminate any options just yet.

I thought if I went to Yale everything would stay the same even though it would change—I could still be Patrick's girlfriend, I could hang out with my best friend in Boston, my family would consist of my mom and dad at home in Chicago.

But John had it right. The more things change, the more they just change. I wasn't the same person I was eight months ago. And that was okay with me. Sometimes change was good. Sometimes it was even exactly what you needed.

chapter twenty-nine

"*I* got into Dartmouth," John told me when he called to ask what he should wear to the theater. It was opening night for *Running Out*.

"That's awesome."

"Thanks." I could tell he was excited. "What about you?"

"I don't know yet. I haven't checked the mailbox."

"Aren't you going to go online and see?"

"No, I think I'm going to wait for the letter to arrive."

"I can't believe you weren't on the computer first thing this morning."

"Believe it," I told him. "I'm going to wait and see what happens."

I knew I wasn't exactly a wait-and-see kind of person, but I'd decided to try it and see how it felt. Like Marnie had said, at least I'd be able to hold the decision in my hands and savor the last few moments of unknown before reading the answer.

"So I'll meet you at the theater, right?" I asked John.

"I'll meet you in the lobby at seven-thirty."

"See you there."

I thought I heard Reed in the bathroom, so I went to see how the newest Bookman actor was doing.

"I think I'm going to be sick," he moaned, leaning over the sink.

"You're not going to be sick. You're going to be fine."

"Then why does my stomach feel like I just ate one of your mother's Swedish soy balls?"

"It's just nerves. Why are you freaking out about this? You've rehearsed it a million times."

"Just because you rehearse something doesn't mean that when the time comes it will turn out perfect. There are all sorts of things that can go wrong."

"That's true, but you can't prepare for every possible contingency. Just go out there and do the best you can."

Reed still looked a little green. I don't think my advice helped very much. But at least he'd stopped dry heaving.

My dad and mom left early for the theater with Reed, so I took a cab by myself. It was the first time in a long time I was actually looking forward to going. I couldn't wait to see the play my dad directed, the scenery my mother helped design, and the character my brother had created.

The lobby was packed when I arrived. It was always like that on opening nights, but tonight there almost seemed to be more of a buzz than usual.

"Vanessa, over here!" I saw John waving his hand at me from over by the stairs to the mezzanine bar. Taylor was standing next to him, talking to a guy who looked vaguely like someone I recognized.

"Sarah's already in our seats," he told me once I'd finally made my way through the crowd. "I brought my friend, Simon. I hope that's okay."

So that's who Taylor was talking to. He certainly had her attention. "That's fine. I'm going to go backstage and see my parents and Reed. I'll meet you guys at our seats."

I started to walk away, but Taylor grabbed my arm and left Simon's side long enough to talk to me.

"Did you see him?" she asked, tipping her head in Simon's direction. "It's unbelievable, isn't it?"

"What?"

Taylor could barely catch her breath long enough to tell me. "He looks exactly like Orlando Bloom."

I recognized Marnie as soon as I opened the dressing room door. She almost looked as nervous as Reed.

"What are you doing here?" I asked, as Marnie made her way over to me and gave me a hug.

"You didn't think I'd miss Reed's first play, did you?"

Reed was taking deep breaths over in the corner and looked like someone should offer him a brown paper bag just in case he started hyperventilating. The other actors must have already put on their makeup and gotten dressed because we were the only ones in the room. "Why didn't you tell me your mom was coming?"

"I didn't know. She didn't want to make me nervous."

"Which is exactly what I'm doing." Marnie took my mom's elbow and led her toward the door. "Come on, Celia. Let's leave him alone."

"You can stay back here, you know," my mom told me. "You can watch from backstage with us."

"That's okay. John and Taylor and Sarah are waiting for me at our seats."

My mom came over and gave Reed one last hug. "Don't be so nervous. You're going to do fine."

"Are you nervous?" I asked Reed once my mom and Marnie were gone.

"What if I said yes?" Reed's voice was a little shaky and his fingers were quivering.

"I'd say you should be."

"What if I suck?"

"You won't suck," I assured him. "Besides, Taylor and Sarah are in the audience. They'll be cheering so loudly for you they'll drown out any boos." I didn't have the heart to tell him that he'd probably lost Taylor's heart to an Orlando Bloom look-alike.

"Boos. Gee, thanks." Reed wrung his hands and started pacing around the room. "Hadn't really thought about any booing."

"Break a leg," I told Reed, and left him alone in his dressing room.

I walked past the saints and led myself to my seat. Simon and Taylor were sitting next to each other, and John and Sarah had left an empty seat between them.

Sarah waved to me. "Over here."

"Did you hear from Yale?" she asked when I reached her and sat down. She handed me the extra Playbill she had waiting on her lap.

"Not yet. What about you?"

Sarah could hardly sit still. I think I already knew the answer. "Yes and yes."

So she'd gotten into Harvard. For the past seven months I thought I'd die if Sarah got in. But here she was, about to send in her deposit, and I didn't feel like dying. I felt like congratulating her.

"That's great. Maybe you and Taylor will see each other around Boston."

"Maybe when you come up from New Haven we can all get together," she suggested.

"That'd be fun," I told her, resisting the urge to make plans. "But we'll have to see what happens."

The house lights flickered on and off, indicating the start of the show.

"Here we go," I heard Taylor tell Simon.

John reached for my hand and I held it in the dark as I prepared myself to be surprised.

chapter thirty

$\mathcal{I}$t was almost ten o'clock when I woke up, but the house was quiet. I figured everyone was still in bed after our late night and went downstairs to get myself a glass of juice and wait for them to join me. I thought for sure my mom would have Glenda come over with a flourless chocolate cake to celebrate Reed's performance last night. I was just hoping it would arrive sooner rather than later.

Usually the morning after opening night my dad got up early and slipped out to get the paper. He wanted to read the reviews before anyone else and my mom and I knew to steer clear if he was sitting at the kitchen table alone, the paper already crumpled up in the garbage can. But this morning the door to my parents' room was still closed, and when I peeked in through the narrow crack, two rumpled figures were still buried under the covers.

So when I came down the stairs and heard someone jiggling the front door handle, a part of me was convinced it was Glenda. As I raced to unlatch the lock, already debating whether or not I had to actually wait for anyone else to wake up before digging into the chocolate ganache icing, the front door opened and Reed appeared, showered and dressed.

"Where'd you go?" I asked.

"I couldn't sleep so I went out to pick up some breakfast. You want a muffin?" he asked, holding up a white paper bag. I noticed he'd also picked up a newspaper. "What's wrong? You look disappointed. I got some bagels, too."

"I was sort of hoping you were Glenda," I admitted.

"I think she's coming over later." He kept his voice low. "But don't tell your mom you know. I heard them talking on the phone yesterday."

Reed walked over to the hall table and placed the bag down while he removed his coat.

Eight months ago I couldn't have imagined this. Reed Vaughn was hand delivering breakfast to me. And I, my hair still in a messy ponytail, my teeth unbrushed, and my eyes probably filled with eye boogers, didn't even flinch.

"Did you read the review for *Running Out*?" I asked, pulling away.

Reed shook his head and took a deep breath. "Not yet. I couldn't bring myself to look at it."

"Hey, did you see this?" he asked, pointing down at the pile of yesterday's mail stacked on the hall table.

"What?"

Next to the electric bill and a Walgreens flyer, I spotted a crisp white envelope with a familiar blue logo in the upper left-hand corner. A small blue Yale logo in the upper left corner. It was finally here.

"Aren't you going to open it?" Reed asked, waiting for me to pick the letter up.

But I didn't. I just stood there looking at my name typed in neat black letters on the front. This was the moment I'd been waiting for. The moment I'd been planning for. The moment I thought would change my life forever.

But it didn't.

That moment happened back in September when I picked up the phone and handed it to my dad.

"Don't you want to know what it says?" Reed asked, watching me hesitate.

"I don't know," I told him. Now that my letter had arrived I wasn't sure I wanted to know what it said. I mean, of course I wanted to know what it said, but I wasn't sure it mattered that much anymore.

Finally, I reached for the envelope and held it in my hands, feeling the smooth grains of the paper, the raised letters of the admissions office's return address. And that's when I noticed another envelope on the table. And it was also addressed to me.

Reed saw me staring at it and offered an explanation. "That's just something from me, but you can open it after the letter from Yale," he offered, pointing to the envelope I held in my hand. "Is a thin envelope a good sign or a bad one?"

Instead of answering, I read the return address for the second envelope on the table: Spotlight Travel Agency.

I looked over at Reed. "A travel agency?"

"Yeah. It's no big deal, just a little something I thought you'd like. Kind of an early graduation gift."

And, for some reason, by the way Reed looked at me, I knew what it was.

I reached for the second envelope and lifted it off the table. Reed stood there watching me as I held the envelope in my left hand, trying to decide which to open first, the letter from Yale or what I figured had to be an airline ticket.

I placed the letter from Yale back on the table and tore open the letter from Spotlight Travel.

"Surprised?" he asked when I pulled the thick computer-printed ticket out of the envelope.

"A ticket to London?" I turned to Reed. "But my parents will never let me go."

"Yes they will," he assured me.

"How do you know?"

"Because I asked them before I bought you the ticket."

"You didn't have to do this." I looked at the airline ticket in my hand and then I noticed something was wrong. "This is a one-way ticket. Are you trying to get rid of me?" I joked, thoroughly confused.

"It's not a one-way ticket. It's an open-ended ticket. There's a Eurorail pass in there, too. I thought this way you could go where you wanted, when you wanted. No need to plan everything so far in advance."

An open-ended ticket. The idea had never even occurred to me before.

"I know you hate surprises, but—"

I cut him off before he could finish. "I think I'm learning to live with surprises. And I love this one. What about Taylor?"

"Your parents are going to talk to hers and see if they can work something out."

He'd really thought of everything.

"You have to be back at least two weeks before you leave for school, though, or your parents will kill me," Reed told me.

I diverted my attention back to the letter on the table.

School. Which might, or might not, be Yale. I was starting to believe it might not.

I stared down at the Eurorail pass still tucked inside the envelope. "You didn't have to do this."

"Sure I did. That's what big brothers are for, right?"

I hadn't brushed my teeth or combed my hair or put on deodorant or anything, but I didn't care. I gave Reed a hug and kissed him on the cheek. "Thanks."

"It's no big deal." Reed almost looked embarrassed.

I picked up the newspaper and handed it to Reed. "Go ahead. Read the review."

Reed hesitated. "You think I should?"

"Absolutely."

He took the paper and turned the pages until he came to the review.

"Well?" The waiting was killing me. "What's it say?"

Reed held up the paper. "See for yourself."

From the grin on his face I knew it had to be good. And it was. You could even say the reviewer loved the play, and the guy who played Thomas, the adopted son of two gay men. Taylor's *Chronicle* column was going to have to be renamed "The Making of a Theater *Actor*."

"You did it," I told him.

Reed seemed a little stunned. "Yeah. I did, didn't I? So what about Yale?" He pointed to the letter on the table. "Don't you want to see what it says?"

I shook my head. I'd planned for this for so long that a part of me already knew what it would say: congratulations. And, for some reason, at that moment, standing next to my brother, Reed, I knew that I wasn't going to jump at the chance to accept their offer. I was going to leave my options open and see what else happened. There were a few more acceptance letters that would be arriving in my mailbox and I wanted to see what they had to say. I wasn't in any rush to make a decision. And I couldn't wait to be surprised.

Maybe planning everything wasn't really what it's all about.

Maybe it's not about having a plan, or even a plan B. Maybe it's about seeing where life takes you and learning to enjoy the ride.

"Maybe later," I told Reed, taking the bags of muffins and bagels off the table and heading toward the kitchen. "Right now I'm starving."

As many as 1 in 3 Americans
have HIV and don't know it.

TAKE CONTROL.
KNOW YOUR STATUS.
GET TESTED.

To learn more about HIV testing,
or get a free guide to HIV and
other sexually transmitted diseases.

www.knowhivaids.org
1-866-344-KNOW

09764

Your attitude. Your style.
MTV Books:
Totally your type.

Cruel Summer
Kylie Adams

First in the *Fast Girls, Hot Boys* series!

Life is a popularity contest...and someone is about to lose. In sexy Miami Beach, five friends are wrapping up high school—but one of them won't make it to graduation alive. . . .

The Pursuit of Happiness
Tara Altebrando

Declare your independence....After her mother dies and her boyfriend cheats on her, Betsy picks up the pieces of her devastated life and finds remarkable strength and unexpected passion.

Life as a Poser
Beth Killian

First in the *310* series!

Sometimes you have to fake it to make it....Eva spends an intoxicating summer in glamorous Hollywood with her famous talent agent aunt in this witty, pop culture-savvy novel, first in a new series.

Bad Girls
Alex McAulay

The name of the game is survival...and good girls finish last. Welcome to Camp Archstone, a bootcamp for troubled teen girls. But the girls' true troubles begin once they arrive....

 BOOKS

Available wherever books are sold.

Published by Pocket Books
A Division of Simon & Schuster
A Viacom Company

www.simonsays.com/mtvbooks

13863